Dead can't talk

By

Alexander Niles

P.E.P.

Published by: P.E.P. Ltd
Berkshire.
First published in Great Britain
1995.

Fiction.
ISBN 0 9525920 0 2.
Printed and bound in Great Britain
by Biddles Ltd.
Guildford and King's Lynn.
Layout and design by P.E.P. Ltd.
Cover design by Peter Brown.

INTRODUCTION.

Warfare, like most events in our lifetime, goes through periods of dramatic change. The eighties have heralded such a change. The early tools of war were clubs and knives, replaced by bows and arrows and the sword followed by the musket, bayonet and the naval cannon. Then came a quantum leap from swords and cavalry to the mechanised mobile armies in the early part of this century, aided by radio contact.

The next two leaps were equally dramatic; the aeroplane and the submarine, allowing for the first time attack from the air above and from under the sea. This produced frightening weapons like the bomb, fire bomb, chemical bomb and the hidden weapon, the torpedo; each time successive generations have claimed that their latest weapon would be the end of civilisation: each time they were wrong. Then came the most frightening weapon of all, the atom bomb, delivering horrific slaughter of civilian population at Hiroshima - it brought a new dimension to war. Yet in another way it concentrated politicians' minds on the horror of modern warfare as never before.

The scientists went on to build a larger, more frightening model, the hydrogen bomb. This bomb has kept an uneasy World peace since its inception, winning the day in the Cuban crisis.

The eighties have seen advances beyond the comprehension of all but the military, wrapping back the boundaries of development into a fantasy World of comic book reality from the fifties. Yes, the modern army is beginning to emulate the characters portrayed in the comics of our youth. The soldiers are slowly becoming an elite force of specialists and the emphasis is firmly towards the space age of 'Star Wars' and of course our own highly sophisticated defence systems.

Electronic defence or Electronic Warfare (EW), as it is called, is at the heart of modern warfare.

Speed and accuracy are the target of the modern army. The central controls at the heart of today's defences are capable of digesting a whole battlefield of information, make over a million calculations a second and present the answer before you can blink your eye. It also takes the decision about deployment away from the high command. They are now given a set of deployments to implement. The old system, of conference decisions both slow and unpredictable, is now redundant.

The new systems can monitor enemy movements while signals analyse the reasons and then the command can react to the situation. For example it can order electronic deception for its vulnerable targets such as weapon bases. It has search, report and respond capabilities. One of the weapons used in this field is the 'Stealth' with its top secret evasion system.

The Air Force use the 'Air defence command information system'. This program has now added a further feature C3i, joining intelligence collection to the existing system.

Developed by Marconi is the 'Improved UK air defence ground environment system.' Costing in estimate upwards of seven thousand million pounds, it will bring our air defence well into the twenty-first century. This program, controlled by Marconi has Plessey under contract for part of its development and also the Hughes corporation of America, displaying how defence corporations collaborate with each other to supply their specialist skills to the project.

The book was developed from within this secret World of defence. For the sake of simplicity we use 'Star wars' or SDI as the focus of our attention, but defence moves on daily and aspects of 'Star wars' have advanced even further. In the UK underwater defence is five to ten years ahead of their nearest rival.

During World war two submarines gave our navy their biggest headache, sinking our merchant fleets and tying up valuable naval power to protect our merchantmen. Marconi has now neutralised the menace of submarines. Their Cosmos system is a simulator for underwater weapons and is a part of the strategic defence initiative commonly known as 'Star wars'.

The two latest torpedoes from Marconi are 'Spearfish' and the most remarkable yet 'Sting Ray'. Stingray is capable of self guidance through its own built-in brain and can be launched from sea or air. Both carry top priority security.

This total system, with its new striking force, can seek, find and destroy any enemy submarine, even under the previously 'safe house' of the ice caps of the North and South poles. This effectively makes submarine defence and attack capability a super weapon of the past. As this is a formidable strength of the Soviet strike power, it can be seen as a serious blow to the future of the Russian might. For this reason alone it would make it essential for Russia to obtain full knowledge of this defence.

To show the speed of change within the defence industry, the Tigerfish torpedo was considered a major advance in weaponry and was being updated at Marconi between eighty-three and eighty-six: by eighty-eight it was obsolete.

The latest development in the air is the Tornado fighter. The plane is a mass of electronic technology developed by a liaison between UK, Italy and Germany, combining the expertise and finance of these three countries within NATO. This fighter is the strike force behind the 'Improved UK air defence ground environment system' and is a top priority security risk.

The defence system is co-ordinated by a program called UKAIR An ICL development that is now the heart of our air defence and links our fighting forces.

This system in turn is linked to and co-ordinated with the UNITER system. Joining all the RAF bases in the UK to all the US bases in Britain: GEC being the main contractor with assistance from Plessey and British Telecom. UNITER is capable of performing analysis at remarkable speed. These systems use the latest technology, including well-placed space dishes to bounce their signals round the World and feed back

vital information for our defence. Again top priority security. Now the British and American forces in England are being linked with the British, American and NATO forces in Europe to provide the largest intelligence network in the World today. The program incorporating all the sectional command and control systems is 'Defence into the nineties.'

This brief description of modern defence boundaries shows that, as well as being expensive, technical and largely beyond the range of traditional military knowledge, defence is moving into the hands of civilian experts to direct its future. Today's defence is vastly different than five years ago.

With this technology, a need for secrecy is paramount. Advances made; bring the ever targeted reward, superiority against maybe larger forces on paper. This is a moving boundary, so its perimeter has to be rolled back constantly because defence development never rests.

The allies in the eighties were on top, thanks to our brilliant analysts, scientists and experts. It is therefore not difficult to appreciate that Russia would be disturbed by this prospect. They had relied on conventional forces to establish World supremacy. It would, therefore, be imperative for them to obtain the secrets of the 'Star Wars' to catch up with, let alone overtake, our superior technology.

'Dead Men Can't talk,' set in this secret area of defence is a fiction investigating the deaths of twenty-three scientists in the defence industry and relating them to actual events within the international forum of politics. It is a frighteningly real story, containing a firm base within reality. The story is more than just

that; it is a fascinating insight into the grey area of politics and it's excesses.

Without the secrets of our defence, governing 'Star Wars' and the 'Defence into the nineties' pragram: Russia, under Gorbachev the realist, knew that they could not catch up with, let alone overhaul, our defence advances. Money was running out and his house of cards was about to collapse. This is a story of power and the abuse of same. Does the end justify the means? Is life in peacetime expendable?

Whatever the truth no-one could have predicted the end result; The democratisation of the Eastern satellite block and Russia through its momentum.

ACKNOWLEDGEMENTS.

A special 'thank you' goes out to the many people who provided the bricks to build this book. Specially those in our defence industry and our Special Air Service, whose valuable contribution made this book possible but through the sensitivity of the information cannot be named.

A very special thank you to my investigative journalist, who inspired the theme for the story and provided necessary information to collate the facts, sometimes at great personal risk. The grey area of government is always dangerous. So all these people took a calculated risk to bring you this book.

Last, but by no mean's least, to my wife and two children who survived my obsession to write this story.

To all these people and to the relatives of the dead scientists and analysts in our defence industry, I dedicate this book.

When the people contend for their liberty, they seldom get anything by their victory but new masters.

The Marquis of Halifax. (1633-95)

CHAPTER 1.

Holder stared in disbelief, as he read the fax from Reuters. Top Russian scientist commits suicide stop Alexi Chernov, head of the Russian nuclear program found dead two miles from his holiday dacha in the Crimea stop His body found face down in a nearby lake stop Suicide is confirmed stop.

For a moment Holder stood in silence; his brain was racing into action, analysing the position. He moved towards the phone on his desk and dialled out.

"Is that you John?"

"Yes, dear boy. The same."

"Can you put the name Alexi Chernov in your computer and see what brews? At the same time, as you speak Russian and I do not, could you ring Pravda and Isvestia and see if they have anything more on his death? While you are connected find out if there have been any other disappearances or deaths amongst scientists in the last year? I need this as quickly as possible!"

"When don't you. I will see what my Russian charm can conjure for you."

Holder impatiently sat back to await John's reply. His mind fixed on the latest news. He started to compare this news with that Easter six years ago, when he was called to investigate the death of Jane Armstrong. Could this be a parallel story? He lay back in his chair and started to recall his investigation into her death.

The air was heavy with the scent of azaleas and wild rhododendrons surrounding the small lake. Lapwings swooped over the smooth surface of the water, snatching insects from the air. A mere hint of a breeze rippled the reeds at the water's edge.

Trout, catching flies, broke the mirror surface and revealed a woman's body face down in the water, her long blonde hair undulating gently on the surface. Her hands held tightly behind her back with a jump lead that protruded from the water in what seemed a last attempt to signal for help. Most of her body lay below the surface and her feet were bound with the other lead.

A person, exercising a dog found her body. The police also found her abandoned black Mini parked in a siding by the lake. At her flat a partially prepared meal lay on the stove, the breakfast table, set for two but never used.

The Major entered his office. He glanced up at the carriage clock, which had just chimed ten o'clock.

The morning sun shone through the blinds casting his well-built shadow on the wall. At forty-eight he

had conquered redundancy from the regiment and formed a highly successful security company specialising in work beyond the scope of other more traditional members of his profession. His hard staring eyes found their target with a chilling threat to its existence, his rugged features complimenting the menace from his stare, but eased by a warm almost hypnotic charm. His physique was superb for a man of his age. His obsession for exercise took care of condition. At five foot ten he showed muscular form at its best, balancing height to economical shape.

Lying on his desk, his note pad displayed a picture of himself in a DPM combat uniform and a caption claiming; 'We start where others finish.' He was a man of iron charm without a conscience.

Now he had to consider his next move. Advanced Laser technology needed to know what price to pay for Micro Technology. They were already in trouble with the Government auditors for overcharging for MOD contracts and they could not afford to overpay for Micro Technology. They had to buy: as an important supplier they could not let the company fall into the hands of the competition, or even worse, a foreign buyer. The Major had gleaned all sorts of confidential material from the area manager's file but still no indication of the level of other bids. He had no other chance of penetration in the time span. He leant across his desk, picked up his phone and dialled.

"Is that you Sir Godfrey? I thought you should know at once. Sadly, we can't complete our contract. Sorry to bring you disturbing news."

David Holder awoke at nine-thirty with a start, fearing he had overslept until he remembered it was Easter and he was having his first weekend's break for months. He could lie back in bed and ponder, a luxury he rarely gave himself. His job was so demanding: a free-lance journalist. While potentially his own boss, in practice the pressures made his work arduous and at times dangerous.

It was seven years since his wife had left him. The job had killed their relationship, not another woman. You can never say when you will next be home. You drink too much to extract information from a contact. Break promises and continually miss out on arrangements, even when you have guaranteed to be present. His profession cost him his marriage.

No successful journalist should marry, he concluded. At forty-six he still missed tenderness in his life. His son Andrew, now nineteen, followed him into his profession. He wondered how he would cope when torn between love and journalism.

Looking at his watch he decided it was time to get up and make breakfast. Andrew, his son, was away for the weekend as usual so he had no reason to rush, the rest of the day was his, he made no plans: a strange experience.

Holder lived in a town house in Twickenham. The style was Neo-Georgian with neat proportions and economic design. On each side of the steps leading to the solid oak front door stood a large stone tree pot with a standard trailing rose tree beginning to bud for its first seasonal flowering. A side path led to a gate at the rear where a well-designed small patio on several levels, broken up with raised flower beds, provided a modern garden.

In the garage stood the only possession he really cherished: his Golf GTI, specially Turbo-charged, Italian red and immaculate.

Having shaved and dressed Holder descended the stairs and entered the kitchen. Dishes lay around unwashed, empty beer cans scattered across the work-surface. The sink was full of greasy crockery. He had no excuse today.

Hunger took the better of him and he set about cooking egg, bacon, mushrooms, tomatoes and fried bread, just cleaning enough dishes to cater for his meal. Sometimes, he recalled, a hot breakfast stood him in good stead all day.

He sat down with his paper, the Sunday Telegraph and began his meal. On page two he noticed yet another suicide at Advanced Laser Technology. Recalling previous cases he made a mental note to look into this death at his first opportunity.

He continued to read his newspaper until the phone disturbed his concentration. Wondering who it could be, he went to answer it;

"Hello. David Holder speaking."

"Oh, is that you David? It's George here."

At that moment he knew his peaceful Easter was in jeopardy. George was a newspaper editor and he never called unless a job was urgent.

"We received a report that a girl's body was found in a lake in Surrey. Could be a big story. We have been advised it might be a sexual attack. Cover for me? I wouldn't ask you but I have no-one else available."

Holder paused a second. Away went the peaceful day ahead. His mind turned to the dirty dishes.

"Yes, I'll cover. It will take me about thirty-five minutes to get out to the scene."

"Thanks David, you are a brick," came the reply. Holder took down the details and replaced the phone.

He collected his note pad and recorder, locked up his house and headed for the lake.

Holder arrived at the slip road leading to the lake at eleven-forty on Sunday morning. The day was wind-free with the crispness of spring in the air.

Parking his car he approached a member of the sailing club for directions. The man, assembling a jib at the time, pointed across the lake.

"The police have found a young girls body, I believe."

"How do I get there?"

"Go back to the slip road and park somewhere. Then climb over the gate on the left and walk along to the lake, past the car park, that is unless they have opened the gate. That is the fishing club side of the lake and the season doesn't start for two weeks."

The gate was open. He parked the car and walked towards the crowd near the lakeside. The body, removed from the lake was now lying inside an ambulance and the area cordoned off from the crowd. Holder approached the Chief Constable and introduced himself, showing his police press pass, his greatest asset in cases involving the authorities.

"Could you fill me in with details of the girl, including the circumstance of her death?"

The Chief Constable, a man in his fifties, thick set with a world-worn face replied.

"The body was found by a lady walking her dog at eleven-forty-five yesterday evening. We have just received details about the girl. We traced her through her black car which was left abandoned in the slip road. Her name was Jane Armstrong. Twenty-six years old. Lived in a flat locally. She worked for a firm called Micro Technology as secretary to the Divisional Manager. She was found up-side-down in the lake eighteen to twenty meters out from the bank. Her feet, bound together with a jump lead and her hands tied behind her back with the other lead. We have now set a study of her life style in motion to see if we can get a clue to lead us to a reason for suicide."

"Surely you don't suspect suicide?" Holder exclaimed. "I was told it was foul play by my editor. He suspected sexual implications."

"The patrolmen mis-read the situation when they first found the body. They mistakenly told a reporter it was foul play. Since then we have examined the scene thoroughly and can find no reason to suspect anything but suicide, however our minds are still open."

He seems plausible Holder thought and was just about to turn and examine the scene, when a man, standing alone, a few feet away caught his attention. It was a man from state security. His staring eyes sent a shiver down Holder's spine.

So this was not just an ordinary death. This involved State security. The answer probably lay where she worked, but since it was Easter, there was no point in rushing over there. He thanked the Chief Constable and started his own investigation. First he examined the area where the body entered the water. There were so many footprints by now that to gain any knowledge from them would be impossible.

He studied the jump lead used to tie her legs and the same type that bound her hands behind her back. They were medium sized with large clips at each end. He could not imagine how anyone could possibly tie them behind their own back, especially with those unwieldy clips in the way.

Holder went back to the car, took his jump leads out and walked behind a bush to try for himself. With all his effort, try as he might, he could not tie a tight knot behind his back and with a loose one he could easily slip his hands through the noose.

After twenty minutes he gave up and returned the jump leads to his car. This was not suicide he concluded. It was a murder but a murder that involved state concern.

He went back to the Chief Constable with a question to dispel his last doubt.

"How tight were the jump leads?"

"Tight enough to stop the blood circulation."

Murder was Holder's final conclusion and no sexual interference occurred.

Holder returned to his car and decided to examine Jane Armstrong's Mini on the way. He found it posted with a single police guard. His viewing was restricted to the outside. The car, parked normally, prompted Holder to ask if they had moved it, but the constable confirmed this was its original position. He thanked the young constable and studied the road tracks for signs.

The slip road, which consisted of loose stones, mud and hard-core, gave very little away. The surface was uneven and full of pot holes filled with water from the night's rain. There were tyre marks, but they were so numerous that no pattern showed with any accuracy. He gave up the idea of finding clues and went back to his car noting the car's registration number.

Once home, Holder phoned a police contact and gave him the car number to obtain Jane's address. Fifteen minutes later his contact rang back.

"Holder, bad news I'm afraid. They have put a block on information for this car. Who the hell owns it?"

"Just a twenty-six year old girl that is dead." Holder replied.

"She must be high security. I have never come across this one before. It could get me in hot water. Sorry I can't help you this time."

Holder thanked him and replaced the receiver. He picked the phone up again and rang another colleague who kept a computer record of all news and supplied it back to journalists on a need to know basis.

"Afternoon John. Sorry to disturb you but I have an urgent requirement. What information have you in your fountain of knowledge about a firm called Micro Technology?" Holder waited impatiently for the reply.

"Not a lot dear boy. They are a small to medium sized company, manufacturing high technology. They link computers to each other, assemble miniaturised components and boards for electronic controls used in the aircraft industry, space projects and defence. There has just been an article about them in the Financial Times. Apparently the Company is seeking an outside buyer. Why, are you thinking of deserting us for industry? Tut, Tut, that just won't do."

"Just be serious for one minute!" Holder replied, "Any mention of bidders yet?"

"No, but they mention Advanced Laser Technology as the firm most likely to loose from such a sale. A high proportion of their expertise goes to them."

"Thanks John. That was the link that I feared would show. It ties in with many other weird things that have been happening. Bill me as usual. I'll leave you in peace with your mistress."

"What do you mean?"

"Your computer, you moron!" Holder replied, putting down the phone.

Why were so many people ending up dead when they became involved with this company? He started the day investigating a sexual murder and found instead a cold blooded silencing job, carried out by a person or persons unknown, to protect information unknown from becoming public knowledge. On top of that the state was winding into gear to cover up the traces and release the usual red herring's.

Could it be that Micro Technology was working on the same secret project as Advanced Laser Technology? If they were, would it be a reason to kill the divisional manager's secretary? Not unless she was passing on information or involved in some way in industrial espionage.

What if one of Advanced Laser Technology's rivals wanted to get in on the act and buy out Micro Technology, leaving their competitors in the lurch? What better way to do it and successfully, than to hire one of the companies involved in industrial espionage? One of the many methods employed was to place a secretary in a strategic position and then compromise them, later to use them from within to feed out confidential information. This system was as old as the hills and often produced results.

Holder thought on and drew a new conclusion. At first it seemed to be a stab in the dark, but it grew on him. Could it be possible that Advanced Laser Technology themselves wanted to buy Micro Technology, however did not want to show their hand before assessing the rival bids? Certainly the best way of doing that was to obtain the rival offer and top it. This would certainly be the work of an industrial spy. They must get details of confidential files, probably only held by the Managers, to get the knowledge necessary to make the highest bid.

Holder knew that Advanced Laser Technology was under investigation by the public auditor for over charging on defence contracts. Buying this company would be a worthwhile outlay for defence, provided the price reflected its worth. This was something the public auditor always checked thoroughly. It would be absolutely necessary to win by the lowest margin. To accomplish that, an inside source was essential. It looked very neat. Indeed taking into account the information that he had amassed from previous investigations, almost conclusive. Next task: find the parents of Jane Armstrong and interview Micro Technology.

He phoned the police and asked to speak to the Chief Constable in charge of the investigation. He was not available, but the Duty Officer answered.

"What can I do for you?"

"I was present at the lake earlier and spoke to your Chief Constable. I was wondering if you had traced the parents of Jane Armstrong yet?"

The duty officer paused; "At the moment this information is being withheld, until we have finished talking to the Armstrong's."

"Can you at least tell me in which town they live?"

"In the Camberley area," replied the Duty Officer, "and I didn't tell you that."

"Don't worry - I'll keep it a secret!" Holder replied and put down the phone. It was now after four in the afternoon, but he had to follow up straight away. He studied the local directory. There were six Armstrong's with the initials J and he employed a trick he had learned from one of his colleagues. He called each one in turn, asking if the inspector was still there. On the fourth call he struck it lucky.

The inspector, he was informed, had left. Holder replaced the receiver and noted the address. After asking a passer-by the direction, he found the house, a semi-detached in a quiet cul-de-sac on the outskirts of town. He knocked on the door and a tall grey-haired man answered the door.

"Mr. Armstrong, I'll be honest, sorry, but I'm a free-lance journalist investigating the death of your daughter Jane. Would you mind talking?"

"You better come in," replied Armstrong. They sat in the small front room.

"First I would like to offer you my sincere sympathy. It must be a terrible shock for you and your wife."

"Yes, my wife is now sleeping under sedation. I can't imagine why anyone would want to kill my Jane, she was so full of life and was very popular amongst her friends."

"So you think she was killed?"

"She wasn't the type to take her own life."

"Did she have a regular boy friend?"

"She had many friends but just recently she seemed involved with an older man. She never introduced him to us - we suspected he was married but she always denied it."

"Did you know his name?"

"No, she never told us. I once overheard her call him Bill when she called him from here - but that was rare."

"Did she ever talk about her work?"

"Not much. She seemed to enjoy it and she liked her boss, but she never wanted to discuss her work. She did say some of it was top secret which precluded her discussing it. You're not a security man?"

"No." Holder smiled. "Did she ever mention the sale of the firm?"

"I didn't even know it was for sale."

"Have you any idea who might have killed or even threatened your daughter?"

"Wish I knew, Mr Holder, as you can imagine. However I am going to try and find out."

"Good luck with your search. Here is my card. Contact me if you find anything, or wish to ask me about my investigations. All I find is yours for the asking. Give my condolences to your wife."

"Thank you, thank you," said Armstrong as tears flooded his eyes. Holder left for home to write a short inconclusive article, just enough to justify his work for the day and keep George happy. Then he went to bed.

On Tuesday he was up early for his drive down to Ascot. He wanted to be the first to see the Divisional Manager. He asked for an appointment when he entered and was ushered into a small but plush waiting room. It was early, so he knew he might have to wait. It wasn't long. Just as he was asked to come to the office the waiting room door opened and in walked the man from the security service. He was five-foot-ten and seemed in the peak of physical fitness. Holder thought, not a man to annoy as he hurried into the Manager's office.

Sitting at his desk, the Divisional Manager, a small bespectacled man, with a bald head and searching eyes, sat reading some papers.

"I won't be a minute," he said without looking up. A few moments later he put his pen down, stood up and held out his hand.

"My name is Peter Weaver. How can I help you?"

"I am here investigating the untimely death of Jane Armstrong." Holder explained.

Weaver looked hesitant then commented. "The police seem satisfied that she took her own life, though I can't for a minute see a reason why she would want to do such a thing."

"Try securing your hands tight behind your back with jump leads and you will see why it was murder."

"What!" Said Weaver, "who told you that?"

"The police team - and I saw the leads. I believe you are in the middle of negotiations to sell the company. May I ask who the contenders are?"

"I would love to tell you but this is confidential at the moment. You know what rumours can do in the city. We can't disclose anything till our attempts are successful or aborted. Tell me more about your role."

This time Holder paused. Yet Weaver seemed honest.

"For the last year I've been investigating a series of suicides - and related accidents. None make sense. They're all people involved with defence from three companies and ministry establishments. I heard you have had a security leak. Has this affected your sale?"

"My my, you have done your home work. I am impressed but also concerned. It could affect the result if it leaked out."

"Don't worry, my investigation is long term, not instant press. I won't be ready to expose it until it is too late to effect your results."

"Can I rely on that?"

"Absolutely. Do you think Jane's untimely death could have been connected to your security leak?"

"I must say it had crossed my mind but I dismissed it. Now you say it is murder it makes me wonder. Could it possibly be that she was the person disturbing the files? She had ample opportunity to do so and it answers my biggest problem. Yet knowing the girl I would be reluctant to think that of her. What is your theory?"

"If I tell you this I want you to undertake not to disclose what I say to any prospective buyer or anyone else. One important caveat: at this stage it is only theory."

"What you say will be between us alone. I give you my word on that."

"I believe Advanced Laser Technology employed an industrial spy to extract information from your personal files. To do this who better to befriend than your secretary. It's the oldest trick. Unfortunately she found out that you knew a leak was affecting your confidential sale and panicked, telling the industrial spy. He knew his cover was blown so he did what comes naturally to them and killed the source that could expose him. You see, dead is silent for ever."

"This is frightening. I must concede - it rings true. I did tell Jane just before Easter that I suspected someone had been tampering with the private files. I never suspected Jane. Against your theory, Advanced Laser Technology have not shown any interest in purchasing this company, despite the fact that we do a great deal of work for them, much of which is classified. I have been surprised by their lack of interest. I suppose that if industrial espionage is their way of gaining purchase, your theory will be proved or disproved sometime in the near future."

Holder sat back in his chair, reflected for a good minute and then replied, "I expect that within a couple of weeks, you will have a bid from Advanced Laser Technology. It will be either just above your other offers or, maybe, if they did not find out the level of your other bids, well above them. For your sake I hope it is the latter. Either way you will know who paid the spy that killed your secretary."

"I must say that when you came in, I thought, must I speak to the press at this time? I was only swayed by my PR adviser, who said our image might suffer if I didn't, so I reluctantly conceded. This conversation has been very enlightening. Best of luck but be careful. I suspect that you are dealing with ruthless people and I admire you for your courage. On my part, I'll respect your confidence."

"In this game we always spit and snarl before we find the real truth! Don't worry." Said Holder, getting up to leave. "Good luck with your sale and your future."

As Holder left he knew he was nearer the truth. One thing still worried him. Who was this ruthless industrial spy and for whom did he work? They were callous that seemed clear.

Two weeks later a news story appeared in the financial times, stating Advanced Laser Technology bought out one of its component manufacturer, Micro Technology for a very generous sum. Holder now knew that his theory was fact and that the so-called suicide had really been murder.

Some months later the public auditor disclosed that Advanced Laser Technology over paid by several

million for the assets of Micro Technology. So the spy failed. A young girl died for nothing: or did she?

CHAPTER 2.

Holder sat up abruptly, the phone disturbed his recollection of Jane Armstrong's tragic death six years ago.

"John here, dear boy. I have not been idle since you spoke to me. Your dead Russian professor is none other than the head of the nuclear energy research institute in Moscow. He is also a senior member of their energy commission."

"He must have been responsible for the Chernobyl disaster."

"He has been a serious critic of the lax standards of safety in the nuclear plants and although his main research was for military purposes, his position on the energy council made him responsible for guidance towards safe production of nuclear power. He has publicly stated, on more than one occasion, that his advice has been ignored and he believes that many nuclear facilities are potential disaster zones."

"That's interesting."

"His warnings were ignored till Chernobyl. At last his advice is being studied."

"Too late for some." Added Holder. "Is it confirmed as suicide officially?"

"Yes, that is what the two main media outlets say. However I have spoken to a free-lance press agency in Moscow that is post Gorbachev and they say their source confirms he was murdered and guess what, dear boy!"

"Try me."

"He is the fourth nuclear scientist to have died in suspicious circumstances and five others have gone missing."

"My god, It's all happening again. What reason do they give for their demise?"

"They say, since the arms agreement their services are no longer required coupled with which the state cannot afford them. They fear they could go to work for unstable leaders like Saddam Hussen. This situation prompted this drastic action by the state."

"The World is sick in mind if that is their solution. Thanks John. This is a nightmare. It smacks of my last epic investigation, the Advanced Laser affair. Be in touch"

Holder sat back in his chair and started to recount the deaths of scientists in that long investigation.

There had been an epidemic of unexplained suicides amongst top scientists and computer experts that first came to his attention eight years ago and even

before this two deaths occured that he had not investigated.

The first was Professor Mather. His speciality, computer related science. They considered him to be one of the top scientists in his field. He even lectured in the States and at forty-six was healthy, reasonably wealthy and seemed to be enjoying his life. His only secret was the one week in six when he disappeared and would tell no-one, including his wife, where he went.

In March eighty-two he met with a tragic accident; his car plunged through the side of a bridge to his death. His wife, not satisfied with the outcome of the police findings, had an independent engineer's report carried out on the car and it was found there were signs that someone had tampered with the brakes.

At the inquest the coroner recorded a verdict of accidental death. As Holder had not attended the aftermath of the accident he could only rely on the coroner's report that strangely found no fault with the car.

Holder's first suspicion arose from the conflict of statement. It made him realise the state was being economical with the truth.

A year later Lt. Col. Peter Taylor disappeared without trace. He was head of defence studies and lectured at defence colleges. His expertise included the future potential for defence against a very sound background in the latest scientific discoveries and computer peripherals. After a period of time he was listed as dead, cause unknown. Then came two more deaths. A radar design expert at Advanced Laser

Technology and a digital communication's expert from British Telecom. At this point Holder recalled he had an open mind to cause, behind which was a nagging feeling he was looking at something big.

The state was so clumsy when it intervened in investigations and left so many trademarks of its presence. He concluded, at this point however, that they also could be curious and it might not be anything more than that. However he would watch and wait, especially as one man had disappeared and could be in the hands of the KGB spilling our defence secrets to Russia at that very moment.

Holder's first in-depth investigation was the death of a twenty-four year old Asian, Vidal Singh. He worked in the underwater division of Advanced Laser Developments, a subsidiary of Advanced Laser Technology. He specialised in guidance systems for torpedoes.

Vidal Singh travelled one hundred and forty miles from his home to throw himself off a bridge into a ravine. The distance he travelled was an unusual feature for a suicide but that wasn't all. The police found a half empty cigarette packet on the back seat and nine cigarette ends in the rear ashtray, all the same brand. On investigation Holder was assured by Singh's relatives he never touched cigarettes.

This posed the question; did he have company and if so, who? There was another enigma, a hypodermic needle mark found on his thigh. Checking with his wife and family Holder confirmed he never indulged in injected drugs. The doctor also stated that he did not administer any drugs by injection.

Vidal Singh's father assured Holder that he had been a happy man, but one thing bothered him. He had just accepted a job outside the defence industry and the family concern was that he died to protect the secrets that he developed. At the time, Holder recalled this seemed a bit far-fetched.

The funeral was postponed once as the coroner, at the last moment, decided to undertake a second post-mortem. The reason given was that a second scientist had just allegedly killed himself in a macabre fashion.

Holder was unsure on five distinct points in relation to Vidal Singh's death. First, the cigarettes found on the back seat in his car. This led him to believe he had company for a substantial part of his journey. Second, the distance he travelled to commit so called suicide. Third, that the relatives had given so many testaments. Fourth, that jab on his thigh. The fifth and most important was in relation to his knowledge. He had a complete understanding of the torpedo 'Seek and Find' system. It made submarines vulnerable, for the first time, to pre-emptive attack; the floating ice caps of the poles were a favourite hiding place for Russian submarines. It effectively neutralised their safe retreat. A very serious blow to Russia's submarine superiority. Britain was way ahead of the Russians and even a few years ahead of the United States in this advanced field of defence.

He also had a profound knowledge of simulators at the heart of modern warfare and responsible for designing the options for defence response and strike power. This top secret knowledge made him a target

for a Russian attempt to gain his secrets or even silence him. Both, in Holder's view, a distinct possibility.

The coroner explained the jab on the thigh after the second autopsy. The statement said that the mark was due to a bone piecing the thigh. Holder was unhappy that the first autopsy had missed the mark and was now suspicious about it's finding. The second attempt even then left four unsolved questions.

Holder recalled the second Asian scientist, Assam Shah, was twenty-six years old and also worked at Advanced Laser Developments at their branch researching underwater vibration simulation. He drove to the West country to carry out his bizarre act, a death too horrible to contemplate. Holder, still haunted by the method of death, could not see it as anything but suicide but the evidence was beginning to accumulate against the theory.

He searched for clues amongst Shah's friends and relatives, but came up with no hard evidence. Yet he had a feeling of unease about the outwardly visual certainty of suicide. It was haunting him that two scientists from the same firm should commit suicide so close to each other. The coroner recorded a death by suicide, but alluded, off the record, to the possibility of a sinister link between the two deaths.

There was no doubt this man had access to top secret defence information relating to sonar guidance development. This was a guidance system for ocean warfare that could pin point a target and guide an attack on its characteristic sonar sound. A system as accurate as laser guidance by air. This information would be a top priority for a Russian shopping list and

placed the idea of suicide by these scientists as an outside runner.

Holder recalled, the pace of deaths accelerated and no less than four defence scientists died between December eighty-six and March eighty-seven. Two were MOD computer experts. One was a design engineer working for Advanced Laser Technology. He was a guidance expert. Another employee of the same company, a space systems engineer, also died.

Although these deaths were all classed as suicide by the respective coroners, it was painfully obvious to Holder this was a cover story for the true reason.

Holder decided to assemble the information that he had gathered about the dead scientists, listing it all systematically.

The first thing that struck him was that the computer was the common factor. However, after some careful deliberation, he dismissed this lead because the computer was a modern fact of life in scientific circles, an essential tool of the trade.

He presented the assembled information to a friend who was a retired defence expert and awaited his response with some curiosity.

The result was surprising. Holder discovered that the dead men, between them, had most of the skills necessary to develop an advanced defence system and program the software to manage it. Together, they could have devised a system that could seek the enemy, pin point the weaponry, launch a defensive attack and guide it to its target with deadly accuracy. In other words, they could have designed a complete defensive command and control system. All that was missing

was a laser expert and a weapons design engineer. The first for laser guidance, a new technology and the second would not be necessary if they used existing rocketry. He also added the point that they could fire weapons under water using sonar guidance or from the ground or by air. He also commented the source of weapons could be under development by another team.

A pattern was starting to form; a picture was beginning to clear in Holder's mind. He recalled his next move. He assembled the details of his findings and went to the ministry of defence to confront them with his knowledge. His accurate analysis caught the ministry off balance. They stone-walled his theory, giving him a tirade of dis-information, their usual practice when concealing the truth for what ever reason. The civil service were experts at this sort of brush off but gave Holder proof positive that a cover-up was in operation. They stated that there was no link, through work, between the dead scientists. This was a successful breakthrough as this statement was not true.

Apart from the clear evidence that several of the scientists worked for Advanced Laser Technology or one of its subsidiaries, the two Asians worked for the underwater research department and were known to have worked together. The authority must know this was public knowledge, so why lie?

Holder's thoughts turned towards his prime suspect, the Russian KGB. In his mind he recalled a drinking session he had with a foreign correspondent from Isvestia. Naturally enough the Russian did not disclose any state secrets but he did impart something

that seemed at the time just a sad reflection on the state of Russia. He said 'you mustn't take Russian treats too seriously, we're running out of rubbles and we couldn't sustain any large scale dog fight.'

At the time Holder had read into his remark a growing despair with his political masters, but perhaps he had read him wrong. Maybe he was parting with a deep state secret. Holder thought on. What if Russia was broke. They would have to steal state secrets to keep up with the West. This was a far cheaper way to attain defence compatibility. It was also a last ditch stand because if it failed the chances of catching up would also deteriorate in the time span.

If this Russian hit the truth, Holder concluded, he could be looking at a concerted Russian attempt, employing their best spies, to steal the top secrets of our latest defence developments which included the full laser guidance program and the sonar guidance weapon to neutralise submarine superiority.

Now it just happened the dead scientists had most of these skills. Holder was now convinced that the deaths were murders. There were three possibilities; the Russians were killing our scientists to slow down our defence program. The Russians were killing our scientists after they had extracted important details of our secrets. The third was unthinkable, that we killed our own scientists to protect our secrets. Holder concluded this was out of the question as it would have been an own goal. So Russia and the KGB were the prime suspects.

Holder's mind turned to the three deaths that he had investigated in depth.

CHAPTER 3.

Holder was attending a press conference at the Hilton when the news broke. Another scientist died. As the conference was half an hour from starting, he left after charging his colleague to keep him up to date with any important developments and headed for Shrivenham to investigate the death of Peter Cable. One and three quarter hours later, arriving at Shrivenham, he stopped at the first phone box to find Cable's address.

The police were there in force. Holder walked up to the senior officer and introduced himself as a member of the press. His great asset was his police pass card. It afforded him, as a contributor to the police force's own publication, access where other journalists were excluded. The Chief Constable immediately directed him to a plain-clothes man standing just outside the garage. This man presented himself as a Press Liaison Officer. Now Holder couldn't be sure but this officer did not seem to be an ordinary policeman. He was five-foot-ten, in the height of physical fitness and his eyes were hypnotic. However his charm calmed the effect from his disarming stare. Holder knew that stare and concluded he was from state security; introduced himself and then asked for some background information on Peter Cable.

"I am able to tell you so far that he was forty-six years old. He worked down the road, at the Ministry of Defence Military College, as a lecturer. He leaves a wife, Pamela. No foul play is suspected. It was quite clearly a dreadful accident." Holder mused; this kind of remark was most unusual so early on in an investigation. There may sometimes be a hint, but never such certainty.

"Did Mr. Cable lecture on highly sensitive defence material or was his work concerned with theoretical and tactical military studies?"

"He did not lecture on sensitive or secret material and had no connection with military secrets," replied the liaison officer, who sounded more than ever like an agent from the internal security service by every word.

Holder thought that was too slick. This guy was trying to wrap an allegedly harmless package with tamper-proof tape and the alarm bells were ringing. There was always plenty to learn from the unspoken word.

"Can I talk to Mrs. Cable?" Requested Holder.

"I am afraid she is not available. She is sedated and is sleeping at the moment," replied the official. Holder knew she was not asleep because just five minutes ago he had seen her through the window, talking to two men inside the house. Either they were getting careless or they thought he was stupid. This security man was annoying him and he had better things to do than stand around listening to a pack of lies. Why did security involve themselves in an investigation for someone who knew no secrets? It didn't make sense.

He decided to go to the military college and ask a few more questions. It took ten minutes to find the college set in its own grounds and protected by a high fence, with a military guard on the gate house. They escorted him to the visitor's car park and ushered him into the press office.

A few minutes later a tall, good-looking officer in his mid thirties came in and introduced himself as the press liaison officer for the college.

"How can I help you?" He asked.

Holder, hoping to drive a wedge between the man and the security officer, asked;

"Can you tell me the sort of work Peter Cable was doing as a lecturer at this college?"

"Yes, Mr Holder. He was a senior lecturer at the college dealing with high grade, classified work. I am not at liberty to disclose the nature of his work. Most of it was covered by the Official Secrets Act. He was the most experienced person at this college in his field, modern weaponry. We have lost an almost irreplaceable man today." The wedge was firmly in place.

"Did he ever visit facilities overseas, for example?"

The officer paused a moment before answering, as if to assess his position.

"He did visit the States, to assess and study the 'Star Wars'defence system, along with a high powered team from our defence industry."

"Why do you think he died?"

Again the officer paused, before answering; "At this stage we do not know. We will all have to wait and see what the police report has to say at the inquest."

"Was he working on any project that could be of interest to a foreign power?"

"This I am not at liberty to disclose except to say, that, in the course of his day to day work, he would naturally be working on top secret projects. It goes without saying all these projects would be of interest to our enemies."

Holder thanked the officer for being so frank and joined his escort who saw him safely out of the gates.

A few simple questions, asked early in the day, before the college press officer received his instructions from internal security man had paid dividends. Should the authorities make a statement that, to their knowledge, none of the scientists were working on classified projects, he would know they were lying. This satisfactory interview delivered instant results.

He did not have to look much farther for clues. His man had been nobbled. By whom? Had it been a KGB contract? Holder could not afford to discount anything. Experience had taught him never to ignore any lead. He drove back to London to record the day's events and to phone Mrs Cable.

A few days later he was at home, writing up an article he had just finished researching; when the phone rang. A friend from Reuters was on the line.

"Holder, I have a flash for you. Another scientist has died at Advanced Laser Technology? His name is Edward Purcell and he lived in Leicestershire. Apparently he died of carbon monoxide poisoning."

"Another one," exclaimed Holder, "the last one was the same. Thanks for the tip, I'll get up there straight away."

He put down the phone, mentally cancelling his plans for the rest of the day: collected his note pad and recorder and headed up the M1 towards Leicester. The traffic was very heavy and it took nearly three hours to reach his destination.

He had no trouble getting to Purcell's bungalow. When he arrived the police were just tidying up before leaving. Holder introduced himself and noted the same man from state security inside the garage. He asked the officer in charge;

"Can you give me details of your findings?"

"Yes, his name is Edward Purcell. He was forty-three years old and worked in Coventry for Advanced Laser Technology. We found his body slumped over the car and a pipe placed over the exhaust and through the rear window. The garage door was closed, until Mr Palmer, the neighbour, came to investigate. We don't suspect foul play. We believe it to be a simple case of suicide."

"Had he any family or next of kin?" Asked Holder.

"Not as far as we know. We have managed to contact a cousin, who should be here any minute."

Holder took a look around the garage and felt the ice cold stare of the security man watching his every move. They had removed the body but the outline mark on the car showed where he lay. Holder tried to imagine the scene. Something wasn't right, why put a pipe inside the car and then die outside the car where the fumes became less concentrated?

Could a man inside the car, stagger out to die over the bonnet? That would rule out suicide. It looked as if he came round, tried to escape, but was overpowered by fumes, the position of the body made a lie out of the police statement. The man still stared at him.

"Are you satisfied?"

"No." Replied Holder and went next door.

A Mrs Palmer answered the door and ushered him into her living room. Mr Palmer was asleep in front of the fire.

"There is a gentleman to see you, from the press." Palmer woke with a jerk and rose to his feet slowly.

"Sorry to disturb you," smiled Holder, "but I am enquiring into the death of your neighbour. Can you tell me something about him - as a person?".

"What a terrible affair." Palmer stared towards the bay window. More police had arrived in a white squad car. "They think it's suicide but I can't believe it. Edward was such a kind man. He was always keen to help other people. He was highly respected in the village. Why only yesterday he completely changed my brake system and serviced my car. I'm getting on a bit. I'm seventy-five you know and I can't do those jobs anymore. Do you know he never took a penny for all this work. The man was so kind. No, he couldn't kill himself. No way."

"How did he seem yesterday?"

"Laughing and joking as usual. No sign of problems. If people have problems, they become quieter than usual. Edward was his normal jovial self yesterday."

"Have you spoken to his family yet?"

"Yes. The police asked me to ring the nearest relative - a cousin, who could not believe Edward committed suicide. It was just not in his character. His cousin suspects foul play because of all the others, but I don't know. I think it may just have been an accident."

Holder remembered the pipe leading into the car. That was deliberate. Two deaths of a kind so close together, that was odd. Holder thanked Mr Palmer and made his way back to his car. He just witnessed the beginning of a cover up again. Why? What was behind it all? Russia? He mused over the evidence so far but found no hint of a motive. Was this a clumsy effort on the part of the state to wipe the egg off its own face? Was the security service just as baffled as he was and attempting to hide the story? Had these men taken deadly secrets to their graves?

Holder drove home to prepare the facts for his verbal sketch of the last two deaths.

Peter Cable was a very accomplished man. He had climbed through the jungle of technical expertise to become a senior lecturer at Military Colleges. Although a civilian, most of the time he worked on highly classified projects. His colleagues often brought their queries to him. His sophisticated analytic approach usually dealt effectively with the most complex technical problems. He had a reputation bordering on the prophetic. This, in his field, was a particularly precious talent.

Prophecy is a valuable commodity on any market, but even more so in a field as vulnerable and as essential as defence systems. Cable recognised the urgency of staying perpetually one step ahead of the competition.

There was, of course, no end to development in the defence field. Space technology had opened new territory to expand into and secure. Most defence experts believed that the leaders in space technology, commanding the spectrum, would dominate the World today and the planets tomorrow.

Cable not only thrived on this immense challenge, but felt it was his bounden duty to imbue the same enthusiasm into his colleagues. They would be tomorrows' leaders, carrying on the relentless search to improve defence. He had seen two important developments successfully completed recently. The laser guidance system, now trouble free and of course its parallel under water, the sonar guidance system. Both programs keeping Britain in the lead in this field of defence technology.

Cable had been to the States to study the 'Star Wars' Defence System. There he gleaned many important leads from developments he studied. One of the most inspiring parts of the program was the simulator, on which the computer buffs played war games with compelling realism. It was there that he realised the potential of laser technology. For the layman, he suspected the technology would be beyond comprehension. Most people would think they were watching a space fiction film. Space was the future and it was his job to make sense of its secrets to benefit the state.

He did not have many interests outside his work. His greatest achievement was in relation to the new laser defence system, under development at Advanced Laser Technology. As an outside consultant, he had successfully married different technologies, from different areas of defence, into a cohesive system of command and control with air attack capabilities. One other man on the project was familiar with all the details. This man had just resolved it's most worrying problem, guidance.

This was Probably the best guarded defence secret, fifteen to twenty years ahead of the Russian expertise, therefore a prime espionage target.

This caused a problem for Cable, who naturally wanted to pass his knowledge to his students. Sometimes he found himself beginning to explain, only to find he could not go farther without breaking the rules binding his work.

He found this most frustrating because it forced him to leave the students in the dark and fob them off with theoretical analysis.

His home was quite ordinary, a four-bedroomed detached house in a quiet cul-de-sac. It stood in its own grounds. The garden was tidy, the wife's pride and joy. The tarmac drive ended in a double garage, half of which he used for a workshop and storage area. The house itself was modern. Its study, Cable's den, was full of technology. An IBM personal computer graced his desk, with a twin hard disc drive unit and a colour VDU screen. A laser printer to the side and modem, connected to his phone, linked him to his work. Cable never really relaxed. His work was his life.

This February evening was a rare exception. He took his wife Pamela to a dinner party given by one of her friends. He hadn't been able to refuse although He hated the fruitless small talk at such gatherings, but he owed his wife this one. They left the house, putting the alarm on and leaving the light glowing for their return.

Before getting into the car Cable locked the garage doors: a neighbour recently had all his tools stolen at night.

Three miles later they arrived for their dinner date. Cable liked the couple well but still had great difficulty in talking on their level and blamed himself for isolating his leisure time from this type of social life. The hostess was a particularly good cook and one thing he did indulge was good food. He was adventurous with food as he was in his work. Once relaxed, Cable was in no hurry and began enjoying the evening, sipping brandy, listening.

At Two-o'clock Pamela hinted they should go. At two-thirty she rose and thanked her host and hostess for the evening, asking them round for a meal soon. Cable also thanked his hostess for the meal and congratulated her on her cooking skill.

When they arrived home Cable parked the car and unlocked the front door for his wife.

"I'll just put the car away Pamela," he said, I will be up as soon as I have finished." Pamela, exhausted, climbed the stairs, undressed, washed and went straight to bed.

Meanwhile Cable walked over to the garage, unlocked the swing door, put on the light and went back to his car. He started it up and drove into the garage, parked, switched off the engine and turned off the lights.

As he left his car he sensed another presence, but he locked the garage. It was impossible. He was about to turn to leave the garage when someone grabbed him from behind and swung him round violently, pinning his arms behind him and immobilising his legs. His mouth covered, he struggled violently but the intruder was immensely strong. A second man put two arms across his neck in a scissor movement. He could feel the blood supply to his brain drying up and dizziness swept across him.

He remembered his colleagues that had died and a feeling of panic overtook him. Was this it? Was he also to die? was this the pay off? His fury made him struggle, but he was as putty in their arms and he fell into unconsciousness. They exerted pressure on his neck for a further minute. The attacker was an expert and knew that this would keep him unconscious while they went to work. It had not been enough to damage his brain or mark his neck, but it gave them ample time to complete their assignment.

One man removed the car keys from Cable's pocket. The other taking his body, still limp and placed it under the car with his head close to the exhaust. They turned the light off in the garage, started the engine, still warm from the journey, closed the garage doors behind them and melted into the night.

Next morning, when Pamela Cable awoke she found her husband missing. Calling out to see if he was already up, the lack of an answer prompted her to investigate. She went out to the garage and opened the unlocked doors, to be met by the acrid odour of burned petrol. She was just able to make out the shape of her husband's head. The rest of his body was under the car. He looked dead.

She felt numb. Her legs wouldn't move. Her brain became blank. The fumes brought her back to her senses. She staggered back towards the house, still not grasping the reality. She stumbled inside and collapsed on the stairs. Emotion overtook her and she wept. Fifteen minutes later, still shaking, she composed herself enough to ring the local police.

Edward Purcell was in his early forties. Unmarried, he lived on his own in a small but spacious bungalow in Leicester and was at forty-three, a fully qualified systems engineer. He had spent the last few years working on flight simulation systems for his firm, Advanced Laser Technology, at their plant in Coventry. His skill at linking his special knowledge to various projects had given him a reputation. The best in the industry.

He was also good at costing out development projects and they used him many times to prepare quotations for customers such as the MOD. He had just done one project for the Ministry on a flight simulator. Unlike most of the engineers working on the weapon, he saw the total concept. His job was to make sure that each section's development would link to the total project. He had never seen such an advanced system and he realised the potential was enormous, bringing 'Star War' dreams to reality.

Strangely enough, although he never gave his own skills a second thought, the expertise of his colleagues always amazed him. Only the other day he met his colleague Peter Cable and discussed this very subject.

What a tragedy that the industries foremost expert on the future development of arms should have died suddenly and in such a horrible manner. Purcell couldn't help feeling that some of the deaths attributed to suicide had more behind them than the company, or the authorities, were admitting. He could not believe that all these intelligent men could be suicide cases. Indeed the few he knew from the defence project definitely did not seem to be the type that would resort to such a desperate act. He couldn't imagine any circumstance that would drive him to an act of such total despair.

Although he had lived on his own, Purcell maintained a very full life. He had many friends and a close relationship with his neighbours. He frequently mended a neighbour's tap, or sealed a leaky roof. He enjoyed helping people.

He also repaired his own car and those of several of his neighbour's. He never trusted the local garage to do the job properly. He had been fitting new brake pads and shoes to his neighbour's car all afternoon and gave it a thorough check at the same time. The car he thought, was in very good condition for its age.

He went into his house, cleaned up thoroughly and went back to the car. It started first time. Parking it in his neighbours drive, he rang the door bell. Mr Palmer, answered the door and greeted Purcell like a son. He asked him in for a drink, but Purcell still had some work to do on his own car, so he excused himself and returned home.

It was now dark and cold, so he drove the car into the garage. Its engine was misfiring and needed tuning. He placed a pipe over the exhaust and the other end outside the garage, so he could run the engine without the worry of exhaust gases. Then he set to work, using an electronic tester, until he traced the fault to one weak plug lead. He replaced the suspect lead from his ample store of spares. He connected his timing light carefully to the battery and the plug lead,

loosening the nut locking the distributor. He started the engine, jammed the accelerator cable at fifteen hundred revs per minute and gently adjusted the distributor until the timing was precise.

He revved the engine slightly to check its accuracy. It ran on a little so he corrected the adjustment to the distributor. Purcell turned off the engine and tightened up the locking nut on the distributor. Finally he removed the timing light from the battery and closed the bonnet, turning he sensed the presence of a man behind him.

Swinging round he found the man standing five feet away from him. He did not speak but swiftly removed a cylindrical object from his pocket. With an outstretched arm he aimed at Purcell's face: gas. He lost consciousness. The man put on a breathing mask and went to work putting Purcell's limp body into the car. Using the opened back door of the car he wound down the window one and a half inches, inserted the loose pipe Purcell had used to clear the exhaust fumes from the garage, making sure of its connection to the exhaust.

He went to the front, starting the engine he checked the fuel gauge. Wasting no time he turned out the light, shut the garage door and disappeared down the road to his parked car.

Fifteen minutes later, Purcell recovered from the knockout gas. Still groggy, with the exhaust fumes choking him, it took all his strength to open the car door. Eventually managing to push it open he stumbled out of the car, desperately trying to get his bearings. The fumes, now released into the garage, overpowered him and he slumped over the bonnet of his car, falling again into unconsciousness.

Next day his neighbour, having failed to hear him leave for work at his usual time, checked to see if he was all right. When he opened the garage door, he found Purcell still slumped over the bonnet: dead. The acrid fumes of the exhaust filling the air with danger.

In a considerable state of shock Mr Palmer rang the police to report the accident.

Those were Holder's first two portraits of facts which gave him a three dimensional view of the incidents. More and more, he began to believe that all these suicides were casualties in a clandestine battle, perhaps the last in the cold war. For, whoever won the race with an armed and working 'Star Wars' system, would rule the planet.

Russia had concentrated too much effort on being in space and not controlling it. America was now in an unassailable position to control space. 'Star Wars' had made sure of that. Could it be that Holder was looking at the last attempt to catch up with Western technology?

CHAPTER 4.

At ten o'clock that day, listening to the car radio, Holder first heard about the sudden death of Daniel Kershaw; it sounded like a bizarre car accident. A few moments later, he remembered that Space Projects Limited, the company where Daniel Kershaw worked, was a subsidiary of Advanced Laser Technology.

Turning his car round, he headed West. An hour later he reached the derelict farmhouse, parked his car and walked over to the crowd of officials standing round the crash scene. The fire engines had gone but a team of fire brigade inspectors busied themselves while many policemen stood around in groups chatting together or examining the debris.

Holder approached the Chief Constable and showed his police press pass card.

"David Holder, free-lance journalist. Can you tell me anything about the accident?"

The Chief Constable looked at him closely for a moment, then replied;

"Sorry, no comment until we have sorted through the debris and had a chance to assess the wreckage. Nasty one this, could take some time; about one and a half to two hours at a rough guess. You're welcome - though please let me finish and stay on the right side of the barriers."

Holder decided to take a closer look at the remains of the car. "What a mess," he uttered aloud. Two petrol cans lay at the back of the wrecked car, badly twisted by the heat. Only the detached rear number plate remained intact catapulted from the car on impact. What the crash had not obliterated the fire had consumed. Surely no-one in their right mind could have committed suicide in this way. They would have to be certifiable. For twenty minutes he searched the scene for anything that could offer a clue. The task was fruitless. He went back to the car to make some notes. In all his working life he had never visited a scene that had so little to offer and he couldn't help feeling that was intended. The presence of the two petrol cans confirmed that and troubled him. Why?

The police ranks increased by two men. Holder recognised one from past encounters: the officer from the security services with hypnotic eyes. He seemed to be available at a moments notice each time. Soon they were having a heated discussion with the Chief Constable. After ten minutes the Chief Constable went over to the Officer in charge and spoke to him. The Officer summoned his men.

The statement was very predictable. Holder had now covered several similar deaths and was quicker getting to the scene this time. The security service must be improving to spread their blanket of secrecy

and dis-information so quickly. Unless they had prior knowledge. Was it really state security?

The Chief Constable began his statement.

"Morning gentlemen. We have had a particularly gruesome task examining the wreckage of this car. As you can see it's going to be difficult to glean any information from the remains. We are trying to get a picture of the events leading up to the crash. We know the car was heading up the road and did a sharp U-turn into the slip road leading to this building. Why it accelerated to around seventy miles an hour before hitting the corner of the building remains a mystery."

"We know the owner's name and address. We are assuming he was the driver. It was Daniel Kershaw. A development engineer working at Space Projects Ltd. of Ascot. His home address, as is usual in these circumstances, will be withheld until the next of kin have been informed. Thank you gentlemen."

Holder thought: his first task was to contact the family, but before leaving he must examine the road where the 'U' turn took place. He walked up the slip road to the junction and there, sure enough, he found a set of skid marks turning into the slip road.

He recalled advice received many years ago from a very wise and respected police officer, on how to read tyre marks. He studied the black deposits carefully and to his amazement he found two distinct sets. One was from a radial type tyre. The other was much lighter, a town and country tyre, fitted on Land Rovers or Range Rovers. Both sets were fresh and made at roughly the same time. This proved his suspicion that the horrific scene was neither an accident nor a suicide.

Holder returned to his car convinced of foul play. He must now locate the family. It was best to get there early. Experience had taught him that it paid him to catch people off guard. Though he hated this part of his job, it was essential, but often wondered how he would feel about such an intrusion were he in their place.

Twenty-five minutes later he arrived in Winchester. Parked his car, went into the post office, looked through the local directory for Daniel Kershaw and to his surprise found him in a village on the city outskirts. Maybe his luck was turning: never before had he found an address that easily.

The house stood on the edge of the village, surrounded by trees and shrubs bursting forth in spring splendour. The gravelled drive was long, leading to a spacious Edwardian style house with a detached double garage. Holder noticed there was no sign of the police so he must break the news gently. He rang the door bell and an elderly lady answered. She dressed well and despite her surprise, carried elegant charm. Holder introduced himself then explained gently,

"I'm afraid I am the bearer of very bad news."

The woman nodded. He read the knowledge already in her eyes.

"Come in. Who do you represent?"

"To be honest I'm a free-lance journalist."

"But the police assured me that no-one was given the address."

"That's true, I found your address from the telephone directory. I am sorry to bother you at such a time, Mrs. Kershaw but I need all the information I can get in relation to your husband's death. May I explain."

"You are mistaken, Mr. Holder. I am not Daniel Kershaw's wife. I am his mother-in-law. His wife is out at the moment and not due back till this afternoon. My name is Mrs. Powers."

"I'm terribly sorry." Holder paused. "This is important."

"It's an understandable mistake," replied Mrs Powers, "but I don't see how I can be of any help to you. I am dreadfully upset by Daniel's death and I just do not know how to tell Janet when she returns."

Holder identified deeply with this dignified woman.

"It usually takes time to sink in. The initial shock is like an anaesthetic and a stiff drink really does help." She was beginning to trust him.

"How wise you are, Mr Holder. I will certainly take your advice."

Holder recognised the tone of her voice had relaxed. He risked a question.

"Did your son-in-law have any obvious problems or worries?"

"He learned recently that his mother had terminal cancer. That saddened him. Other than that, he seemed to be on top of the World. He was enjoying a lot of success at work on a top secret development that he could not tell us about."

"Did he have any close friends at work?"

"There was one he always called his father confessor. He used to have a drink in a pub just outside Camberley with him on his journey home from work on Friday's. His name was Jack; Jack Farr or Parr, something like that." She thought before adding, "Daniel always said it relaxed him so he could enjoy his weekends."

This was the information he needed. Holder thanked Mrs. Powers, comforted her on the way out and started his drive back to Ascot. He arrived at Space Projects by Two-fifteen; gate-house security was tight. No-one entered unless invited. He showed his press pass and asked to see the personnel manager. He waited at least ten minutes to hear that he was not available. Holder then asked to see the press liaison officer. Two minutes later the gate rose, he entered the visitor's car park and his escort took him to his office.

The press officer was aggressive, young and too sure of himself by half. Holder spoke first.

"I am here to look into the death of one of your employees, Daniel Kershaw, killed on the way to work this morning in unusual circumstances."

The press officer curtly replied, "I don't think so. The police have advised us that it was an ordinary car crash. It's a great shame. He was a top rate development manager. "

"There seems more to the accident than meets the eye. What I have come to establish is details of his work and a description of the project he has just finished."

"I'm afraid I am not in a position to tell you details. This firm works on highly sensitive material and it is all classified information covered by the official secrets Act."

The curtain had fallen. Holder avoided any mention of Farr or Parr. He thanked the young man and left. He would have to find 'Jack' the hard way.

Hunger overtook curiosity. He drove into Camberley and parked. Taking his map book with him to study the area carefully, he found a Kentucky fried take-away to satisfy his appetite.

He pondered over the map, remembered that Kershaw met Jack in a pub just outside Camberley. That narrowed the likelihood to four main towns. Bracknell, Wokingham, Reading and Basingstoke assuming Kershaw drove towards home.

He decided to take the route that Kershaw used, the A30 to Basingstoke. Fifteen miles and twenty minutes later he arrived, found the nearest phone box and thumbed through another directory. No Mr Jack Parr or Farr. It was near the end of the working hours at Space Projects; he decided to backtrack and call in each pub. By the time he reached the outskirts of Camberley it would be opening time. The third pub was an inn that looked inviting from the road, between Blackwater and Camberley. He ordered a pint and struck up a conversation with the barmaid. When the moment seemed right he asked her;

"Do you have a customer called Jack Parr or Farr?"

"Jack Parr, I'll say we do, this is his home! He'll be in any minute. Always dead on six is our Jack. He has two double scotches and then he goes. Except on Fridays, when he meets a friend."

She was right. Three minutes later Jack entered, looking grim, took a seat at the bar and ordered a double scotch.

"Have this one on me," said Holder.

"Thank you," he replied. "I need this one badly. Today I learned that a friend met with a horrific accident. I fear it was a ruthlessly planned and executed murder."

"What makes you think that?" Asked Holder

"I can't explain."

"Try telling me." Holder reached in his pocket and pulled out his press pass card. "I'm a grizzled hack-worse, a free-lance-if you can convince me, well, you'll convince anybody." He hesitated.

"Let's find a quiet seat."

"Where shall I begin?" asked Parr, trying to gather his thoughts. "You may or may not have heard the news today, but there was a dreadful accident this morning. My colleague, Daniel Kershaw, an associate from work was said to have committed suicide, but I know that he was murdered for what he knew." Parr shook as he spoke, driven by emotion and rage. His drink was disappearing fast.

Holder rose and reached for his empty glass. "I'll get us both a fill up and then you can tell me all about your friend." He ordered a full bottle of scotch and a soda siphon. He did not want to have to get up again during this discussion. Parr's eyes opened wide when he saw the bottle, then gratefully accepting its presence half filled both glasses with whisky and topped them up with soda.

"To give you the background," Parr continued. "I work at Space Projects. Daniel Kershaw was my projects manager. Over the years he became like a younger brother to me. We used to meet every Friday night, at this pub, for what Daniel called his unwinding chat. It was most important to him. He was a lively man, full of drive and energy. About six months ago he hit some snags, not with his work here but with a project he was managing for the parent company. The company use Senior staff for other projects because of their specialist knowledge. He worked on this one for nearly two years. Then they hit a snag. Daniel solved it eventually...but that day he was very low. He had a lot to drink which loosened him up more than usual. For the first time, he began to tell me about his work down at Advanced Laser Technology. This major development involved a very sophisticated, mobile laser defence weapon that is adaptable. It is suitable for use on a moving transporter, a submarine or a ship and guided onto the target by laser and satellite diversion.

"Keep going," smiled Holder.

"This was the firing power behind a very elaborate command and control system. It occupied Daniel, this was his specialised area. He was probably the best in the World. Before he joined the team they tested several guidance systems. Apparently early on they had some pretty nasty accidents, while tests were being carried out, somewhere in Wales."

Holder seemed to remember reading an article about a house that had lost its roof. There hadn't been a storm or any other apparent explanation. He must look into this later.

"When he started on the project he realised that the workers making up this immensely sophisticated weapon knew little of the details relating to the next man's work. The whole operation was segmented. Passes were required to go from one segment to another. None of them knew much about the entire program."

"Did that apply to everyone?"

"The only exceptions were a few top scientists, computer analysts and senior managers, like Daniel, who had carte blanche access, but had been sworn to complete secrecy."

"OK."

"The problem that confronted them when he joined the team was simply that of directional firing. It seemed amateur radio signals diverted the beam, impairing its accuracy. The accidents happened several years before he joined the project, during its early testing period. This fault delayed the development for the want of a solution to this problem. Four top analysts and computer guidance experts had already tried and failed to tame the beast. One was a brilliant young Asian, a computer systems analyst.

Daniel came along, changed the whole direction of the research and in two and a half years came up with an answer."

"Did you help on this project?"

"No, he received help from a lady scientist from America who brought over a remarkable discovery. When I tell you what it was you won't believe me."

Parr sat back, drank deeply from his glass, leant forward and continued;

"If I said she came from America with a hand held laser weapon straight out of the comic strips what would you say?" Before Holder had time to answer he continued, "you would say I was mad or drunk or something but that was exactly what she had. This happened before Daniel came onto the scene, but none of the other experts could make anything of it. Daniel was something quite special. He had a very logical advanced mind, combined with a vast depth of knowledge. About six months ago he had this soul searching talk with me. What he said next frightened me and has prompted me to say what I did when I met you at the bar."

"What was that?" Questioned Holder.

"An American lady professor. A member of the previous research team, who tried to solve Daniel's problem, died in a mysterious suicide. That brilliant Asian I told you about was another. Daniel suspected foul play with at least two of them. He thought that when their usefulness ceased someone, killed them.

"Are you saying he thought once they were no longer any use to the project, they were killed?"

"Yes. That's what it seemed like at the time. After a few weeks he recovered from his depression and perhaps decided that he had been over emotional at the

time, but his last remark has haunted me all day and I cannot get it out of my mind."

"What was that?"

"He said, I could never commit suicide, because what ever seems bad today looks totally different tomorrow. So if they say I have, don't believe them."

"That was an amazing prediction. Do you think that statement meant he was frightened?"

Parr took another long sip from his drink, "I don't know."

"Your secrets are safe with me. Don't worry."

"If you are ever in the area you will find me in here early every weekday evening. Good luck with your story! Thanks for your shoulder."

Holder was convinced the elaborate plot to kill Daniel Kershaw was executed by a specialist team from a private security company with skills equal to the highly trained members of the special air service. All the signs of thoroughness led him to this belief.

He remembered the first alarm when he heard the ten o'clock news that morning. If his radio had been off, today may never have revealed its secrets. Journalism was, he concluded, ninety per cent luck and ten per cent intuition. He had a story. Could he make it stand up and also live to tell the tale?

Holder once again sketched all the known facts relating to Kershaw's death. Parr gave him enough details to work out a mental replay.

Kershaw was an early riser who loved to take his dog for a walk before breakfast. He found it cleared his mind for his day's work, using exercise to keep himself alert. His job was very demanding, having climbed to the top at a remarkable pace. Nevertheless there was always someone else ready to pounce if he showed any sign of flagging during working hours. He was very successful with his latest defence project. It won him acclaim and the promise of an even brighter future. The only cloud on his horizon was news recently received, that his mother had terminal cancer. It saddened him to think that she would not live to see him rise even higher. After all she showed great pride in her son's success, ample payment for the sacrifices made to give him the best education.

His job, a satellite project manager at Space Projects near Ascot, brought its rewards. He had a lovely wife and a beautiful old house in three acres of land set in the depths of Hampshire countryside. He was lucky.

At six-fifteen he was back home and devouring the large breakfast his wife prepared while he walked. He found a good breakfast set him up for his mentally strenuous day. He survived on coffee until he returned home for dinner.

His only indulgence was his drink with Jack Parr on The way home, every Friday evening. Parr was an assistant at Space Projects, working closely with him. Not an ambitious man, he was happy to follow orders, but a good engineer. Kershaw confided in him like a brother. He had no-one else he could talk to about sensitive material without breaking the Official Secrets Act. Jack, acted as a stop valve for his silent frustrations.

Having finished his breakfast Kershaw collected his briefcase, kissed his wife good-bye and started on his long journey to Ascot. He took a twisting, turning road through beautiful countryside. On a fresh spring morning, the sun was still below the horizon, but its imminent appearance created a glow through the early mist. After twenty minutes, he passed some road repair lights. Suddenly coming round one of the sharpest bends, he braked hard; a Range Rover was parked halfway across the road with its bonnet open.

The two occupants were examining the engine. Kershaw asked if he could help. The tall man smiled.

"I am afraid we have had a bit of a mishap. Could you possibly take my friend to the nearest garage?"

"Of course," said Kershaw, "jump in and I'll give you a lift down the road." He unlocked the door.

The stocky little man entered. Kershaw was about to engage gear when his head was forced back and in the same movement a blow struck just under his Adam's apple. It hit the hypoid bone causing suffocation in seconds. The man crossed over to the driver's side, while his partner bent into the passenger side to move the motionless body. They propped him up in the passenger seat.

The tall man returned to the Range Rover while the shorter one started Kershaw's car, ready to move. There was just the diversion sign to collect half a mile down the road. They cancelled the road lights by remote control, leaving the equipment to be removed by a third man.

They stopped at the diversion. The morning rush hour was still three quarters of an hour away. They disassembled the sign and put it in the back of the Range Rover. While it was open they transferred two cans of petrol to the boot of Kershaw's car, then they drove off in convoy for three and a half miles until they came to a slip road on the right. At the bottom was a disused farmhouse. They did a fast U turn and stopped behind a small hedge shielding the slip road from the main highway. The Range Rover stopped with Kershaw's car slightly to the rear, but along side.

Kershaw's body was quickly transferred to the driver's seat with his legs carefully on one side.

The engine still running, the hand-brake was released. They opened the driver's window pushing the car up parallel so the window was directly below the front passenger side window of the Range Rover. The well built man then transferred himself into the Range Rover, picking up a broom handle from the back, while climbing across into the front passenger seat. Opening the window he lent out with his full upper body, steadying himself by hooking his feet round the passenger seat.

"Move." He shouted, as he pressed the pusher to the accelerator pedal, controlling the steering with his other hand as they moved.

They accelerated together towards the diner, building up speed gradually: thirty, forty, fifty, sixty, seventy miles an hour. About twenty-five yards from the building he gave the steering a sharp tug to the left, directing the speeding car straight at the building and withdrawing himself and the pusher simultaneously. The Range Rover swerved to the right avoiding the impact and seconds later the car crashed into the side corner of the building. Bricks and rubble from the building spread everywhere. What was left of the car, a twisted wreck, burst into flames reaching above the dilapidated roof of the building.

The Range Rover disappeared into the distance to rendezvous with the third man.

CHAPTER 5.

Holder knew he had to decide where to go next. He spent the rest of the day looking at his notes and assembling the facts. By doing this he found it easier to plot a way forward. His greatest guides were his verbal sketches built from the bricks of his research. It was escalating into a mammoth inquiry and taking up more and more of his time. That didn't earn money. Unless he made a break-through soon, very reluctantly, he knew that he must tackle some stories for which editors pay! Holder cleared his dining table, laid out all his notes and began to map the path forward.

So far he had counted fourteen deaths, including Jane Armstrong. This death was not in the same style nor perhaps for the same reason, although the assassins could possibly be the same persons. He felt sure the killings were done by a team.

He was also sure at least six of these deaths were not suicide but murder by persons unknown. His most pressing task was to unmask the assassins. Setting it as his number one priority, he decided to investigate security companies involved in industrial espionage, specially those having dealings with large companies or governments both national and foreign. These companies were the most likely base for his assassin.

His second priority was to trace the details of the American scientist involved with Daniel Kershaw's development. This might involve going to the States.

His third priority was to check out the rumours in Wales about strange events in the Newhaven area and the American occupation of Brawdy airport. Sightings had taken place that could tie in with the details Parr disclosed in relation to the accidents that happened while testing the laser weapon. In its early stages there had been complete secrecy about the activities at Brawdy. Once a coastal patrol air base, now it had a two mile long run-way to accept the largest US military aircraft, in a place where weather is often a problem for planes. There was something secret going on and it might tie in with laser development. It was the sort of remote area used for such research and the American involvement was in line with Anglo American co-operation.

The fourth priority required a visit to America to check out Parr's evidence relating to the laser weapon used to further development at Advanced Laser Technology. This, if true, was going to be very difficult to investigate. The majority of people now accept the possibility of laser warfare, but governments in most countries, for reasons best known to themselves, have suppressed even basic information on its use.

themselves, have suppressed even basic information on its use.

Holder then listed his second stage priorities. He wanted to visit Daniel Kershaw's wife, Parr and Armstrong; then prepare and submit a summary to the MOD.

At this point he had the basis of a very exciting story with far reaching political implications. Political interference was not his aim, quite the opposite. However if his suspicions were true it must lead to some serious bloodletting in political circles, followed by a string of denials as the mandarins of power struggle to pass the buck. All this occurred because of their incompetence in controlling the Russian intrusion.

One question was answered - the thrust of his story. Somebody, perhaps a large corporation or national agency, not necessarily British: felt at liberty to hire assassins and the government - unless also involved - seemed powerless. Worse, it seemed under instructions to wipe clean the killer's trail after each fresh victim. Either the government was involved - or the government must stop the murders. How many lesser crimes were committed by these 'security' companies?

Despite this danger he would write his story to stop the type of ruthless business that offers its services unlimited to anyone who can pay. His aim was to neutralise these so called security companies who specialise in criminal acts for financial gain while protected by governments.

Holder decided to concentrate on his priority, tracing the assassins. This was going to be a difficult

He was not looking for ordinary security companies but for those few specialists who undertook work of a highly clandestine nature: phone tapping, confidential file photography and industrial espionage in all its forms. He was looking for companies prepared to handle extremes. Even covert operations for governments. They might traffic in mercenaries for private armies and on the legal but specialised side, protect oil rigs or provide anti-subversive experts. He was looking for a company who employed men conforming to SAS levels of expertise and ruthlessness.

Holder knew that these firms use ex-SAS men to carry out many of the more specialised demands of their clients. Ex-SAS men already possessed the skills to cover all eventualities. Most ex-soldiers busied themselves with perfectly legal contracts such as training staff for company security and were a good source for free-lance journalists, not to mention TV script-writers. However this looked quite different.

He decided to consult the computer bank and find out the names of the firms involved in this type of work. John answered the phone with his usual opening remark;

"How can I help you, dear boy?"

"I have an unusual request. Can you scan your files for all security firms involved in company espionage, phone tapping, bugging and supplying specialist services such as oil rig protection and mercenaries? I need as much information on these companies as you can give me."

"What's up old boy? Girl friend giving you trouble? Can't be that bad, can it?"

"Can't you ever be serious, John? It is to do with my investigation into the deaths of the scientists if you must know."

"I'll search my files. Can you give me about half an hour? I'm in the middle of another job at the moment."

"That's fine, but get back to me as quickly as you can. I'm waiting to get on with it."

"You are all the same, you guys. Yesterday is too late. I'll do my best."

Holder sat down and pondered his next move. He could interview each company until he found a lead but that was a clumsy approach. He must not expose himself at this stage. He could ask around amongst his SAS contacts and see if he could find a lead that way.

This had its dangers, but if he stuck to the SAS man he had cultured he covered himself against enquiries getting back to the wrong people. He might try to infiltrate Advanced Laser Technology and gain information. It was such a large and diverse company that the chance of contacting someone who possessed the information was remote and much time would be wasted in the meantime.

A simple and safe way to do some research without exposing his identity was to use a little bluff. If he phoned the various companies saying that he was from Advanced Laser Technology's accounts department and asked the right questions, he could judge by the reply whether they invoiced their services to that company. If the bluff failed he would lose nothing.

He decided to try his SAS contact first. Then, if that failed to produce the answer, he would go for the fourth option. The success of this ploy depended upon the remoteness of the account's department from the main operation.

The phone rang and John's cheerful voice was heard to say;

"Is that you, old boy?"

"Yes. Thanks for getting your skates on, what have you found for me?"

"Quite all right old thing, all part of the service. I have four names for you. They have all been involved in one or more of the activities you listed and are all contenders for your jackpot.

First we have S.S.S or Sarison Security Services. Listed under surveillance, they have a record of involvement in industrial espionage. They featured in a case last year when they allegedly used an ex-SAS man to crack a nut, escaping prosecution due to lack of evidence. They come from South London. The boss is an ex SAS man called Major Pearlman."

"Doesn't seem our type."

"Second we have O.S.S. or Operation Security Service. They seem to specialise in operating off shore. They do most of their work in the North Sea. No record of any misdemeanours. One firm tried to sue them for industrial espionage, but the case failed in court. Their office is in Southall. The boss is unknown by the fountain of knowledge."

"Probably too specialist for our man."

"Third we have S.O.E. or Security Operation Executive. They are a sinister organisation. They have reportedly hired mercenaries for Angola and lately Nicaragua. They have a record of involvement in industrial espionage on five separate occasions and use ex-S.A.S. men as bodyguards for their clients. Their office keeps moving. Our latest records show

Richmond but this may now be out of date. The boss is a man called Major Smythe, who claims to have been in the S.A.S."

"That's more hopeful."

"Fourth we have SAS. or Sentinel Armed Securities. Their sales line is: 'Any security problem undertaken'. Their name appears several times in relation to mercenaries. It is a known secret that they work for governments. They have a very clean record in the courts. The boss of the firm is Major William Strange and their headquarters is in London."

"They seem promising too. Thanks John. You have done a marvellous job. I'll mention you in dispatches."

"I'd rather you didn't, old boy. I can't stand the sight of blood, especially mine. Good luck with your search, but for Christ's sake be careful! You are playing with the big boys now and they know how to play dirty. I don't want to see you as one of my statistics in the fountain of knowledge."

Holder took twenty minutes finding the phone numbers of all four firms. He then decided to go down to the Admiral Codrington, in Chelsea where he usually met his contact for a drink and a chat. He knew it would be a long session because this guy only loosened up when he had a few and that usually took at least an hour.

As he entered the bar he spotted Michael Neville sitting in his usual spot, chatting to the landlord. Holder pulled up a stool and asked Michael what he would like to drink. A ritual he performed even knowing his friend's tipple, in this case a Bloody Mary.

Neville, in his early thirties, was clean shaven with military style short cropped hair. He was five feet ten inches tall, trained to the peak of physical fitness and well dressed in a casual way. His face was extraordinarily forgettable, a mutable mask. That was an asset in his business.

He was in a particularly melancholy mood, as if he had the weight of the World on his shoulders. Holder sat with him for half an hour chatting about nothing in particular. Then, when the pub seemed to be getting busy, he suggested that they should move to a more comfortable table in the back room.

The garden room was an old extension furnished with white tables and chairs. It was slightly tatty in its decor. In the summer the glass roof gave it a certain charm. It was not very popular with the customers, at this time of the year used only as an overflow if the pub became very crowded. They found they were alone which suited Holder's purpose well. Neville was a trooper in the twenty-first SAS. He never married, knowing that the type of work he did was not conducive to family life, but sometimes he became broody. He was a deep thinker. This was his flaw. The S.A.S. system requires complete control of the mind. Holder sensed that Neville wanted to spill out his thoughts and encouraged him, plying him with drink till it relaxed him.

"You know David I have known you for five years and although you are from the gossip department, I feel I can talk to you as a friend. God knows I need to talk. I'm knackered at the moment. We are kept on a constant state of alert. We are ready at any time for anything to happen throughout the World, from high-jacks to surveillance."

"You mean that you are kept on a state of alert constantly?"

"Yes. Our training is such that we are taught to react rather than to waste valuable time weighing the decision. In our trade a split second can be the difference between life and death. We have to be prepared for instant reaction at any time. We live on an adrenaline high. There is no relaxation while training. This pub and my bed are the only escapes I have. I've given up any thought of finding a steady girl let alone a wife - and I'm thirty."

"Life can't be that bad?"

"Despite this, I am very happy in my job and would not have missed it for the World. I have just been back to Hereford for re-assessment. For the first time, my reflexes have deteriorated. They are not yet below acceptable levels, but dangerously close. It is only a question of time before the service will no longer require me. I accept their reasoning. Anyone sub-standard can be a danger to the team."

"I can understand that."

"Nevertheless, this has made me think about the future. You see, the service is the best when it comes to training, but when it comes to putting us out to grass, it's hard to switch off."

"I can see that. What about a job in the real World?"

"For the first time I have realised there is no other job that will satisfy my adrenaline addiction. It's like a drug and our training makes sure we get regular and adequate supplies. The only jobs available that could generate that level of energy are as a mercenary, or working for one of the shady security companies. A lot of good men end up there."

"At least you can make a use of ten years' soldiering," ventured Holder, knowing there was a

chance of obtaining some answers without arousing suspicion.

"Depends on their operation. One I know specialises in oil rig work and its protection. This would be an acceptable job, but I can't see myself pinned down on a oil rig for long. Not my life style. Two others I know do all sorts of dirty work. They are not above murder for political or financial ends. Who wants to tackle this dirty work for them? One is a firm called Security Operation Executive and the other is Sentinel Armed Securities. They are both run by ex S.A.S. men and they both work for governments. I haven't told you that, remember. We are not meant to know that, but the word gets around."

"Not a word will pass my lips!"

"These firms recruit direct from the S.A.S. and according to rumour, have open access to all retired troop records. They also recruit at places like Aldershot, where there used to be a particular pub called the Queen's Head, well known as a recruiting centre for Mercenaries. That is another side of their business. They supply personnel for places like Angola and lately Nicaragua. Rumour has it the CIA is behind the recruiting campaign."

"Do you mean to say the ministry of defence know about this and turn a blind eye?"

"Yes. My Christian belief does not allow me to work for anything but a legal army and I despise these firms and the manner in which they operate. They are not doing my fellow ex-troopers any favours by employing them. They turn them into the best spies and the foulest murderers. Where else can they go to get their adrenaline addiction satisfied? They are Service junkies that the Service has conveniently

forgotten. For the first time in my life I feel displaced."

Holder realised that he had never thought of the assassins as anything but murderers. Sitting in front of him was someone who could easily be branded that way. Yet he was a likeable human being with justifiable fears for his future. He could jump either way. The State was about to discard him just as a council tips its waste without first defusing the time bomb they planted inside him. This was not just tragic. It was lunacy. Surely the State, that had used psychology to produce his mental discipline, should be able to de-program him when he retires?

Holder talked for another hour trying to reassure Neville that everything would work out, but he couldn't say it with conviction. There was no answer, unless Neville wound-down, or spent a small fortune on psychotherapy.

He almost forgot the information he came to obtain. It had come out during conversation, but Neville's personal story was so powerful that Holder had, for once, allowed his work to slip to the back of his mind.

Next morning He woke with a hangover, rose, showered and cooked his breakfast, then decided to ring the two security firms mentioned in their rambling discussion. First he rang Security operations Executive. The operator answered with a change of number but Holder recalled that they moved frequently. He rang the new number.

A woman answered. "Can I help?"

"Yes, Accounts department, Advanced Laser Technology. I have your invoice to hand, but it does not quote our project number. Could we please have this? We need to know which project to charge it against."

"Just a minute, I check out the records."

Holder prayed that he had sounded convincing. Four minutes later the girl came back, sounding perplexed.

"I can find no record of an invoice to your company. Are you sure you have one from us? "

"Yes", said Holder, "dated the twenty-fifth of the fourth eighty-seven."

"Well, we have no record. Could you send me a copy and I will check it out?"

"Yes OK, thank you." Holder put the phone down and breathed again. That was lucky. He was now certain that it was not that firm.

Next he rang Sentinel Armed Securities in London and asked exactly the same questions of their accounts department. This time the girl asked;

"Which office are you from?"

Holder thought for a moment. "Head office."

"Just a minute." The girl left him on hold.

"I can't find the invoice, but if it is from your head office, I'm told that it is charged to the Managing Director's account and no project number is quoted. You should know that. Who am I talking to?"

"I'm new here. I haven't quite got the hang of all the rules yet and there never seems to be someone around to ask when you need them. Sorry to bother you."

Holder put down the phone. This firm killed Jane Armstrong. Secrecy did not seem to extend into the accounts department.

CHAPTER 6.

"Morning John. It's me once more, wanting the impossible - yesterday."

"What's new? Don't you always, dear boy? What can I do for you this time?"

"An American scientist, supposedly on holiday in this country, died in North Wales. I seem to remember she fell from the balcony of her holiday home. I don't know the date, or her name. Will it be possible to trace this story?"

"Dear boy. We do the impossible immediately. Miracles, that's a different matter. They take longer. Leave it to me. I'll cast my spell and see what comes up. Ring you back as soon as the crystal ball clears."

Holder put the phone down and remembered that this was the second death involving a fall from a balcony. The other one was abroad. Was there a link? He waited over an hour before John rang back.

"Sorry old boy, it took a long time, but the crystal ball refused to clear. I can find no mention of your lady doctor. Without the date or her name I am chasing shadows. Failure is miserable, but I shall have to bear it. Why don't you try the American Embassy, or go to North Wales and ask a local paper?"

"Thanks John I'll do that." Holder put the phone down and headed for the American Embassy.

He booked in to see the press liaison officer and they ushered him into a waiting area. Twenty minutes later they called his name and escorted him into a large office. There was a huge desk at the far end of the room, behind which hung a picture of the President and an assembly of flags. Sitting behind the desk was a man in his mid thirties wearing a designer suit, with heavy check patterning and a vulgar tie.

Speaking with a slow American drawl, he appeared polite and courteous;

"How can we help?"

"I am trying to trace details of an American scientist who died in North Wales between two and four years ago. Unfortunately I do not know her name. I know that she had a doctorate and that she was reported to have committed suicide while on holiday in North Wales by jumping from the balcony of her holiday house."

"I see. You are not giving me much to go on. What is your interest in this matter?"

"I am doing research into suicide." Replied Holder, hopefully.

"Just a minute." He pressed a button and a small man with horn rimmed glasses came into the large room. They spoke so quietly that Holder could not isolate their words.

"He will try and find the information you require but your details are sketchy to say the least, so I can't say for sure that we'll be able to help."

Holder sat talking to the press liaison officer until the researcher came back into the room. He walked up to the desk with a file in his hand and started talking again in a very low voice. Holder just made out the wording on the front of the file that said 'classified': he was about to hear a tall tale.

"We have searched our files containing all American deaths in the U.K. over the last five years and there is no record of a lady scientist dying in Wales. Sorry. Might I suggest that you try the British police."

Holder thanked the press liaison officer. A military guard escorted him back to the main hall.

As he left the building he sensed he was being followed. Instead of going to his car, parked in a side street off Grosvenor square, Holder decided to walk round Mayfair and see if he could shake off his tail: try as he might, he could not lose him. The little man stuck like a limpet, at a respectable distance. Holder headed for the bustle of Oxford street where he calculated it must be easier to lose him.

After half an hour the tail was still there. In desperation he tried the tube station. Running down the escalator he dived onto the train just as the doors were closing. Emerging at the next station, he walked down Park Lane to his car, this time without escort. The investigation he was pursuing had international implications. The secrets must be important to afford them this degree of protection. Next day he started early to avoid the rush hour traffic on his long journey. Llanrwst, in the centre of North Wales, was his first destination.

As the tourist season had not yet started, guest houses were less than half full. He found a quaint, old-fashioned eating house, with waitresses dressed in traditional Welsh costumes and decided this would make a welcome change from fast food. The gentler side of Holder took a moment to regret the scarcity of such luxuries in his life.

He complimented the waitress on the meal and asked for directions to the Gazette offices. Entering the office he asked the receptionist for a meeting with the editor. She ushered him into a small office to wait.

Twenty minutes passed bye before a slight, grey-haired man in his middle forties introduced himself as Gareth Davies. Holder gave him his card and explained all that he knew about the American scientist.

"I seem to remember something about it," remarked Davies vaguely, "but I cannot for the life of me remember her name. That must have been three or four years ago. As far as I can recall she rented a holiday cottage down by Llyn Brenig. Definitely reported in our Local Gazette. I tell you what. Use this office and you are welcome to look through our back issues. They are all filed in date order. Sorry I can't be more specific but a lot of news passes through this office you know."

Holder thanked Davies and set about the laborious task of searching front pages. He started five years back; It was a monotonous task; he realised while reading the headlines that Wales, so remote from the capital, had exactly the same type of stories in their papers. The local scandals in Wales seemed more intense if anything. Perhaps that was just the telling.

For the rest of the afternoon he fingered through copy after copy, fearing that through monotony he might miss the vital article. When he reached closing time, only having covered a quarter of the back copies, he called it a day and walked back to his Hotel.

Next morning he was at the office when it opened to resume his necessary task. By lunch time he had reached February eighty-six, still without a result, he decided to invite the editor for a wet lunch at the local inn. Pleasant and genuinely friendly, Davies had come up the hard way in the press World, but had never been ambitious. His life style satisfied him, which he described as being the conscience of the community. He bore this label with respect for his fellow men and took an active and responsible interest in the local community and its issues. He rarely bothered with National politics. Yet as Holder related the outline of his investigation, he seemed to become quite engrossed.

"Keep reading," said Davies, "because, if my memory is right, that American girl rented a cottage. People don't move much round here - the owner is probably still there."

"You can't remember where?"

Davies shook his head. "Down by the lake is the best I can do."

After lunch Holder resumed his search. Around four o'clock he came across the article under the heading; 'American scientist plunges to her death.' Her name was Dr Merle Steiner. She lived in

California city, near the base of Muroc known as Edward's Air Force base, about seventy-five miles from Los Angeles. The paper described her as a systems analyst working under a Dr Bush, at Edward's Air Force Base in California. She had reportedly been on holiday in North Wales, where she rented a holiday house overlooking Llyn Brenig, a large lake in the middle of North Wales. The cottage belonged to a Meg Morgan and was situated on the West side of the lake.

He thanked Davies for his kindness and drove towards Llyn Brenig. He arrived there at five-thirty and found, to his surprise, three cottages. Not the traditional white washed walls and thatched roofs that adorn all holiday brochures, but modern, purpose built houses with large balconies overlooking the tranquil surface of a magnificent lake. What a beautiful place to live, he thought. No wonder nobody moves.

Megan Morgan answered the door. She ushered him into the front room and offered him a cup of tea. She was round faced, grey-haired and in her late fifties with rosy cheeks that balanced her pronounced Welsh forehead. She spoke with a gentle Welsh accent and Her nature seemed to blend with the tranquillity and beauty of the setting.

She came back into the room with a hot pot of tea and poured a strong brew.

"Now what can I tell you?" she asked.

"In August eighty-six an American scientist, Merle Steiner came to one of your houses for a holiday and met with a terrible accident. She fell from the balcony to the concrete patio below. I hope you can tell me all you know about her?"

She frowned for the first time.

"Well there isn't much to tell, really. She was a lovely lady. She came to me for the last three years, maybe three times a year, always alone. She seemed to like the solitude and peace. We're lucky really - living in such a beautiful valley. The year she met with that terrible accident she seemed so happy and contented. She told me her work was going well at last and she really seemed to be enjoying her break. She worked on secret defence work, you know. I have never told anyone that before."

"Was she on holiday from America?"

"Goodness me no, she was working at Advanced Laser Technology. That much I know. She did say she was on loan from her boss in America. I never believed she committed suicide as the papers said. She wasn't the type and she certainly was not outwardly depressed. It was either an accident or something worse."

"Why do you say that?"

"She loved just standing leaning on the balcony, soaking up the peace and beauty around her. If she became dizzy she might have fallen by accident. However earlier that day I saw two men around her house. One stared at me with hypnotic eyes. It put a chill down my spine, I can tell you. At first I thought they may be friends so I did nothing. It seemed as if they were watching the house so I went out to approach them. Just then they walked off down the road and I decided not to follow them. It could be nothing, but I have a feeling they had something to do with her death."

Holder recognised the discription of his man from security. Now he had reason to question his status.

Was he really from security? This was the first sighting before a murder took place and put his presence in a different light. Yet he had official access.

"Did you ever see these men again?"

"No I never did, but I still have an uneasy feeling about them. They were up to no good. I do hope you can solve this mystery. There is one other thing I must tell you. When this all happened, as you can imagine, the place was swarming with police and officials. After they had completed their search two plain clothes police came and spoke aggressively to me. Well I'm not used to that and in my own house as well! They didn't impress me one little bit."

"Were they local?"

"No - sounded from London."

"Foreigners?" Smiled Holder.

"We chapel folk can dig our toes in and I did. They wanted me to keep quiet about everything I knew relating to Dr Steiner. They said it was a security matter and therefore vital that nothing be said. Later I had a visit from an American who said virtually the same thing. I did not have any of their secrets. So why the fuss? Are they paranoid or something?"

"I suppose so," said Holder laughing. "Meg. I hope you don't mind me calling you Meg. You have been most helpful. Thank you. May I see the balcony before I go?"

"Just a minute I will get my coat. It gets a bit chilly in the evenings."

They went to the back of the third house and round to the patio directly under the balcony.

"It was here she fell," Meg Morgan pointed to the spot where the body was found. Holder then looked out over the lake. The sun was setting, changing the clouds from grey to pink to orange and it really was like heaven on earth. No one could wish to kill themselves here.

"Thanks Meg. If I can get some time off one of these days I would like to relax with this view. It's so peaceful, but not from this balcony."

In the morning he went to the morgue to check on the official details of Merle Steiner's death and found the records showing that the coroner judged her as having committed suicide.

There was no mention of the two prowlers in the report. Could this be another case of the authorities ignoring facts they didn't want to hear? the man with the hypnotic eyes was an important new lead.

Holder was now a step nearer to appreciating Merle Steiner's connection with Advanced Laser Technology. Would those with hard information talk? Experience from the last weeks made it clear that, on this side of the Atlantic, given suffocating government pressure, not to mention the risk of a car accident or suicide, nobody working for one of these high technology companies would talk with a free-lance reporter, unless they were morally shocked like Jack Parr. He would have to go to America to understand completely.

CHAPTER 7.

Holder wanted to find some connection between the strange reports from Wales and the testing of the laser weapon. Locals claimed that unidentified flying objects passed over a small area around Littlehaven. The quality of witnesses and number of sightings was, to say the least, impressive. Brawdy air base was just up the road. A squadron of the air force, mainly covering coastal patrol, occupied this air base, with some air to sea rescue helicopters. Due to the frequent poor weather they found their flights were constantly grounded.

When the government were looking for cut-backs, this base seemed a natural candidate for closure. The local population, although not large in numbers, derived their livelihood one way or another from the activities surrounding the air base. They put up a concerted fight against its closure.

Then suddenly, without consultation, the runway at Brawdy increased, making it two miles long, capable of accepting the largest transport planes in the World. At that point a command of the American air force moved into the local population: the authority passed it off as a response to local demand and after a while, the objections subsided. The local communities were again benefiting from the wealth generated by the air base.

This much Holder knew from articles written at the time. The strange thing was that the Unidentified Flying Objects had not created more interest. He concluded that acceptance was not part of life's rich pattern then as it is today. Coupled with this, people tended to be quiet about sightings because of the fear that others would think they were mad. Everything ultimately had an explanation. It was just a case of cutting through illusion, to the hard core of reality. What he was looking for in Wales was a definite link between the sightings of the craft and the use of the laser beams. Such a link would show some of the other happenings in a different light.

He arrived in Little Haven and asked for the location of the Cliff Top Hotel, booked in, went up stairs, unpacked and had a good soak. Much refreshed he came down to the bar for a well-earned drink. The bar was empty. He walked over to the long windows. The hotel had once been a stately home, made of solid stone, rather in the style of a small castle. It had large grounds and a car park with stables.

Holder looked towards the raging sea. In the distance, rocks stood proud, continually pounded by breaking waves. There was a gale blowing up with some force producing the sound of the wind and rain cascading in waves against the large bay windows of the bar room.

He sat on a stool at the bar, ordered a pint of lager and started to talk to the barmaid, who smiled, "I can tell you're not from around here. This is a normal end to the day, nothing like a storm. You will really know what a storm at sea is when you see one here."

"Tell me. Someone in the town was telling me about strange happenings in this area. He said some people saw strange space craft. Is that true?"

"Well, I myself have only been in this part of Wales for three years so I cannot speak from experience. I have heard it said that they visited this very hotel on several occasions. One landed in the car park! Goes back several years."

"Always interested me, so I have studied it in my spare time," encouraged Holder.

"People were seeing strange flying objects all over the place but particularly at the farm three miles away. A whole class of children, including their teacher, saw two people get out of a disc shaped object, inspect something in a field, then get back into the craft and fly away. The teacher still talks about the incident. I have a friend who heard the story first hand. The farm down the road frequently received visits from this craft and they experienced all sorts of other interference. Electrical faults were common. Their television kept burning out and wires in the house melted for no apparent reason. Eventually they decided to leave. Couldn't stand it any longer."

"Do you believe that - doesn't it all sound rather far-fetched?" Holder smiled encouragement at the girl.

"I don't know what to believe. The previous owner of this hotel was the same. He tried to make a business here but strange things kept happening. The electrical supply overloaded and fuses were blowing everywhere. He saw the craft on several occasions they say."

"Is that so?"

"One theory was that they came from the rocks out at sea. There is a piece of land that goes with this property. Rumour has it there is a tunnel under the sea, from this hotel to the rocks which dates back to smuggling days. A few people saw the flying objects disappear into the rocks and doors seemed to open to accommodate them. A report from a policeman in Little Haven mentions seeing an object come out of the rocks, fire beams across the sky and then retract again. Several people witnessed this happening."

"That is convincing."

"The worst two incidents occurred at roughly the same time. They build houses round here to withstand storms. On this occasion the weather was very calm. Yet this man came home to find the roof completely missing from his house. He also found that the wiring in his house was in a terrible mess." She paused.

Holder remembered the report on this incident.

"The second incident happened a few months later. The wife of this household was at home cooking her husband's evening meal, when a blinding flash occurred. When she recovered she found all the wiring in the house melted; the television burned out and even the car in the driveway was smoking! It had to be re-wired and never really worked properly again."

"Where can I find these two houses? I would like to talk to the owners. This intrigues me."

"Well there have been a number of people that have wanted to do the same, but shortly after the accidents at their homes the families both disappeared completely. They did not leave changes of address or contact any of their friends. They just left. There have been many rumours. Some suggested they were scared off by their experiences. Others that they were kidnapped by the craft. No-one really knows what happened to them."

"Mystery always builds fantasy to replace reality. Tell me, you said these flying objects were seen by several different people disapearing into the rocks. Are those the rocks out to sea in front of the hotel?"

"Yes, the very same. They're called Stack Rocks. Something else happened just before the sightings. They heard Strange rumblings all over this bay. They came at the same time each day and persisted for several weeks. Then they ceased. Again people offered many theories, from earthquakes to underground explosions. The government inspectors came down and after several months, presented an evasive report to the local community. All waffle!"

"You spoke about a policeman witnessing an object projecting out from the rock and firing beams. Does he still work locally?"

"No, he also disappeared without trace, just like the owners of the two damaged houses. It really is mysterious. When my parents bought the hotel I was dreading the thought of this place as a prison but now I'm enjoying the mysteries."

That explained her educated manner and the knowledge she possessed. She was twenty-five with auburn hair falling over her shoulders. Blessed with a clear complexion, she looked almost boyish and had a strange depth of beauty that attracted Holder.

"Has anyone been out to Stack Rocks to look for an entrance to the cave?"

"Not that I know. The weather is so bad. There are probably only ten days in the year that are calm enough to land on the rocks. A helicopter cannot get near enough to have a good look without the danger of being dashed against the rocks by a sudden gust. It really is unfriendly out there, you know."

Holder resolved to go to the cliff's edge and use his very powerful binoculars to get a better view of the rock face. That would have to wait until tomorrow.

"What do you know about Brawdy air base?"

"Now that's an interesting subject. Some of the local people reckon it was all put on by the US Air Force, to detract attention from what really was going on up there at Brawdy.

"Do you mean it was not the Nato base it was dressed up to be?"

"It was certainly very secret. When the Americans came, the place became secure, with a high level barrier and a constant patrol. They allowed no civilians onto the airfield and local business men needed passes even to enter the offices. You know that they lengthened the runway?"

"Yes."

"That was to take those enormous freight planes we see now and then. They seem to be doing underwater research in the ocean off the coast. It's a fact that the Americans in the base do not mix with the locals. Now that's odd, isn't it?"

"Yes." Holder knew that he must visit Brawdy.

"Tell me, have any strange craft been spotted recently, or were they concentrated around the time that the US air force moved in to Brawdy?"

"No, there have not been any trustworthy sightings for some years. The activities at Brawdy seemed to have slowed down too. I am told the local trader's supplies have been halved which indicates a large drop in American presence. I suppose it could be that the construction team have gone home and left the operators behind to man the base."

Holder thought for a minute and then asked.

"Do you think it is possible the US air force deliberately posed as spacemen from another planet to distract attention from their activities at Brawdy?"

"Now that's a thinker's question. I don't know. The base is being used, as far as local reports affirm, for oceanic research. Yet how do you explain away the presence of the craft in sightings by several people?"

"That is the million dollar question but many years of experience has taught me that there is always a logical answer, if only you can find it."

"I often thought it might have been a diversion planned by the Americans. However I always come back to the certainty of the craft existing."

"You certainly have the mind of a reporter. Ever thought of coming into the business?"

"Not really. I just like getting a good look at things and finding the facts. It's a sort of hobby of mine."

"Well, you have just come up with a lot of the ideas that I have been digging deeply to obtain and I have been in the business twenty-five years."

"I was sure you were a reporter. Are you famous?"

"I'm known in this business but you are only as famous as your last article. I think both our instincts are correct. Now we have to prove it. The difficulty is to find someone who has actually been inside that air base. There must be a tradesman of some nature, maybe a plumber or a central heating engineer. We need someone that has been in that hanger and observed its contents. Somewhere there is sure to have been a flaw in their security system. It is my job to find it."

"Really, this is quite exciting. I am glad you have come to stay. Can I help you on my day off?"

"Why not? Two thinking heads are better than one. We will plan a campaign and start tomorrow. When is your day off?"

"Tomorrow. It's not the busy season yet."

"Great. Do you have a car?"

"I have a motor bike, actually. They all think I am a tom boy round here; however, it's cheap and it gets me where I want to go most times."

"What I want you to do is to go round all the tradesmen in Little Haven, Broad Haven, Roche, Newgale and Penycwm. Ask if any of their employees ever went inside the air base between, say seventy-four and eighty and if so, did they ever enter the hangers or see anything peculiar?"

"This is going to be exciting. I'll need for ever to get round that lot."

"You can't get a week off can you? We could cover a lot in one week."

"I'll ask my Dad when he gets back. It will leave Mum on her own but I dare say she can cope." I'll say you are researching for a tourist magazine - don't want them worried."

"What's your name? We have not introduced ourselves."

"Lynn Taylor. What's yours?"

"David Holder. Free-lance journalist."

"An adventurer! This is going to be great."

"While you cover the tradesmen, I am going in by the front door. I want to get the feeling of the place. Before I go I am planning to have a closer look at those rocks. I must eat now, I'm famished."

Holder went into the dining room and sat down to his meal. To his surprise it was Lynn who appeared to take his order.

"Kind sir, I am here to serve," she said with a hint of a smile.

"Are you indeed? I could swear I just left you in the bar."

"If only I could lie, I would tell you that was my twin sister. Damn it, I can't. What gourmet's delight can I offer you? May I recommend the fresh trout, followed by the beef stroganoff."

"Is that all you have?"

"No sir, how dare you! Those are just my own favourites. Anyway I caught the trout myself. I have many talents you know."

"OK, I will be happy to bow to your expertise and follow your recommendations. May I have a bottle of wine of your choice to go with the meal?"

"Yes sir," replied Lynn disappearing towards the kitchen. The trout appeared ten minutes later steaming hot, complete with cream of leaks and sauté potatoes. Holder found it delicious. The cream of leak sauce was unusual but complimented the delicate flavour of the trout perfectly. Ten minutes later Lynn came back with the main course and a bottle of red wine.

"Why don't you sit down and have a glass of wine with me. You aren't busy so you have no excuse to refuse me."

She needed no prompting. She sat down, poured two glasses of wine and sipped enthusiastically at hers.

The main course was even better.

"Congratulate your mother on her cooking."

"It's not my mum cooking. It's Dad. That's his profession. He is a chef, but he helps out at a local restaurant in the low season to earn a bit extra."

"This evening I think I will do a bit of exploring, just to get my bearings and a feeling for the area."

"That's great. I'm off at nine. I'll show you round, if you like."

"That will be wonderful."

Lynn guided him on a tour of the local villages right up the coast, until they reached Brawdy air base. On the way she pointed out the school in Littlehaven where the craft landed and the farm that experienced so much trouble with its electrical power.

A double wire fence eight feet high surrounded the base. Warnings against trespassing strategically placed at intervals. A mobile patrol was busy inspecting the perimeter. The night was dark and cloudy. The wind was gusting and driving the rain in waves against the windscreen. There was no moon, so it was difficult to make out the shape of the hangers, but the runway was well illuminated and seemed to stretch into the distance.

At the main gate pass control operated behind a bar-lift manned by the usual marine guard. The administration block and the control tower were just visible. There was not much more they could do that night so they drove back along the coast to the hotel.

Upstairs Holder started to assemble the bricks he had gathered so far. There was the presence of a strange, previously unknown flying machine: sighted by responsible people though yet to be interviewed. A rock that bore secrets hidden by its inclement waves and an air base publicly attributed to NATO command yet undertaking oceanic research hidden from sight perhaps by using Stack Rocks as its base.

More and more, this looked like a deception tactic designed to hide a truth, an instinctive feeling Holder had already voiced to Lynn. Question marks still hovered over the Laser weapon and its connections, but he must take the police sighting seriously. Maybe, just maybe its testing took place from this rock as the rock was almost unapproachable by the public and hidden from view and protected by nature. This made sense as all weapons under development had to be tested and this was as remote as you can get: highly suitable for a testing site. From here they could be testing the sonar guidance system under the water and the laser guidance system above; the latter being responsible for the unexplained accidents.

Why were they testing in Wales and not America? Maybe it was linked with Advanced Laser Technology and their underwater development? The craft, as he called them, could have possibly served two purposes: transport to the rock and as a decoy to distract attention. He favoured that theory as it seemed logical. Holder fell asleep pondering on his brickwork.

Next morning he was down to breakfast at eight o'clock sharp and Lynn was waiting to serve him.

"I've been given time off for good behaviour, so I start my new job today."

Hc gave Lynn money for fuel and food to last the day.

"Gosh, that's enough for a month." Exclaimed Lynn.

He enjoyed her naiveté and her youthful exuberance.

"Good luck partner. We'll compare notes tonight."

Lynn waved good bye and drove off on her first venture into journalism.

Holder went back to his room, picked up his binoculars, then set off towards the cliffs. It was a clear dry morning with a brisk wind. He saw the rocks clearly one and a half miles out to sea. Taking care not to form a silhouette against the skyline, he focused the binoculars on them and scanned the rocks, helped by the light coming from the East.

He could make out a flat platform, just above sea level, which seemed to be man made. He scanned the surface again for some sign of a door. There were cracks that could be a door's edge, but nothing conclusive. He was just about to leave when a man in a silver suit appeared on the ledge, threw something into the sea and disappeared into a dark part of the rock.

"He waited another half an hour to see if the man would return but nothing happened. Holder then drove to Brawdy air Base. At the gate he asked to see the Press Liaison Officer and was escorted into an office. A lieutenant entered, six feet two inches tall with a well balanced body to complement his height. He had crew cut hair and large penetrating eyes.

"How can the US air force help you, Mr Holder?"

"I am writing a history of air bases. I've found this one has changed hands and I am curious to find out why."

"Well, Mr Holder, your government was going to close it and we needed a facility for our NATO forces, so we took it on."

"Why do you need such a long runway?"

"To take the large transporters used on NATO exercises."

"But according to the locals they very rarely see the large transporter planes. They were only seen when you first moved in here. Can I inspect the air base?"

"Sorry. It is strictly out of bounds."

"But I can inspect other NATO bases anytime I like. What secrets have you here to protect?"

"I am sorry sir. With terror threats, we can't be so accommodating nowadays."

"Are you doing some secret oceanic research off Stack Rocks and using the rock as a base?"

"What you are suggesting about our work is news to me, sir!"

"I just saw a USAF man on Stack Rocks with my own eyes."

"You what?" The lieutenant checked himself but nevertheless showed surprise. "Maybe he was on leave fishing."

Holder knew that it was the last place anyone in their right mind would go fishing. Furthermore, no fisherman ever dressed like that. He smiled, "I have been told a local once saw a flying saucer in one of your hangers."

"If that is so perhaps you could give us his name so we can interview him. Really! Some of the locals do have a vivid sense of imagination."

"I have been reliably informed that you used the saucers to divert attention from your real job, in the early days, when you set up your operation."

"Your informants seem to be mistaken. We co-operated fully with attempts to find an explanation for these strange sightings. Nothing came of it."

Holder knew by now that he was pressing the right buttons.

"Can you tell me anything about the laser weapon you have been testing?"

"What? I know nothing about any laser weapon."

"A laser weapon has been fired from Stack Rock and its beams have been seen across the sky. Your men seem to have the ability to land on the rock, so it is reasonable to assume they control the laser weapon."

"Mr. Holder, I do not know how to convince you that we know nothing about any of these fanciful ideas. You don't write for a science fiction comic do you?"

The curtain had fallen, a young airman escorted him to his car and off the base. Reactions to his questions had told him more than the answers. He decided to spend the rest of the day checking out the tradesmen in a few of the villages around the air base. At five-thirty, exhausted by his efforts, he drove back to the hotel to meet Lynn and compare notes.

Lynn was still out working, so he went up to his room, washed, changed and returned to the bar to quench his thirst. He sat sipping his lager in front of the log fire until Lynn came in with a broad smile. She went to the bar, poured herself a sherry and joined him in front of the fire.

"Well what did you find?"

"You first"

He told her about his day. Lynn gasped when he mentioned the man on Stack Rock. She laughed at his cheek when he described how he levelled his questions at the lieutenant.

"Now" said Holder, "Your turn."

"I've spent all day going from place to place. Seventy five percent of the people I visited were sole traders and most were out. I could only ask questions of their wives. Not the same, really. However, as luck would have it, just when I was cold, depressed and about to throw in the towel, I made my break. I called on a small ventilating firm in Roche and guess what?

on a small ventilating firm in Roche and guess what? The boss was called in to sort out a ventilation problem in one of the hangars. I have invited him over tonight to tell his story to you direct. I hope I did the right thing?"

"Not only have you done the right thing, you have performed an admirable job, my fellow journalist. Tell me more."

"When?"

"Dinner tonight I hope"

"Is that the payment for a job well done? Meet you in an hour at the bar. Oh, by the way, David Jones is his name. No, really. Don't laugh! Coming around at nine-thirty. Now for the transformation."

Holder stopped for another drink while he pondered over the days work. This space machine was a front for activities the American air force wished to conceal. He knew that his theory was becoming more plausible. Some highly secret work was going on, both at the base and under the rock. The rock was unapproachable by normal means, so he could not view it closely. He must ask Lynn about that tunnel.

The US air force used UFO replicas to divert attention from the main thrust of their work. It appeared possible they were using the base to test them as well. It was even a probability, through zero gravity, if that was their special feature, they were the most obvious choice to overcome the inclement weather problems out at stack rocks. Holder finished his drink and went up stairs to prepare for dinner.

Half an hour later he saw Lynn enter the bar. She walked straight up to him and said;

"I believe I have a dinner date with you?"

For a moment Holder stood transfixed. Then led her into the dining room and they sat down to eat. He looked at her steadily for a few moments.

"Is my mascara smudged or something?"

"You look stunning."

"Thank you, kind sir. You don't look too good yourself. Are you OK?"

"Never felt better," Smiled Holder, feeling slightly foolish, but incredibly privileged.

They relaxed together, forgetting the day's work, just talking and laughing, between the food and the wine. Holder ordered a bottle of champagne and asked Lynn's father to come and share it with them. Her mother also joined them and for half an hour they enjoyed the break. Then another guest came in and her family resumed their work.

Ten minutes later David Jones entered the bar. Seeing only Holder with a companion he came up to them and asked for Lynn.

"You are looking at her." Lynn replied, enjoying every second. "Don't worry - I'm off duty tonight. This is David Holder the journalist I told you about."

"Glad to meet you." Holder said, settling him down with a drink.

"I hear you saw saucer shaped objects in the hanger at Brawdy. Can you tell me in more detail?"

"Well, as I told Lynn, I was called in to repair the air conditioning unit in the hangar. The security being very strict, I was escorted everywhere I went. The job took three days. On the first two days nothing out of the ordinary happened, except when I tried to go to the other side of the makeshift curtain covering the left side of the hangar. My escort stopped me politely. Apparently there was some secret NATO project behind it. Anyway, on the third day I was up on the air conditioning motor, out of sight of my escort and working away, when some USAF pilot came in. He climbed into one of the small aircraft in the hangar. The doors opened to let the plane out. It was then that a strong gust of wind blew into the hangar momentarily lifting the curtain and exposing three saucer-like objects on the other side."

"Go on," said Holder, leaning forward.

"I am guessing, but they looked twenty to thirty feet in diameter and they each had a bulge on the top. They stood on legs but I could not see how many because I was seeing them from above. I had to laugh after all the local stories about UFO's. It was the Yanks all the time. I kept quiet about it in case my experience found its way back to the base. I couldn't afford to lose their custom."

"When did you do this job?"

"Ten years ago."

"Did you ever see light darting across the sky from Stack Rocks?"

"No, but my son used to go night fishing off the rocks about a mile up the coast. He saw flashes several times. I told him it was probably an electronic storm. You have something else in mind?"

"Yes, I do. Was it straight or jagged edge light?"

"My son said it was straight flashes like aircraft trails in the sky but much thinner."

"Sounds like laser beam light. Thanks David. You have been a great help. How about another drink?" However David Jones declined and left for home. Once more they were alone together.

He was getting stronger feelings for Lynn but he knew he must resist. It would not be fair on the girl, who was young and perhaps impressionable. They finished their drinks and walked to the foot of the stairs. As Lynn bade him good-night, she lent forward and kissed him. At that moment he knew that the attraction was mutual. Yet he would have to leave soon and he could not take her with him.

Next morning he was down early for breakfast. Lynn was already half way through hers. The evening princess was in her working clothes ready for a long day.

"Something I have to see is the entrance to the passage that leads to Stack Rocks." Said Holder brightly.

"Well that will be in the cellar. We'll have a look after breakfast. Thanks for my pay cheque. I loved it, especially the champers."

"It was my pleasure and more than earned. After the cellar we should take another look at the rock from the cliff to see if there is any form of life on it today. Then I would like to see the school teacher just to confirm her story."

"Right sir, your word is my command. Can I come with you and study the master at work?"

"Yes of course," said Holder, pleased and concerned with her request. After breakfast they went to the cellar, armed with a lantern.

They found a wall instead of the passage. That put an abrupt end to his search. He could hardly knock down the wall. In the darkness, Lynn clutched him tight and he felt an irresistible urge to kiss her.

She was only slightly older than his son. Age did not seem to matter. Compatibility was the stronger force driving them naturally together. Lynn was beaming when she reached the top and Holder realised his life had changed. He went up to his room and collected the binoculars to study Stack rocks again. It was not clear like the day before. The sea was rough, but the weather fair. They watched for an hour. Nothing happened. They decided to call at the school in Little Haven during the morning break and found Miss Palmer supervising games in the playground.

"We are interested in the strange events you and your class experienced several years ago."

"Well I thought I had exhausted all curiosity on that subject. Yes, I did see a saucer shaped object halfway up that field. Two tall men came out of it and went over to something. They bent down as if they were examining it. Then they went back to the saucer and disappeared very quickly towards the North."

"What did the craft look like?"

"It was a flat, circular shape with a raised centre, about thirty feet across. When it took off it moved almost without noise. There was just a very faint hissing sound."

"What did the men look like?"

"They wore dull aluminium-coloured suits with helmets and visors. They were both tall, about six feet-two inches but walked just like us."

"Could they have been American air force personnel from Brawdy?"

"How would you explain their craft?"

"If I could, would you believe it to be US airmen rather than aliens?"

"Yes. After all, it would seem to be a far more logical explanation."

"Thank you Miss Palmer, for your time. You have been most helpful."

As they left Holder knew he must tell Lynn he'd finished his investigation in Wales for the time being. He drove along the coast road and parked overlooking the sea.

"Lynn I have got..."

She put a finger across his mouth. "Don't say a word. I know what you were about to say. You mustn't spoil our last hour together." She bent across him and gave him a long meaningful kiss, as if to say that this is not the end. Holder knew inside that it wasn't, but it would take him time to admit as much. They stayed in each other's arms for over an hour, talking about everything and nothing. The World had changed for Holder. He had someone he cared for again. Eventually he drove back to the hotel, packed, paid his bill and walked to his car with Lynn.

"Look after yourself and don't let them get you. Give me your address in London so I can write."

"Lynn I don't know how to say this, but I never thought anyone would get under my skin again, till I met you. Take good care of yourself, and when you come to London look me up." He wrote out his address, tore the page from his pad, and gave it to her.

"Thanks for treating me as an equal on my first story. I'll keep watch for saucers and lights...and I'll see you soon."

His thoughts repeatedly turned to Lynn as he drove towards London, leaving a part of himself in Wales.

CHAPTER 8.

Now he had time to deal with some of his less urgent Priorities. He wanted to visit Daniel Kershaw's widow, Jack Parr and Jane's father.

He drove down to Winchester and found the long drive to the elegant Edwardian house. When he rang the bell, a woman in her late thirties answered; not wishing to be caught out for a second time, he asked to speak to Mrs Kershaw.

"I am Mrs Kershaw. What can I do for you?"

"I am a journalist. May I ask you a few questions about your late husband."

"You'd better come in."

She led him into the living room and asked him to take a seat.

"How can I help you?"

"I visited your mother here on the dreadful day of your husband's death. She was so courteous and extremely helpful, but I have one or two questions which remain unanswered." She nodded consent.

"Firstly, did your husband ever have two petrol cans in his car?"

"We didn't own one, let alone two."

Holder nodded then continued. "Did he show any signs of tension or depression, unrest or possibly discomfort, or any small signs at all during your last few days together?"

"He was normal, perhaps a little tense, yet happy and was reluctantly, as usual, planning our summer holiday."

"Did he ever mention anything about his work, or who he was working with, at any stage?"

"I have been told by the security services not to answer any questions about his work. It was top secret. Therefore I feel they have the right to demand that."

"Fair enough. Have you yourself any doubts about your husband's death? Whether it was suicide?"

"I live from day to day trying to answer that question. I can't believe suicide. For a wife - there were no money problems - But suicide that's too horrible for adequate words. Who would want to kill a man who was considered so valuable by his company? He was recognised throughout the industry as a genius. One day I think that it must have been suicide, the next I am not so sure. Maybe our enemies had him taken out"

"If I told you that I am sorry, but after lengthy, thorough investigation, I am sure that he was murdered, what would you say?"

Mrs. Kershaw paused for a good minute before answering. Fighting back tears she replied;

"I would say that it was more in keeping with what I knew of him as a man."

"I am determined to prove that something is dreadfully wrong in our defence industry with relation to the deaths of all these scientists. If there is anything that you know that will help, I beg you, please tell me. I need all the help I can get to crack this one."

"I certainly will."

"This whole business stinks. What drives me is the lies I have been told in the name of national security. These have had nothing at all to do with official secrets. It seems to be a complete cover-up for the incompetence of our security service who cannot find the source of the tragic deaths. Somewhere tangled in this mess are actions executed by private firms maybe for foreign powers."

"Mr Holder, thank you for your efforts on my husband's behalf. I know he would be pleased to have you fight in his corner. I myself cannot really be much help at the moment. It is as if I am in purgatory, unable to forget. If I can think of anything that might be of interest, I'll contact you. I will need your phone number."

He gave her his car phone number because this was more difficult to trace.

"Mrs. Kershaw, I will keep in touch. I hope I can clear up the mystery of their deaths. I also hope that you will soon come out of this terrible state of hopelessness. I do know how you feel at the moment."

He left and drove towards Camberley, arriving at a pub outside the town just before six. Sure enough, dead on six o'clock, Parr entered and walked up to the bar next to him.

"Get my friend a double scotch." Said Holder.

"Now there's a coincidence," replied Parr, "I was only thinking of you today, about how you saved me from insanity." They moved over to a quiet corner.

"Jack, I must tell you the truth. As you know I am a reporter but I am covering the deaths in the defence industry, but don't worry. I am not about to expose you. On the contrary I am after the people that killed Daniel. With your help I will crucify them."

"I am glad you told me that." Parr replied. "I felt by the way you treated me that something lay behind your interest. How can I help you to bring Daniel's murderers to justice.?"

"Has anyone approached you to stop you talking to the press?"

"Not directly, but we were all ordered not to speak to the press about Daniel, or his work, indeed anything associated with the company. It is the first time I have been unable to respect their wishes. I won't tolerate what they have done to Daniel."

"I think I know who killed him now," said Holder, "but I don't yet know exactly why. I also think I know who gave the orders, but again I don't know why. Because, frankly Why remains the big question. There are several possibilities I can't seem to isolate the right one. Can you shed any light on it?"

"First tell me who did it and who you think gave the orders?"

"A security company carried out the murder and I think maybe the KGB gave the orders."

"A security company? That is a bit vague. I can imagine the KGB behind it. Going back to the central question, I can only say that the development that I told you about is hot and that it is protected at all

costs. What other possible explanation can there be for your, Why?"

"That we killed our own scientists for silence but that is unthinkable. I'm going to America shortly to investigate the background of the American scientist who was working on the project. I now have her name. Dr Steiner from California. She worked under a Dr Bush at Edward's Air force Base."

"That rings a bell. Daniel mentioned that base, when referring to his colleague, an American scientist. That must be the base where the Americans keep their top secret development for laser warfare"

"Do you know if the Americans are involved in any other laser development?"

"We have been told there was a joint venture between America and Britain. That's only informed hearsay."

"Does your firm do much work for the American government?"

"Nothing on the scale of this project. Daniel told me that this was a massive development that would ensure our superiority for some years to come."

"What you seem to be saying is that the project was so hot, it became a target for the Russians to obtain. that is a firm belief of mine."

"By the way, before I forget, Daniel told me he was followed once on his way to work. He gave me the car number in case something happened. It may be nothing, or a vital clue, but it's worth checking. He wrote it on this used envelope."

"That is certainly worth a check. Thanks. When I get back from America I may want to contact you again. Don't worry though. I will go to gaol rather than disclose your name to the authorities."

"Holder, I want to help, but your assurance is gratefully accepted. Good luck. I am sure Daniel would want to thank you."

Holder rose to leave, knowing that he had a staunch supporter in Parr.

On reaching home, Holder found a message on his answering machine, giving him details of two more deaths. One was a young post graduate working for the Royal Military College of Science, aged twenty-five: Peter Laing died in a car crash just before Holder went to Wales. The second was another systems analyst, from Wales. He also died in a car, which ended on its roof in a river bed, shortly after Peter Laing's death. His name was Tony Webb. Holder decided to keep his focus on finding the motive, so he withheld his usual energy for each investigation. He resolved to focus his attention on the heart of the matter.

His next task was to phone Jane Armstrong's father.

"Mr Armstrong. David Holder speaking. Hope you remember me. You were kind enough to give me somc time when I came to see you about Jane's death. I wonder if you could answer a few more questions? I can be available at any time that suits you."

"I am afraid I can't talk now. Can I ring you back?"

He noticed a tension in Armstrong's voice.

"Of course." Holder gave him his car phone number and sat back to wait. Ten Minutes later his phone rang. The man on the other end introduced himself as Inspector Brian Formby.

"You rang Mr Armstrong this morning and harassed him to give you information about the suicide of his daughter. I must warn you that if this happens again you will have to answer to the crown prosecution service."

"I am a free lance journalist investigating a suspicious death. I have the right to information."

"I am telling you. Drop the case if you know what's good for you."

Holder put the phone down shaking with fury. Did he really expect him to back down at this point? That sort of attitude was like a red rag to a bull and proved beyond doubt that his investigation was right on track. Their heavy handed authority was not going to distract him.

How had Mr Armstrong been nobbled? The best plan would be to interview the neighbours.

He drove to the entrance of the Mr Armstrong's road and walked the rest of the way hoping to stay unnoticed. There was no reply from the house to the left so he tried the house on the right and rang the bell. A curtain in the front window moved and shortly after the door opened. A stout woman asked him his business.

"I am a journalist investigating Jane Armstrong's death."

"You'd better come in. How can I help you?" asked the woman.

Holder found himself sitting amongst cats and cushions. The room was not yet warm, his hostess wore a thick woollen cardigan.

"What can I tell you that I haven't told a hundred reporters?"

"I am most interested in Mr Armstrong. Have you noticed any change in him recently?"

"I'll say I have. You are the gentleman that called the day after it happened, aren't you? I can always remember a face. After you called I went down to see if I could help in any way. He told me how kind and helpful you were and he was so grateful for my offer. A couple of days later two men called to see him and ever since then he became irritable, withdrawn and rude. His behaviour has been completely out of character."

"Has he got any other children?"

"Yes. Two"

"Thank you. You have been very helpful. I am afraid you've confirmed everything that I feared."

Armstrong had been nobbled, it was that simple. At least he had got there first and gleaned some of the truth from Mr Armstrong. The two men must have been from Special Branch. They were very persuasive. They probably threatened to do something nasty to his other children if he spoke. No wonder he was irritable, withdrawn and rude. It was unthinkable that the police would support that level of corruption, but that was the indication given by the phone call, unless Formby was not a policeman.

Holder was growing very angry. This was interference with his freedom to investigate.

He arrived home to find a woman sitting on his doorstep. As he closed his car door she leapt up.

"I thought I would have to wait for ever. I couldn't bear the thought of you getting all the glory, so I decided to come and help you with the story. Hope that's OK?"

Holder smiled broadly. "Missed you, partner."

CHAPTER 9.

They talked till late, not even noticing the passing of time, until Holder, feeling drowsy, suggested it was time for bed. He offered to make up a bed for Lynn in the spare room.

"Don't be so old-fashioned. I didn't come all this way for my health," she retorted. "I love you and I want to share your bed."

Holder was taken aback by her forthright approach, but she disarmed him with a passionate kiss. They showered together, discovering their sensuality, until the physical desire became too great to delay their first union. Once in the bedroom the urgency of their purpose became compelling. Holder's hand reached between Lynn's thighs bringing an electrifying delight to her senses. She turned to mount him in feverish delight.

They rose and fell in harmony, ever trying for deeper, closer union, until they climaxed together with a burst of energy that seemed beyond the limits of their combined strength. Satisfied, they lay back in each other's arms and fell into deep sleep.

Next morning, when he awoke, Lynn was missing. Then he heard the clattering of dishes and went down stairs to find her in his kitchen. She had cleaned and tidied weeks of accumulated dishes and empty bottles. The place was unrecognisable!

"There you are, David darling. Now we can have breakfast." She impressed him. It might have stayed like that for months if Lynn hadn't happened along. Could it work? He hoped it could. Working together the relationship would stand a much better chance. Although he didn't want to admit it to himself he was in love with her.

As Holder made plans for his trip to America he decided that Lynn should come with him. It would be a good experience for her and she would be safer at his side. He phoned his bank and sent Lynn round with authority to collect the spending money.

Next he rang his travel agent and asked for details of all available flights to Los Angeles. There were seats on a flight Thursday, leaving Heathrow at midday. He asked for an open return and booked the tickets. He was not in the market for cheap flights. He accepted the price for flexibility. At that moment Lynn returned.

"I've got the loot. When do we go?"

"Thursday. Is your passport up to date?"

"Yes Sherlock, it is in order, but don't I have to get a visa or something for the States?"

"Thank god you mentioned that. You are not just a pretty face."

"Perish the thought!"

Holder drove to the American Embassy to get Lynn's visa but decided to wait in the car. He had the visa stamp from his last trip and he didn't want any trouble with embassy security. Lynn returned after only three quarters of an hour and they drove home to prepare for the work ahead.

The first task was to process a check on the car number given to him by Jack Parr. Having put that in motion he rang the fountain of knowledge to get information on all laser-weapon related press coverage.

"Hello dear boy, how can I help you?" Asked John's unmistakable voice.

"Can you compile a file of all laser stories that have hit the press and give me two print-outs?"

"Thinking of going on holiday, dear boy? Where is it to be, Mars, Saturn, or the Moon?"

"No, America. I need that today. Can I collect it later?"

"Yes that sounds OK. It should be well catalogued. Your word is my command."

"Also, could you enter Dr Merle Steiner and see what you come up with in your records. Lastly, enter Dr V Bush, an American space scientist and see what your data base can deliver on him."

"My god, you are a busy bee. Do I take it you are going forth into the wilderness, on research into the unknown?"

"Yes, you hit it in one. What time shall I come round?"

"Give me two hours and I'll have it gift wrapped for you."

Holder put down the phone and started to pack. He always travelled light so it was an easy task. Lynn, however, couldn't decide what to leave behind, until he intervened.

They sat down for a coffee and toast. Holder could not remember when he last indulged this luxury. Things were certainly changing for the better. It was time to go to the fountain of knowledge. On the way he explained John's background and warned Lynn about his humour. John opened the door of his flat and greeted them from his wheelchair. He was born crippled, but made a good life for himself.

His dark hair fell around his face merging with his beard. A jolly smile peered out from behind the hair. He was like a character from Dickens, the eyes, never still, darting and searching everywhere lest they should miss anything important.

"Hello dear boy. Who is this vision of Venus that honours us with her presence?"

"That John, is my boss, Lynn."

"This angel of charisma is your boss? She whose charms transcend logic and confounds male hearts, including mine, is your boss?"

"I see you are speechless again."

"That will be the day, dear boy."

"Is she the reason you are flying off into the sunset?"

"You see what I mean, Lynn? He can't be serious for one minute."

"Lynn, I hope you keep a tight rein on him. He gets very wild, but today, obviously, he is the luckiest man in the World."

"I thank you sir, for your kind words. I am also a journalist's apprentice and I must learn the trade from my master."

"Oh what obedience! I am so jealous, Holder. Here, dear boy, are my findings. Two copies of each. I can see why now. Good luck and God speed."

Lynn gave him a kiss and John feigned a faint. They both left laughing with the pleasure of John's company. He was a truly remarkable man who had overcome great personal tragedy to become an independent character.

Holder explained to Lynn how he had first met John working for charity at a local bazaar; John's magnetic personality attracted him instantly. When he knew him better he realised that his masterful brain was being grossly under-used.

John once told him about his childhood. Parents and teachers alike had underrated his mind, because he was a cripple. He overcame their lack of care by reading everything he could borrow, later spending all his pocket money on books. Other children hadn't helped, they had ignored him, or teased him with taunts like mindless cripple. At first he felt hurt and abused, until despite all this, he reached top of his class in most subjects.

Yet John found great difficulty in getting jobs when he left school, not because of any lack of ability but because firms didn't want disabled staff. He drifted between small jobs and charity work. Holder and some friends set him up with a professional computer so he could work from home. They put him in touch with colleagues and John supplied them with the details of past stories that they often needed. Now he was an indispensable resource within the World of

Journalism and received a very good income from his service. After listening to the story in silence, Lynn said:

"That is one of the nicest things that I have ever heard. You are both quite something."

"Now, now, the first thing you should learn as a journalist is not to be sentimental."

"That's good coming from you."

Arriving home, they started to plough through all the articles that John supplied, relating to Laser weapons. At nine-thirty Lynn stopped to cook while Holder opened a bottle of wine. They sat and talked over the articles, some of which confirmed details of the incidents in Wales.

When Holder reached the information about Dr Merle Steiner it again confirmed most of the details he had found in the local paper. There was one interesting addition.

"Lynn, I want to illustrate how journalism is built out of bricks. This article from the Times states that Dr Merle Steiner was a laser expert. This is new information that we have to add to the picture. All the work we have done this evening is worthwhile, just for that small snippet of information. It confirms our finding in Wales and part of Parr's statement."

"What if you had missed it?"

"He grinned slyly. "The difference between a run of the mill reporter and a top investigative journalist is simply that! but, seriously, A professional does not miss the smallest brick. He knows that he will need them all to build his house."

"David, I am going to take you away from your bricks for an hour or two. Come with me." Lynn picked up the bottle of wine and two glasses and led

Holder upstairs. Later they lay basking in the afterglow of warmth and affection. Eventually Lynn remarked; "Just think, if you had gone to another hotel we would never have met!"

"That's fate." He yawned and they both drifted into sleep, waking up the next morning in each other's arms.

During breakfast the phone rang as they discussed their plans.

"Is that you Holder?"

"Yes."

"The name of the car owner you required is Ivan Karovski investigations. It sounds like a private investigator to me!"

"Thanks, I owe you one. Be in touch. I'm off to America today."

"That's interesting Lynn. The car that followed Daniel Kershaw shortly before his demise was driven by a Russian private eye!"

"What does that tell us?"

"It lends credence to my Russian theory. He will almost certainly be working for the KGB, probably checking on Kershaw's exact movements. We will run a check on him when we get back."

At ten o'clock Holder rang for a mini cab to take them to Heathrow.

After booking in they browsed round the duty free shop, passing time until their flight was called.

CHAPTER 10.

During eleven uneventful hours in the air Holder and Lynn lost all track of time, engrossed in their research. He brought her up to date with details of the investigation answering many questions, but failing to satisfy her insatiable curiosity. Hostesses kept interrupting, offering them food and drink.

Before they knew it, the plane was landing, as they left the craft they felt the intense heat rising from the tarmac below. A tunnel led into the passport control hall where queues moved at a snail's pace. It took over an hour to clear customs, while every passport was examined as though time was expendable.

Once out, they headed straight to the Hertz desk to collect a car: having paid by credit card, they drove North, looking for a suitable hotel.

Settling on a Howard Johnson, Holder paid for two nights and made it clear that they might want to stay longer. The hotel wasn't busy so that was not going to be a problem. They went up to their room and crashed out, exhausted by their journey.

Next morning Lynn awoke first and looked around the sunny room. There were two double beds, a large dressing table and two armchairs. A freezer and a security safe stood next to the wardrobe area. French windows led onto a balcony. She rose and went into the bathroom to find a combination bath and shower unit with a special light outside the shower doubling as a warm air blow drier. She started to shower and noticed the water was bubbling out of the tap through a special filter, giving it an exhilarating freshness.

The attention to detail impressed her. As she came out of the bathroom she noticed a trouser press on the wall and of course, the obligatory television. Holder stirred. She sat on the edge of the bed and gave him a lingering morning kiss.

"You've just started something."

"Nothing I can't finish," replied Lynn rolling over him to end up alongside.

"Now lets see who fails from jet lag first."

They played around for a while, decided it was a draw and after a few minutes rest, showered, dressed and went down to breakfast to plan their campaign. They needed to prove the existence of laser research at Edward's Air force base and the far-fetched possibility of the saucer story. Holder's mind was certainly open but suspicious.

He decided they would need a good map of California but also another, covering the rest of the States. They needed to have a look at the locations of other air bases involved in similar military operations. There might be more than Edward's Air Base involved. Holder asked Lynn if she would get the maps while he made the phone calls.

"Consider it done, my Teacher." Lynn replied.

"Buy some bottles of wine and anything else you fancy. We have a long day's planning ahead. I don't think we can go up to Edward's Air Force Base till tomorrow. Make the best of civilisation."

Holder reflected that, if it was all true and the USA had found and duplicated alien craft, then it put America in an unassailable position. It did not take much imagination to see how this edge could develop farther. The technology could be the basis for the design of a new breed of space weapon; a laser beam weapon, computer controlled to home on its target. It would revolutionise the whole of the Western defence system, giving it a crushing advantage over Russia and China.

Possession of simulated craft, must now become the primary thrust of his research: could he find definite proof of their existence at Edward's Air force Base? That must be his goal, because everything he seemed to have learned so far hinged around the laser development.

He rang an organisation called Zero Gravity Space Research of Garberville, California. The head of research was Tom Bowen who was the author of a book about Edward's Air Force Base. A friendly voice answered the call. When Holder explained the details of his research, Bowen invited him over to discuss, in detail, the focus of his investigation. Holder agreed, adding that since it might be ten days before he could make it up to Garberville, he would ring before he came.

Bowen's organisation was within a day's drive of Los Angeles, roughly three hundred miles away. The sheer size of this continent was beginning to impress Holder, who had never given it much thought before. California was only one State and it was larger than the whole of England. It was sobering to realise the size of America. It put her massive power into prospective.

At that moment Lynn came back into the room, looking like a parcel trolley. She had maps tucked under her arm and all sorts of goodies stashed about her person: food from a delicatessen to keep away pangs of hunger for the rest of the day. Wine to quench their thirst. A large, mysterious parcel dominated. She gave it to Holder to open and out fell the largest Mickey Mouse he had ever seen.

"Lynn what on earth..."

"Don't you dare say a thing against Mickey. He is very sensitive." She tried to cover the toy's ears as best she could. "I have always wanted one and he smiled at me in such a way that I couldn't resist him."

Holder laughed and started to study the map books of Southern California that gave good coverage of Edward's Air Force Base. It had developed around two dry salt lakes. The larger lake was some thirty miles long and twelve miles wide. For the first time he realised the magnitude of the task he had undertaken. He knew of no base approaching this size in England.

There was a security fence around the perimeter and three main entrance points. One to the South, one to the North and one on its West side. The main complex of the buildings was strategically placed roughly in the centre of the base, above and between the two salt lakes. Seven small towns existed within fifteen miles of the perimeter. It was in these towns that he would commence his hunt for information. On the left, above the Bissel Hills and Lake Rosamond, was the flight test centre. Just above and to the right of the main complex, NASA had a flight research centre. At Roger's Lake, he seemed to remember, was the salt strip where the space shuttle landed after its flight. Centre right was a rocket propulsion laboratory. Dotted all over the place were observation towers and radio towers.

North-East, not connected to Edward's Air Force Base, was an even larger naval reservation, farther East, a naval weapon's centre larger than Edward's Air Force base. All filled an enormous valley ringed by mountains. It was a perfect place to locate and establish a base, away from the view of curious eyes. They guarded the base well but around there somewhere was a needle. He just had to sort through the chaff to find it.

"David darling, lunch is served," came Lynn's voice from the balcony. He rose and went outside. The hot air caressed his face. The sun was high in a pure sky. He sat down at the table and opened a bottle of wine. Pouring, he looked around at the spread that Lynn had prepared.

"This is enough food to feed an army!" he exclaimed. There were three types of bread, each looking fresh and inviting. He counted eight different kinds of meat, several cheeses and fruit to finish. They ate well and enjoyed the fresh hot air, discussing details of their morning's work. They needed to combine forces in formulating a strategy for finding that needle.

Time was precious and they must concentrate in the areas most likely to succeed.

Lynn cleared the table, just leaving the wine and the glasses while Holder collected his notes, the two map books and paper on which to plan their next moves.

"The target is our needle. Where do we find it?"

"In one of the towns around the base?"

"Exactly. So let's list them. I'll take the distant ones, as I have a car and you can tackle the three towns nearer the base; Rosamond, California City and Boron. I suggest you start at Rosamond and then California City. Logically we are most likely to find our man there.

"You mean California City?"

"Yes. My towns will be Lancaster, Palmdale, Victorville and Bartow. Our first target will be to get an interview inside the base. To do this our cover story is that we are writing a book on military airports throughout the World.

How to find the needle. What is he? What does he do? What experts would have the knowledge that we require?"

"He is a specialist in metallurgy, fuel, aerodynamics, or a computer analyst."

"Yes, that's good thinking. You can add to that avionics, very necessary as it covers all instrumentation and don't forget senior managers. We have to be particularly careful at this stage. We do not want to arouse suspicion. You must get to know them before pumping them. Americans tend to be very patriotic and this could go against us if we are not careful."

Lynn nodded that she understood, this was no game.

"We have probably missed many professions. Your first decision comes when you find out their job. At that stage you must decide whether to develop the relationship, or move on to another prospect. If you decide to go for it, the next stage is to get to know your subject. Analyse his character - without making it too obvious! Just slip a few questions into the general conversation. Eventually he may disclose a weakness. It may be women. It may be a bad marriage, or trouble at work, but everyone has something worrying them. As you get to know about it you can pull closer. Ask questions. Only sound caring, because coming from a beautiful woman like you, most men will weaken."

"You are not asking me to be bait?"

"Not quite! Walk away if it is getting out of hand. But, if it isn't, once you know their weakness play on it. Get to know everything about them and then use it to prise open the shell and look inside. From there onwards you are homing in on the needle. By then you will know, from what they have said, whether they are likely to work in one of the areas we have targeted. You can bail out at any time by using the age old ruse of another appointment. If you get close remember there is always tomorrow. Don't push too hard. The more you see of your subject the more he will confide in you."

"What if he becomes amorous?"

"I can't help you. You will be on your own. You must judge each moment and judge it well. You can always say that you are interested, but it is too early in your relationship. You won't believe this, but as a working hack I have often had to deal with that one and I have always managed to wriggle out of it."

"What if it is a girl scientist?"

"I'm no help."

"Thanks a million."

"Seriously - if it feels wrong, get out, you are worth more than this case to me."

"Thank you very much. I feel better for that."

"Now how on earth are we going to find these specialists? Where do the top people go when they go out in public?"

"Clubs, pubs, health farms, gyms, golf clubs, saunas and bridge clubs."

"Very good. Those are exactly the sort of places we will find our person. Bars here are not frequented by our sort of person. In America they tend to be for the rougher elements. There is possibly a society or two worth investigation. The music society, maybe a fertile hunting ground, or a German group, something brainy. Many immigrants have come here. It could be a Shakespearean society as he is very popular over here. All we have to do now is to list our hunting grounds in order of preference and we have a plan of action."

Holder and Lynn talked until five o'clock in the afternoon. Then, work finished, they decided to have a swim followed by a Jacuzzi, sauna and a cold shower. They both came up stairs feeling fresh and invigorated. Holder wanted to see something of Los Angeles. With nods of approval from Lynn, they changed into fresh clothes and hit town, drove down avenues of palm trees to the water's edge, parked the car and strolled along the golden sand.

The warm evening breeze touched their bodies and the scent of the Pacific filled their lungs. The work of the day forgotten, they were alone and completely happy. The sun, now low in the sky, took on a reddish glow casting its beams across the sea. They stopped, kissed, with tender passion, at peace with themselves and the World as the sun slipped below the ocean.

They walked on and on, stopping for the occasional embrace, until hunger reminded them to turn for the car. They ate at a bistro by the waterfront, on a patio enclosed on both sides by stone walls, covered in vines. Darkness was falling as their diner arrived; fresh lobster with a salad, followed by Irish coffee. They lingered for a while after their meal watching the lights from the boats and counting stars.

Returning to their hotel Holder called room service. Minutes later the waiter arrived with an ice bucket and Champagne.

Holder slipped his arm round Lynn's waist and kissed her, only to jump away as Lynn dropped a loose lump of ice down his back.

"Cool it," she said, "let's shower together first."

They raced to get undressed and into the shower throwing clothes everywhere in urgent abandon. They settled to soaping and gently caressing each other, until mutual desire took them back to the bedroom and more than champagne.

CHAPTER 11.

Next morning, hot and muggy, they checked out of their hotel and set off for Edward's Air Force Base. Leaning forward Holder switched on the air-condition unit and headed towards the Soledad pass. The road went through spectacular mountain forests, before winding down to the Soledad canyon, twisting and turning down the steep pass. The sun's rays filtered through the trees cascading magical light, while to the right, forest surrendered to rich pastures and rocks in the canyon below.

Eventually they came down into the Soledad Pass between Mount Emma Ridge and the Sierra Felona Range. As they drove along the valley, mountains towered above them, like two green giants at rest. In front lay the vast plains of the Antelope valley that were hunting ground for the next few days. On their right there was a large lake with the town of Palmdale on the far side. It was fifteen miles before they reached their first stop, Rosamond.

The small hamlet lay on the West side of Edward's Air Force Base. One of the main gates to the base was just to the East. The town was meagre. They decided to move on and make their base in California City, on the North side of the base, approximately thirty miles. Forty-five minutes later they entered a modern, purpose-planned town, with little character, found a suitable hotel, with the obligatory swimming pool, Jacuzzi and sauna where they booked in for five days, with the option to stay longer.

On to the central boulevard they found a Burger bar that claimed to serve the best pure beef-burgers in California. The burgers were enormous and they helped themselves to as much side salad as the plate would hold. A long walk round the centre to find their bearings showed the town was built for the residents, who mostly worked at the base. It seemed to exclude visitors, as if the place was a fortress and they, unwelcome intruders, knocking on the gate.

This atmosphere could hamper their research. Only time would tell. They made note of likely looking venues as they roamed the streets and finally ended up back at their hotel exhausted and ready for a swim. Holder questioned the hotel receptionist about leisure activities and all the facilities the town boasted, until she began to wonder how he would fit so much activity into a five day stay. Armed with their list and some notes Holder and Lynn went to the pool for an afternoon of planning. Relaxed by a long swim in the cool water they sat by the pool sipping Californian orange juice, discussing their next day's search.

Holder phoned the base to book an appointment with the press office, arranging a visit at ten-thirty the next morning. Their escort would be Lieutenant Bud Walters. They should report to the Rosamond gate, leave their car at the gate compound and be prepared for a body search before entering.

"Sounds like James Bond," responded Lynn," isn't it exciting?"

"It could be, if we make a wrong impression. We must remember our cover story and believe it. Don't worry, we'll get through. Come on. Last in the pool buys dinner." They both raced to the pool, but he slipped and Lynn, laughing, claimed victory. They had a quick swim and a Jacuzzi. The joy of being pummelled by iridescent water was satisfying. Next the sauna drew all the impurities from their skin and left them relaxed and exhausted. A cold shower revived and refreshed.

It was a fifty-five mile drive to Lancaster and they arrived as the sun was setting over the distant mountains. The town, though older than California City, appeared similar in layout. Its inhabitants, busied themselves with their evening activities.

Holder decided to concentrate on the East side first. They spent the evening listing interesting activities and clubs in the town and then, in a state of fatigue collapsed in a fast diner for rest and sustenance. Finally they drove back to California City.

Sunlight filtered through the blinds, heralding the start of another hot day. Holder arose first, showered and dressed while Lynn lay motionless, trying to will herself out of bed. Eventually she emerged and stumbled into the bathroom.

After breakfast he collected his note book from his room, removing his tape recorder in case of trouble, and left for Rosamond. They parked in the perimeter compound and made their way to the gate house for a strip search. Having suffered this undignified experience they were handed visitors passes and were escorted to a waiting jeep.

The drive was much longer than expected, past the corner of salt lake flats and twelve miles farther to the office complex.

The marine escort directed them to an office on the ground floor, just past the reception area. On passing through the lobby they noticed that everyone wore an identification pass with a photograph. Holder had a brief glimpse of a technician using a palm imprint identity machine, to gain entry to a door. The whole area seemed totally protected, with TV cameras to pick up any suspicious intruder and each entry armed with a buzz alarm to identify anyone carrying any metal objects. The security was tight. Behind lay many things he still couldn't imagine.

Everywhere marines, in full military dress, guarded strategic points with automatic colt 45's and M16 carbines slung over their shoulders. Their presence filled the air with a threat to all that passed however innocent their mission. Holder and Lynn entered a waiting room covered by video surveillance, controlled by the security Team who were on constant look-out for any abnormal movements. It would be foolish to act out of line here and easy to become a statistic.

Ten minutes passed, until a marine entered and ushered them in to a large office. Sitting at the desk was a man, thirty-eight years old. He had a rugged complexion, crew cut hair and piercing grey eyes. A scar on his left cheek, highlighted by the rays of the sun stealing through the blinds, looked menacing and enhanced his generally aggressive appearance. He rose and greeted them formally, offering Holder a cigar, which he declined.

"My name is Lieutenant Bud Walters and I am the press liaison officer for this base. On behalf of the United States Air Force I would like to welcome you. I will answer your questions as far as I am allowed to within the confines of the law governing security. Would you like to talk first, or have a tour of the facilities that are on show?"

"Perhaps it would be better to see the base first and then talk. It will be easier for me to ask the right questions with a broader knowledge of the base."

"As you will appreciate, there are parts of this base where even I can't go. This is one of many bases where we carry out development of several different projects for the space program, as well as others for military purposes. We have for example developed new models of flight control and aerodynamic structures. We have made great progress in avionics. Our aim is always to improve and our technicians are constantly breaching new boundaries. Unfortunately much of this is out of bounds for security reasons, because in enemy hands our advantage would be lost."

That, thought Holder, sounded reasonable. However, it might also allow somebody to cover up much that was not nearly so reasonable.

"If you follow me I will take you on a tour of the base." They seemed to walk down miles of corridors. A palm check unit appeared outside most doorways. There were video cameras at every strategic point. No intruder could pass unnoticed. Guards covered all entrances and controlled their territory by radio. Eventually they came into a car park area where a jeep waited to take them on a conducted tour. Looking around he realised the sheer size of the complex that he had just left, stretching into the distance were hangers and workshops.

"As you guys can see it's quite a massive operation. We cover a large sphere of work, from normal service maintenance to experimental work and development. This place has mushroomed over the years. It is a hive. We have our own hospital to the South East of the complex. For recreation we have a golf course, base-ball and net-ball fields, swimming pools and a gymnasium. First I will take you to the airstrip and show you where the shuttle lands. Where do you folk come from?"

"London," said Holder amiably, "but Lynn comes from Wales, near Little Haven."

"I don't believe it. I was just down the road from you at Brawdy Air Base. Oh, it must have been ten to twelve years ago. Small World. Though then you must have been in school."

"I only moved to Little Haven three years ago." Lynn flushed.

"Oh really," said Walters, not at least aware of his guest's embarrassment. It's still an amazing coincidence."

"What were you doing at Brawdy?" Intervened Holder.

"Same as I'm doing here. I was the press liaison officer for the base when the US Air Force moved into Brawdy."

He resisted asking further questions. He wanted to see and hear as much about the base as possible without showing his hand. Walters drove towards the East and stopped by a large complex.

"Inside that building is NASA's research department. That is where the space program is planned." They drove on towards the runways where all the shuttle flight's land.

"This is the flight test centre, controlled from the tower. There are two main runways. One is for take off and the other for landing. You will see we angle the runways slightly away from each other for safety reasons. Now, if we drive to the edge of the salt lake, you will see the landing sight for the space shuttle running roughly North to South."

A vast salt flat was an impressive sight, sixteen miles from North to South and at least five miles wide. Down its centre a clear marker system operated for landing that stretched across the shimmering salt flats and blurred into the morning haze.

"Perhaps you guys would like to come and see a shuttle landing next time round. I can arrange it if you can make it."

"Thanks. That would be great." Holder replied, genuinely excited. They drove on round the salt flats and East towards the perimeter, stopping outside another complex though viewing it from a distance.

"This is our rocket propulsion laboratory. All the space rockets are fuelled by developments from this complex. We also develop aviation fuels for civilian and military use. It is the most advanced plant of its kind in the World."

Holder looked around. The complex gave way to open space. There was an observation tower in every strategic position. No intruder could move around the

open terrain, even if he could penetrate the fence. He could not remember seeing a base so secure.

Next Walters drove North East across the top of the salt flat to the North base. This had a smaller airstrip and seemed to specialise in fighter planes. There were several F1-11 fighters standing on the tarmac. They stopped outside a hangar. Two fighter planes stood within its shade undergoing an overhaul by ground crews.

"As you can see these guys have the skill to take one of these kites to pieces and then rebuild. They are vital to the success of any mission."

They continued on their journey past a hangar that was larger and more securely built. Holder asked if they could take a look but Walters informed him that this particular hanger was out of bounds even to the President. The hanger was numbered twenty-seven.

"Surely the President can go anywhere he wishes?"

"No sir, our government's policy is to restrict certain areas of top secret information only to those that need to know. Even the President does not qualify on that basis. Neither do I because what we do not know, we can't tell."

That concentrated Holder's mind. This meant that a small clique of military personnel who controlled the 'need to know' policy could, if corrupt or politically biased, hide all sorts of weapons and activities for their own purposes. This could easily put all the power in the hands of the military. He thought of the Iran Contra affair and a shudder went down his spine. Oliver North was appearing before a congressional committee, accused of controlling a similar closed ring. He contemplated the danger that America courted by this policy. America, effectively blindfolded, could fall

under the control of a handful of ruthless people in a strategic position of non executive power. People, never elected to office, answerable for their actions to no-one.

Walters noticed their silence as they drove South back to the main base, past the hospital and down the side of the golf course.

"This is where our personnel relax in the sports hall and on the golf course. We have all sorts of equipment from exercise machines to weights, in a fully stocked gym and facilities for sports such as fencing, boxing and basket ball. Now I am going to invite you to our canteen to have lunch with me, complements of the USAF."

They stopped roughly in the centre of the complex, outside a large building looking rather like a low level hotel. When they entered Walters showed the press passes.

"You can come in and just have a coffee, or, at the other end, you can have a five course meal with service, depending on your appetites."

Holder counted five different food halls. Walters took them into a plush diner with table service. The decoration was modern with partitioned tables to create a more intimate atmosphere.

They ordered rump steak with side salad and French fries with a bottle of Californian wine. Walters was good at his job. Soon Holder must really start to work. Walters talked to Lynn about his time in Wales. He had not, he told her, been allowed to mix with the locals, though he escaped to North Wales for the odd weekends. He seemed to have an affinity with the British pub. Holder judged that the time was right to start probing as Walters showed signs of dropping his guard.

"Can you tell me why Dr Steiner was murdered in North Wales?"

"Murdered? As far as I can recall she committed suicide while on holiday in North Wales. She was a great loss to our team, a very talented lady."

"I believe she was murdered. I have done a lot of careful research. She was on holiday, but not in the sense you imply. She was on loan to Advanced Laser Technology, for a project of mutual interest to the American and British governments."

"Well you've told me something that I didn't know. The British police covered her death thoroughly and suicide was their verdict."

"What job did Dr Steiner do at this base?"

"She was a systems analyst. One of the best."

"Could you be more specific?"

"That's all I know."

"Wasn't she a laser expert?"

Walters face tightened. "Hell," he responded, "not that I recall. Why is it so important to you guys? What's the big deal? She was our loss, our friend, not yours."

"She's a part of an investigation I've been conducting in Britain, into suicide. As we found evidence to the contrary, I thought you might have some information that might help me."

Walters relaxed. Holder had scored.

"I guess I can't. I don't know a hell of a lot about her work."

"Do you have a laser department on this base?"

"We use laser power for all sorts of modern technology, like cutting metals accurately. So we are continually carrying out development in this field."

"Can I see your laser development area?"

"Sorry. That's top secret." So the laser research wasn't mainly for tools as Walters inferred. He had scored again.

"Let me explain my present research. There have been many rumours over the years that Unidentified Flying Objects found in America were brought to this base for analysis. Is that true?"

"You read thc wrong comics. That is just what you called it, rumour. No Sir, we are not invaded by the third wave or any other kind."

"Then it's nonsense that President Eisenhower paid a visit here in nineteen-fifty four and viewed alien craft?"

"It was popular press, however, it made us famous!"

"Reports say that you have analysed and reproduced saucer shaped objects at this base and that you tested them at Nellis Air Force Base in sixty-five and again in seventy-four after modification. Are you telling me this is unfounded rumour too, despite the fact that there are several reliable sightings by witnesses?"

"Most certainly I am."

"Can you tell me what you do in the underground workshops in this base?"

Walters flushed, "I don't know, but they are top secret and the highest security passes are needed to enter. I suggest you forget them for the sake of peace. We don't talk about everything, Mr Holder, we have a duty to the American people who pay us to do a job. Now that's friendly advice, so be warned."

At that moment Lynn felt uncomfortable. She looked round and saw a tall blonde man, sitting alone at a table across the diner, staring at her. She blushed and turned away.

"How much of the operation at this base is covert? I mean secret from the American people at large"

"Before I answer that, I think you should understand that the American people trust their government to do the right thing. It makes no difference which political party they support. This is why we are allowed to develop, in secret, the defence necessary for our protection. Most of the work at this base is secret; there are levels of secrecy. The underground work has the highest classification. There is nothing wrong with secrets. They are necessary for our country's development."

"In the right hands I agree, but in non executive control they can be dangerous."

"Don't get me mixed up in politics. I am a simple airman doing my job to the best of my ability."

Holder drank the last of his coffee. Ammunition exhausted, he rose and thanked Walters for his time. Their escort took them to the waiting jeep.

"Well I hope you guys enjoyed yourselves. Remember we are all on the same side."

"Thanks for your hospitality Bud. By the way, before we go, how did you feel about fooling the people of Little Haven with your American made Zero gravity craft?" Walters winced, but recovered quickly. Holder scored once more but still needed to know if they really worked within zero gravity.

"I don't know what you are talking about. Good bye friend."

With that parting shot, they drove to the gate and Holder's car, checked out and headed towards California City. Once they cleared the base Lynn, who had been silent, turned to Holder and said;

"So that's how you operate. You outsmarted him. How did you manage to remain friends?"

"Do it with a smile," replied Holder, "few resist that."

"I thought he was going to blow a fuse when you mentioned the underground workshop, but you said it so convincingly that he conceded to your knowledge instead of denying it. How did you know about them?"

"I didn't. It was a long shot that paid off. Knowing they are there is a start. Finding out what's in them is now a priority."

"Wooh. You are a poker player."

"Life's one big poker game."

CHAPTER 12.

From a cloudless sky, the sun beat down as they lay beside the pool, soaking up energy for the arduous task ahead. Holder's mind kept returning to the dangers he had perceived for America and the World.

If the executive did not have total power, as written into the American constitution, then who did? It appeared easy for power to pass into the hands of a small group of extremists or unscrupulous business men interested only in personal gain. What havoc could they create in the World for their own greed?

If idealists controlled a non executive group all the secrets at that base were at risk. The idea was horrific. Could this really be the case? Could the executive restore true democracy, or would it be another white-wash job, hiding the real truth from the people? Holder did not want to get too involved in American politics, but he saw this as a very important part of his investigation. What he had learnt bore serious implications, particularly for super weapons developed at Edward's Air Force Base or any other base with blanket security. He could not believe that non executive control had extended to the secret's business, but how long before they were cocky enough to try?

He decided to contact his friend Danny Fisher on the Los Angeles Times before they returned to England. He wanted to discuss the matter in full with him and gain a better understanding of the whole affair. Danny himself, involved in a long investigation into the Iran-Contra affair, would be able to give him a clear opinion.

"Lynn, before you hit the road, remember, if you get into trouble I won't be around to sort things out, if in doubt, pull out."

"Thanks David I'll be all right, honestly. I am looking forward to doing some ground work."

"OK - but take care. Before I start looking for the needle I am going round to Dr Steiner's flat to see if I can get any leads. Then I'll start on Lancaster. Good luck with your search and may the best man win."

Holder arrived at the complex of well-appointed modern flats. Each one had a large balcony, overlooking landscaped gardens, tennis courts and a large swimming pool. On entering he noticed the manager's office to one side of the hall. Holder asked to see the manager and they directed him into a small office. Behind the desk a short tubby man in his late forties sat drinking a coke.

"Hi, what goodies are you selling today?"

"Sorry to disappoint you but I'm a visitor from England. I am trying to trace someone who knew Dr Merle Steiner. She used to live in this complex some four or five years ago till her untimely death."

"Sorry, but salesmen are all we seem to get in here. Yes I remember her well. She was a strange woman, you might call her a loner. She didn't have many friends but one lady did seem to get through to her. Her name is Mrs. Osman. She lives in a flat on the first level. As this is a protected building I must ring her and see if she is prepared to talk to you. Excuse me a minute." Holder waited three minutes before getting clearance.

A well-dressed lady in her late forties answered the door. She was tall and slender with a sympathetic, expressive face, which revealed elegance and grace.

"Please come in Mr. Holder. I hear you are interested in my dear friend Merle. How can I help you?"

"First I must make my position clear. I'm a British journalist, Mrs Osman and I am investigating a series of unexplained deaths, mostly young scientists with great futures. I do not believe she committed suicide, rather she was murdered, perhaps to stop her work. Did she ever give you any insight into her work at Edward's Air Force Base?"

"She was a loner. She never spoke much about her work but when I began to know her well, she opened up, though it was only a couple of times, when her boss upset her. On one occasion she told me she worked on a major development that would put the States way ahead of the rest of the World in relation to defence."

"Did she say what it was?"

"No, but she was excited. The work provided scope for her to use her special understanding of laser power. She always joked that the comic books of our youth were now becoming old hat. Just before she went to England she told me she was going there to help solve some problems on a parallel development and that she was taking some secret equipment along."

"Did you ever find out what it might have been?"

"No. It must have been laser based. That was her speciality."

"Going back to Merle. Do you think she could or would commit suicide?"

"Never in a month of Sundays. She loved life. I know she had a strange life style, but she loved loneliness. She always needed solitude to do her best thinking and she was dedicated to her work. It was everything to her."

"Did she have problems with men?"

"Not that I know, but she avoided love affairs. She felt they would get in the way of her work and that was her first love."

"Any financial problems?"

"Lord no! Why she never spent half her salary. she was well covered financially" A huge pay-cheque for somebody her age."

"You say her work was successful?"

"According to Merle - yes - definitely."

"Then the three most likely reasons for suicide are discounted. I regret you have only convinced me all the more that I am right."

"You haven't come all the way from England to investigate one murder? What is behind all this?"

"I suspect foul play in a series of deaths which involve the defence industry and in particular laser development. It includes both the British and American governments. I do not know who actually assassinated Merle, but she worked with many other scientists that have since died in questionable circumstances."

"Why would they kill her?"

"I can only say that, after an exhaustive investigation, I believe that the scientists died because of their work and particularly their knowledge."

"Who was responsible?"

"I suspect the KGB compromised them."

"My god Mr Holder, that is an awesome conclusion."

"I fear so. However, there is still a vast gap between what I believe and what I can prove."

"He thanked Mrs Osman and went about his nights work. It was Sunday evening and he wanted to cover half the town that night. Some base personnel were at work and others off duty. Sunday was just another day round this town. The health clubs and gyms were all busy and he found no difficulty at all in moving around asking questions. When he showed any interest in the base they seemed to clam up. He persisted until eleven o'clock, when he called it a day and drove back to California City. Lynn was already in the room and preparing a long cold drink for his return.

"Well how did you do Lynn?"

"Everyone seems so friendly till you mention the base. Then they shut up. I found one exception, but as soon as he started to talk, it was obvious that he knew very little of importance. How did you fare?"

"About the same. My meeting with a neighbour of Dr Merle Steiner was very successful - but we're nowhere yet." He sipped his drink suddenly exhausted.

For the next three days they planned by day and searched by night for a lead, to no avail. The attitude of the local population did not help. On the fourth day they decided to target health clubs. Perhaps tongues may be a bit looser after the sauna. Late that night, he arrived back at the hotel exhausted, after hours in the gym, two saunas and the plain truth of how unfit he was - but he still had no lead.

Lynn was irrepressible;

"Darling it's a bit early to be sure, but I think I may have found the needle. Do you remember when we were in the restaurant at the base, I had a funny feeling that someone was staring at me. That tall blonde man was looking straight at me and I just looked away. Well, I was in the gym of this health club and who should be there but this man. He was on the next exerciser. He obviously recognised me and introduced himself as Reinhold Weisner. He said he was a first generation American, but his father was a scientist who worked at Peenemunde, on the V1 rockets. His father was brought to America after the war and worked for the USAF and then NASA, until he retired. The funny thing is that he seems to talk freely about the base. I think he believes I work there - and I have done nothing to disillusion him. Guess what his job is?"

"A test pilot?"

"No."

"A fuel scientist?"

"No. An avionics expert."

"That sounds promising. Did he say where he works?"

"No, but he intimated that he had to come up for air, so I reckon he works underground."

"Lynn you are a marvel. Here am I, exhausted from exercise with nothing to show and you, looking as fresh as a daisy. To top it you may well have found the needle."

"Well, don't be jealous, but I have a date with him tomorrow. He is picking me up outside the gym at seven-thirty for wining and dining. The things I have to do in the line of duty!"

"Careful. He might be a wolf in sheep's clothing."

"Do I detect jealousy getting the better of your journalistic objectivity? Tut, tut."

"How could you? I am thinking only of your safety."

"That's all right. Come to bed and prove it."

"What, in my state?"

"Reinhold would."

"That settles it." He growled wearily. "Just you give me two minutes."

Next morning they both found their movement restricted by aching muscles. They had hot and cold showers to ease the pain. After breakfast they went to the pool to plan the important meeting that evening. They wanted to minimise the chances of a hitch in obtaining the information from Dr Weisner. They went through the plan repeatedly, rehearsing it as if it was happening. Eventually Lynn was reacting automatically to the various circumstances. That was the level of preparation she needed.

After lunch they drove to Victorville to plan Holder's evening work, arriving back in time for Lynn to dress for her dinner date.

She didn't have to wait long outside the gym. Reinhold Weisner arrived at precisely seven-thirty, dressed immaculately and driving a Mercedes sports car. He was six feet tall with a well-constructed body. His neatly trimmed long blonde hair gave him a Viking look and his large blue eyes were definitely intelligent.

Holder felt alarmed as he watched him kiss Lynn's hand, help her into the Mercedes and drive away. He had a job to do in Victorville. He found he could not concentrate. His mind kept imagining what might be happening to Lynn. Meanwhile Lynn arrived at a luxurious restaurant in the mountains. She was looking down on the valley below. The sunset was casting a romantic rose hue over the countryside. The Aryan Romeo took Lynn inside to a secluded table, quiet and intimate, where he ordered their meal. Lynn showed schoolgirl interest in his work.

"What is avionics?"

"It's about The design of flight instruments. As planes fly faster and become more sophisticated, they require all sorts of accurate information to keep them on course, at the right height and the correct speed. Planes travel at supersonic speeds nowadays. They need to have accurate warning of other planes in the vicinity. All this lies within the field of avionics."

"That's fascinating. What about the Laser project?"

"That has opened up a whole new field for avionics research into areas which are irrelevant to atmospheric flight. It is fair to say that we lead the World in this field, thanks largely to a stroke of luck we had in the fifties"

"What was that?"

"Lynn, I can't tell you that. It is top secret."

"You mean your zero gravity craft?" She prompted, hoping he would open up.

"Yes, so you know."

"News travels."

"We developed replica craft in our underground facility, far from inquisitive eyes. We first flew them in sixty-five and then again in seventy-four, after modification. We used them as decoys in England, or to be precise in Wales after these tests to overcome bad weather. That produced a whole flood of UFO spotters hyping themselves into a frenzy but it did the trick."

"So you used them in Wales?"

"Yes. The instrumentation for this craft was the biggest challenge I have ever undertaken. It was so totally different from anything conceived before within the boundaries of conventional flight. We worked very hard on the control system. They are quite easy to fly. Tell me, how did you come to know about the zero gravity craft?"

"I guessed, from information I have heard around."

"Which department do you work in?"

"I don't. I'm a visitor."

"My god! I have told you all that. They would shoot me for less. You are not a spy are you?"

"Don't be silly. Your secret is safe with me. It's fascinating. Tell me about the craft."

"Sorry. I have said too much already. I thought you already knew because you worked at the base. Please change the subject. I was stupid."

His concern was so intense that Lynn decided to desist from further questioning for the rest of the evening. They talked about everything but work. He was a very interesting man and Lynn enjoyed his company. Reinhold, attracted to Lynn, became romantic in a formal way.

They drove back to California City and sat outside Lynn's hotel talking for half an hour. He lent over, kissed her tenderly and asked her if she would spend the weekend with him. They could do a tour of California. He would love to show her around. She left it open, she wasn't sure of her company's plans till later in the week, then parted with a kiss. One of the hazards of the job, she thought smiling. She entered the hotel room, jubilant, to find Holder pacing up and down in a state of high anxiety.

"Are you all right darling?" Lynn exclaimed.

"Of course I am. I was just worried about you."

"Jealous, huh? Well, you'll be more jealous when I tell you that I have found the needle and picked it up."

Holder forgot his worries and rushed over to Lynn, picking her up and swinging her round. After this spontaneous bout of euphoria he went over to the phone.

"Don't you want to know all about it?"

"First things first," he said, "could you send a bottle of champagne to room three-two-four. Thanks." He put down the phone, sat Lynn down and heard about her triumph. She taunted him with details, expecting him to show some jealousy. He knew her game and smiled. The champagne arrived and he opened the bottle. Pouring two glasses, he proposed a toast;

"To a top class investigator. She has the eyes of an eagle and has performed the impossible. She has found the invisible needle. To her health, I love her."

Lynn smiled, enjoying the thrill of this moment. Beckoning she said;

"Lets celebrate."

For the next hour their minds were diverted from work by the power of sexual response. It swept them up in a whirlwind of urgent desire into the vortex, where fulfilment was ultimate: leaving them floating on a cloud of contentment.

CHAPTER 13.

They rose late after their celebration. Their work at the base was now complete. Their next appointment, Garberville, with Tom Bowen, the new president of Zero Gravity Space Technology.

Before leaving the hotel Holder rang Bowen to say they were on the way. They packed their bags, paid the bill and drove back towards Los Angeles through the Soledad canyon, then diverted North along the Pacific coast towards San Francisco.

The warm salt air from the Pacific made the journey relaxing. After three hours they approached the outskirts of San Francisco and stopped for a bite to eat at a burger bar. Refreshed, they continued their journey towards Garberville, arriving at four-thirty. They went straight to Tom Bowen's office.

Bowen was in his early thirties, of medium height and build, with a smile that advertised a cheerful disposition, very gregarious by nature. His office was something of a mess, strewn with paperwork and unfiled letters. He seemed more interested in research than management.

"Great to meet you. Come on in and find a chair. Tell me how I can help you?"

Holder summarised the relevant parts of their research to date and Bowen intervened with questions.

"Right. I take it you want facts rather than rumour or wishful thinking. Our research, being of a strange nature and delving into territory unknown, tends to leave most people in a state of total disbelief. I will discount the more ambiguous sides of our research, which we believe implicitly and give you proven fact from the records relating to Zero gravity craft at Edward's Air Force Base."

"At Edward's," repeated Holder, "then someone has managed to spot craft on that enormous base."

"It all started back in nineteen-forty-seven after the reported crash of a saucer shaped object near Roswell. The whole story leaked out before the authorities had time to kill it. They transported parts of the wreckage to Edward's Air Force Base, under armed guard and kept it for examination and analysis. In those days, you must remember, the base was much smaller and security, though present, was not as thorough as it is today. The base was then called Muroc."

Holder nodded thoughtfully.

"Suddenly they tightened security at the base and restricted movement around the area to certain top technicians only. They banned personnel from the vicinity round the hangar. This included the President himself. Several personnel have spoken of their experiences."

"So you have substantial evidence."

"Yes. Now we come to the period between February seventeenth and twenty-fourth nineteen-fifty-four. President Eisenhower, having just arrived back from a vacation in Georgia, went on a trip to Palm Springs. During his stay, on the evening of the twentieth of February, he disappeared. The press went wild with rumour. There were even reports that he had died. James Haggerty, the White House press secretary, scotched the rumours with a broken tooth story. The truth was the President visited Edward's Air Force Base to see Zero Gravity Craft for himself."

"So they are propelled through a zero gravity field?"

"Yes, I will come to that later."

"He decided that the World was not ready for such news and a cloak of secrecy has remained on this subject ever since. There are several interesting facts that expose the dentist's story for nonsense. First, in seventy-nine, the widow of Dr Purcell, was asked simple questions such as the time of day the treatment took place. The nature of the treatment and if the dentist went to the President or the President went to the dentist's surgery. She was unable to recollect any details. When asked about the barbecue party given by the President, the following evening, her memory seemed faultless. Other factors lead us to believe that the dentist theme was a cover up."

"You have further evidence to back up your dentist theory?"

"Yes. Careful research at the Eisenhower library uncovered an interesting point. Although the library has an extensive set of records relating to the President's health there was no record of dental work being performed in February fifty-four. The file on dentists in the President's personal file also contained nothing relating to any visit to or from Dr Purcell."

"That seems to add weight to the theory."

"Copies of all sorts of acknowledgements and 'thank you' notes sent by the White House to everyone who had something to do with the Palm Spring trip are available. These included offers of golfing partners and people who just met the plane. There was no note to this dentist in any shape or form."

"You mean they kept records of all events however seemingly unimportant?"

"Yes. The cover up failed in some details, not unusual for that period when the press was less sophisticated. A top test pilot confirmed the presence of President Eisenhower at the base. Dr Robert S. Richardson, an astronomer at Palomar and Mount Wilson, wrote an article for 'This Week', in June fifty-four, entitled 'The Mysteries of Mars.' He stated clearly his strong belief in the existence of intelligent life on Mars. Had he seen the saucers at Edward's Air Force Base?

"That's interesting."

"Air Force General, Nathan Twining, wrote in May fifty-four: 'The best brains in the Air Force are now working on the mystery of the UFO..... which continues to baffle them.' If it did come from Mars

and they are that far ahead of us, we have nothing to fear."

"That is reasonable."

"Another Astronomer, Frank Halstead, of the University of Minnesota, stated in late fifty-four: 'Aircraft of some sort have visited the earth from outer space. The best scientific minds in the World agree that some planet out there is sending these things to look at us.' That's part of history."

Bowen paused then smiled. "It fell to an Englishman to find the best evidence. Desmond Leslie was researching the UFO story in June fifty-four. He found an Air Force officer that saw the craft in hangar twenty-seven at Muroc."

"That's the hangar I asked if I could view only to be told even the president could not enter."

"Leslie disclosed that a saucer about one hundred feet in diameter landed at Muroc near hangar twenty-seven. All personnel returning from leave found themselves barred from entry and restricted from the base even to retrieve their personal belongings. Their Personal effects were brought to the gate by guards. There was a considerable amount of evidence pointing to the activity of Zero Gravity Craft around the base. Gradually the base has become a huge complex. It was interesting that it developed into a centre for space technology despite being so far from the launching pad."

"Yes, that surprised me till you added the logic."

"It was because they had their main source of information being analysed right there." Bowen confirmed, "it made sense that they were using information from the saucers to conquer new horizons.

The country who conquers space first will control the World. Russia concentrated her efforts on getting men into space, while America has occupied it by remote control."

"That makes Russia far more vulnerable to attack and annihilation."

America's 'Star Wars' program controls space from the earth and can use thousands of dishes she has already in place to fire at and obliterate anything she chooses. Would that make Russia ready to disarm if she can't catch up with Western technology?"

"I doubt if anyone outside the centre of power really knows the answer to that question." Answered Holder.

"As you know, Edward's Air Force Base has simulated the real thing. All this work is carried out in a secret underground factory."

"Yes" said Holder. "I trapped their press liaison officer into confirming this point, by treating it as gained knowledge."

"That's great. Another substantial witness. What you say about Wales worries me a bit. You think they used Zero Gravity Craft made at Edward's as decoys?"

"Yes, we had that confirmed too. They had three in one hangar. They were seen by an air-conditioning engineer."

"So the sightings were USAF Craft?"

"That is so." Said Holder.

"This makes our job that much more difficult. We must re-appraise what has been seen. It will clearly influence our judgement in future. We knew that they had test-flown simulated craft in sixty-five and seventy-four at Nellis Air Force Base, but we did not know it had gone further than that!"

"Sorry to complicate the formula!"

"The shame is that President Eisenhower had the opportunity to make a name for himself, a name unparalleled in history. He could have extended the hand of friendship to these visitors on our planet. He could have been the first leader of a great nation to do so, but he remained steadfastly loyal to the sixties' Military-Industrial complex. The church had a lot to do with it too. They all put him and kept him in power. They all remained silent."

David thought a moment and asked;

"Why do you include religious leaders in this context?"

"A politician needs the support of many factions in his quest for power. A President must appeal to all religious factions, but particularly to the Roman Catholic Church, which is very strong in America. The Catholic church believes that if the secrets of the universe become known, the strength of their power, as guardians of the unknown, will diminish. They are afraid of losing control of their flock. The church wants to remain powerful, so it resists the publication of any knowledge which explains creation in rational terms."

"That's rather severe."

"The church is a reactionary force in the World today. The whole purpose of our research at Zero Space Technology is to open men's eyes to other dimensions. There can be no understandings of space technology until we accept other dimensions. We meet with massive resistance."

"So how do these craft operate?

Suffice to say that these craft operate, as far as we can understand, in an area of zero gravity that they create around themselves and are powered by self generated electromagnetic forces. That is the reason for its damaging effect on electrical circuits in close proximity."

"That answers some questions left open in Wales."

"Enough shop talk. We can continue later. In the meantime my wife has prepared a meal for us. I would be delighted if you would both be our guests."

Bowen lived on the outskirts of Garberville, in a spacious bungalow, or 'one level home.' The rooms were large, specially the living room and kitchen, but the garden was much smaller than the usual English equivalent. Bowen's wife was a charming, expressive person, having the same manner and warmth that he displayed. She showed delight with her unexpected visitors. They ate and talked until late at night, each learning from the other about the differences between America and Britain and gaining a new understanding from the sharing. It gave them valuable insight into each other's psyche.

At one o'clock, having completely lost track of time, Lynn and Holder bade Bowen and his wife good-night and returned to their motel. Next morning they rose early to drive back to Los Angeles.

CHAPTER 14.

On reaching the outskirts of Los Angeles the following afternoon Holder called his friend and fellow journalist Danny Fisher of the Los Angeles Times.

"Danny? It's David, David Holder. How is life treating you?"

"Fine. What brings you to the playground of America?"

"Can you spare some time this afternoon? I want to pick your brains about the Iran Contra investigation."

"Meet at five o'clock, we'll take it from there."

"Your office? By the way, I have my fellow journalist, Lynn with me. I'm teaching her the ropes."

"I'll bet you are, you dirty bastard. See you at five." They entered the massive offices of the Los Angeles Times. Everything in America seemed so large. The only exceptions were the cars that were generally somewhat smaller since his last visit. He asked the receptionist to tell Mr Fisher they had arrived.

Ten minutes later Fisher approached. He was rugged; worn and torn by the rigours of journalistic life; his dark hair turning grey at the sides but still covering his head. His skin was tanned and his large, grey eyes, penetrated yet, seemed friendly. He wore casual clothes with a designer jacket.

"Hi friends, great to see you. This must be the terrible handicap you told me about. Hi, Lynn. How would you guys like to have dinner on me? It's not every day I get visitors from another planet."

They walked two blocks, to a small Italian restaurant in a side street.

"Here you get the best spaghetti in Los Angeles."

They tucked into spaghetti washed down with Chianti and followed by zabaglione and coffee. During the meal Holder informed Fisher about the investigation and voiced some of his fears. After dinner they sat and talked over coffee and brandy.

"Now what I want to understand are the details and implications of the Iran-Contra affair. Although it has no direct bearing on my investigation, the action and reaction of the United States has a direct link to the course our government adopts."

"Well, you are in for a long session. That is a complex subject with many different facets and tentacles going out in all directions."

"Where did it start?"

"Cast your mind back to the summer of nineteen-eighty. Reagan was an actor and a State Governor putting in his pitch for President. His running mate

and chosen candidate for vice-president was George Bush. He supported Reagan through thick and thin during the primaries, where we choose our Presidential candidates. Remember that at this time Reagan was putting up for the office of president for the first time."

"I seem to remember the opinion polls showed Carter was weak and likely to lose the race."

"Yes but, Jimmy Carter was the President and the democratic runner for re-election. Reagan's election managers became very worried that Jimmy Carter was going to steal the limelight by getting the American hostages released from the American embassy in Iran before polling day. The Reagan campaign headquarters decided to act to stop any chance of the release of the hostages before the election."

"Thereby hoping to deprive Jimmy Carter of glory and victory at the polls." Commented Holder.

"Yes. Two meetings took place with high ranking officials of the Iranian Diplomatic corps, one in Washington DC and the second in Paris, in October eighty. The republican delegation consisted of Richard Allen, Donald Gregg and guess who? George Bush. To cut a long story short, they struck a deal. It was a particularly important deal for the Republicans. They guaranteed Iran a multi-million dollar payment and as much armoury as they needed for their fight against Iraq. The condition was they would guarantee to hold the hostages until the election was over and release them on inauguration day for Reagan."

"If you could prove that...it would be sensational."

Fisher smiled, "Then They agreed the deal and as you know, Reagan won the election. The Iranians honoured the third part of the deal and the release of

the hostages took place on the twenty-first of January eighty-one. Reagan denied consistently, for five years, that he had struck any hostages-for-cash or arms deal. He was under so much pressure about a year ago, that he retracted. There was a phenomenal weight of evidence but he still denied knowing what had gone on."

"If the evidence was so substantial how could he ride the storm?"

"This whole affair poses serious constitutional questions. Was Jimmy Carter cheated out of an election victory by an illegal deal? Did the Iranians hold the hostages beyond the time they would have released them because of a deal? Did the President lie to the American people for five years, before being forced to concede part of the truth?"

Holder volunteered. "The answer to the first is probably yes, as the American people love success and the return of the hostages would have been a great victory for Carter." Fisher continued,

"The answer to the second question is most definitely yes. The answer to third is that it is inconceivable that Reagan would not have known at least the main details of this illegal act. Indeed he should have known right from its conception unless he was President in name only. To support this we have one of Reagan's top campaign aides, Barbara Honegger and the ex Prime Minister of Iran, Abul Bani Sadr, attesting to what took place at the time. Thus started the Iran Contra affair, encompassing numerous wrong doings by our executive and I suspect, some by yours."

"What do you mean by wrong doings by our executive?"

"I'll come to that later. The scene has been set for the next stage and it gets more ominous as it goes along.

Now, the Reagan camp had to fulfil their side of the agreement and supply arms. His first big blow came when Congress turned down his move to supply arms to Iran. He promised arms to Iran, so he turned to a contingency plan. They formed a company in Israel to handle all the arms' transfers. Its name was Kendal Holdings Ltd. They started arms transfers to Iran by the second half of eighty-one."

"That's only one and a half years after his inauguration."

"Yes that is so. Again congress turned down Reagan's effort to supply arms to the Contra rebels. Defying their wishes he consulted his senior military adviser, Admiral Poindexter and his adviser Lieut. Col. Oliver North. We assume he asked them to find a way around the decision by Congress. Oliver North was to turn out to be the fall guy for the politicians. He was young and politically naive being a professional soldier. He was placed in charge of executing orders that did not have the blessing of Congress. So started the most terrifying drift from executive power we have ever witnessed in the Western World."

"The implications, I suspect, are particularly far-reaching as you lead the World in democratic government!"

"They formed a loose league of entrepreneurs in the arms, drugs and revolution business. Its purpose was first, to obtain money for the contra cause. Then, second to supply arms and mercenaries to support the right wing groups who were working to overthrow the government in Nicaragua.

Frankly, I cannot say that the Nicaraguan government impress me, but that doesn't give anyone the right to interfere.

The league consisted of right wing entrepreneurs dedicated first to making money and second to whipping the asses of the left wing government of Nicaragua."

"This was the non-executive government?"

"Yes. From this moment, you must realise, there was no incentive to solve the Iran-Iraq war. America was financing their efforts to help the Contra rebels through profits made on selling arms to Kendal Holdings Limited, in Israel, who in turn sold them to Iran. America made no real effort to end the war until it became apparent that their scheme had failed."

"From what you say, they had a financial and political reason to let it roll."

"Exactly. Three of the league had, meanwhile, formed a company with another ruthless partner. These wars then became an extraordinary source of personal profit for them."

"So they gained from their covert operation?"

"Yes and how. They began dealing in anything that would disrupt the Nicaraguan government, like drugs, weapons and mercenaries. Active support from Washington brought assistance from the CIA. John Hull, a rancher in Costa Rica and a CIA agent himself, took part in supplying drugs and arms through the new company, Eastcote, to the rebel forces."

"So the CIA was actively involved?"

"You bet they were. They formed a non-executive power house dedicated to two principles, making money for its directors and crushing a democratic left wing government. It was not answerable to anyone, as long as the arms kept flowing and the mercenaries received their pay. They recruited mercenaries here, in Belgium and in England and indeed anywhere else that they could find well-trained redundant, front-line troops."

"They recruit internationally?"

"Yes. One of the English groups went into a hospital in Nicaragua to kill officials. They blew up a whole ward, killing many children and wrecking a wing of the hospital. These are the type of animals they use. Take a look at the American government's record for supporting democracy in the smaller states of the World. You will find, specially in Africa and South America, nothing that will give any self-respecting American one shred of pride. Our aid mostly goes to help rebels to overthrow democratically elected governments, where they have shown interest in nationalising mineral reserves owned by multi-national companies based in America."

"That's pretty heavy criticism!"

"Examples of this have been seen in Guatemala, Brazil, Ghana, Angola and now Nicaragua. Far from being Russian satellites, these countries are among those which have tried to manage their own affairs, with great hindrance from us. There has been no sign of the drift towards Communism that is an all-purpose justification for everything the American government does. If Communism in these countries exists it is an organic form of Communism born of circumstance and necessity."

"You mean that it is more local community action to protect their own interests?"

"Yes. This has all left America looking rather shabby. She has been jumping in all over the place to protect mineral rights that have made her wealthy. These countries should have been the ones to get rich. Instead their natural resources became abused and ruthlessly exploited. The CIA has spearheaded this war of protectionism, assisted by the league. They have all been lining their pockets with the spoils."

"Surely, minerals sales are at a low today? We'd need another fifties boom to make those mineral rights active mining again."

"I'm giving you the picture in outline. There is a third aspect that I am now investigating and that is state controlled drug dealing. Later this year I am going to South America to do some digging. I'd love to have you along if you are interested?"

"I would be very interested. I am involved in a drug case in August and I would like to get a prospective of the other end of the business. This has nothing to do with my main research. When will it be?"

"About September or October, I hope, but it will be far too dangerous for Lynn I am afraid. These boys don't like snoopers. One wrong word and you are dead meat."

"That will be fine." She smiled. "I'll stay at home."

"Very wise. I have heard say that your government supplied mercenaries for Nicaragua through a private security firm, Sentinel Armed Securities."

"Well if that is so it adds another tentacle to their list of devious activities. Our government would not be outwardly associated with such a move. However this firm seem to crop up in everything I investigate, they're like a bad penny! I sometimes wonder if the government aren't behind them, pulling their strings."

Confused by the lack of accountability Holder questioned; "Tell me, how can a President survive with such a conclusive case against him and his colleagues?"

"To understand that you have to understand the American constitution and political system. Without that knowledge, the best way to explain it simply is that the enquiry system for impeachment itself is long, drawn out and complicated. The media is hasty and easily misled and confuses public opinion. The end result is that the people are so misinformed and confused that they cannot decide for themselves. When that happens they usually split down party lines, it is another case of divide and rule."

"Are you implying that politicians deliberately confuse the issues to avoid impeachment?"

"Do bears shit in the forest?"

"Then what you are saying is that they can form a non-executive government and use the system to support it!"

"Yes. That just about sums it up, each nail we put in their coffin is useless as long as they can still escape. They laugh at us. Only if we drive the nails home all at the same time can they be caught, which is just not going to happen in reality."

"So that is why you never get passed the threatening stage where impeachment is concerned."

"My main worry is what's going to happen when Reagan retires at the end of his second term in December. If the Democrats don't get their act together, it seems we could get Bush and you know what he has done. That worries me more than anything. The confidence of these right wing entrepreneurs is unassailable."

"Surely the American people will see through this hollow pretence?"

"I'm not so sure. Oliver North is now doing a highly profitable lecture tour around the States. He is extolling the virtue of everything he did for the country he loves. He boasts about carrying out his orders for the good of America. He even brags that Isvestia knew all about his Iran Contra deal. I hope the committee ask why he kept it from the American people when they start their interrogation. I am sure that he will get off lightly, as he has destroyed mountains of evidence in the shredder."

"I think he has admitted to shredding the evidence. What arrogance." Holder intervened.

"The American people are suckers for cheese cake boy colonels. He is playing to the gallery, giving it all his best shots. He has Script writers, production managers, image makers, the lot according to reports. He's acting so cocky he must know he'll get off. Reagan is sure to refuse to give evidence at the inquiry and without the help from important documents in the President's possession, he will go free or serve a short sentence."

"That's terrible."

"In my opinion Reagan, Bush and a whole lot of other people should go down as well. Mark my words, by the spring of eighty-nine Bush will be President and Oliver North will be free or under a light sentence and very, very rich."

"You said the British government was also involved in some way. Can you explain?"

"What I am about to relate has not been substantiated, but never the less I take it as read because of the end result. Iran needed help to keep her military equipment on the field. She had inherited all the Shah's equipment. Among this was a substantial number of Chieftain tanks. During the war these needed spare parts. Reagan's administration pleaded with the British government to send the parts required, but met stiff opposition. So it is assumed that the two heads got together and struck a deal, because the parts were sent from Britain, via a roundabout route, to Iran. Their tanks were kept on the battle field."

"That sounds like another devious dealing. Probably tied up so tight the truth will not out."

"When the Iran Contra scandal eventually broke and the source of funds to support the contra rebels dried up, other funding replaced the shortfall fast. This is where the drug dealing came into play, organised by the CIA in South America. When you come there with me, I think you will get a clearer understanding of how those operations work. The CIA pays for all sorts of clandestine operations through drug dealing. Because of their structure and protection from investigation, they get away with it."

"Reports state that seventy-five per cent of the drug dealing in South America come under the control of the CIA." Remarked Holder.

"I believe that this is quite possible. They have certainly used drugs to de-stabilise countries they have targeted. They have also made vast sums of money from trading in them. So I believe have the British government. Hiding behind a private security company."

"What you are saying is that both our countries are hypocritical in their so called crusades against drugs, as they peddle them themselves?"

"That is precisely so."

"You have given me a lot to digest. It is going to take me some time to come to terms with all the possible implications."

The waiters were showing signs of impatience and Holder knew they must leave. Fisher and the LA times paid the bill. They walked into hot, muggy night air.

"Thanks for that excellent dinner and your insights, Danny. Keep in touch and when you come to England you must stay with us. I'll tell you more about my investigation when we tour South America. Let me know in good time when we'll be going. I don't want to book anything that might interfere with our plans."

"Bye Dave and good luck. Make sure you teach Lynn good, you lucky bastard. I wish I could find a trainee like you."

"Thanks, kind sir. I'll follow your advice and leave out Latin America from my lessons."

Lynn and Holder walked the two blocks back to their hotel in silence. The details they had just heard overwhelmed them. Their minds grappled with the magnitude of the story and the implications lying behind the truth. American democracy received a body blow that may take a long time to heal and it has roll on effects for Britain.

Lynn had been largely responsible for breaking the silence surrounding Edward's Air Force Base and he knew that she had been a great asset to his endeavours. Now it was time for a reward. They had earned a break and that was just what they were going to have.

"Lynn darling, how about a three day rest at the resort of your choice before we go home?"

"Can we go and see Hollywood and then spend some time on the beach at Santa Monica?"

Their first stop was Sunset Boulevard then Rodeo Drive, one of the avenues to the North, towards Beverley Hills. The first was unique but it had a seamy end as well which they avoided. The shops were extravagant in display and decor, frequented by famous stars, living in Beverley Hills and working in Hollywood. Harrods would have looked old-fashioned and out of place in this Boulevard.

As they arrived in Rodeo Drive Holder spotted a name he knew from London, Cecil Gee, a leading fashion house. They had a large store catering for exclusive clientele from Hollywood. The whole atmosphere was expensive and outrageous. The staff seemed intent on service. Lynn's eyes opened wider as they toured the shop. She spotted a blouse that even Holder agreed was uniquely beautiful. When Lynn saw the price her heart dropped. Holder, feeling her disappointment, asked her to try it on for size.

He took the opportunity of her absence to pay for it. He knew it would fit her perfectly. As she came out of the changing room Holder gasped in surprise. She looked stunning.

"Right, leave it on. Can we have a bag for her old blouse, please?" He asked, turning to the assistant.

"Of course sir, no problem. Thank you. Come again, have a nice day now."

They browsed around the rest of the store. Feeling more part of the place having purchased a piece of the action. There were extravagant clothes and designer shoes, the speciality of the vice-president of the store,

not forgetting a jewellery department of outrageous designs and exquisite taste. Everything a star could ever wish to own. Having taken in the atmosphere they wandered up and down the boulevard and avenues for two hours, spending millions in their minds.

When they became too tired to go further, they footed it back to the car and drove up to Santa Monica and booked a room in a large hotel overlooking the golden sands of the Pacific. It was late afternoon and very hot. When they reached their room, with a panoramic window on the playground of California, Lynn gave him a long kiss and whispered in his ear;

"And now I am going to thank you properly for this exquisite present. Lets take a shower, then I will show you some real Californian hospitality."

For three days they did little other than sun-bathe and swim. Occasionally they visited the Jacuzzi and sauna, followed, of course by a little more Californian hospitality.

Their time went too quickly. Thursday came and they packed reluctantly and made their way back to Los Angeles Airport.

CHAPTER 15.

Their flight left at seventeen-thirty American time. Suffering a slight delay at take-off they landed at Heathrow the next day. They slept for a good part of the journey arriving quite relaxed, if slightly jet-lagged. As a precaution Holder put his notes into Lynn's luggage. They went through customs separately and Lynn passed through without trouble.

"Have you anything to declare sir?"

"No."

"Could you please open your case?"

They searched his cases thoroughly, feeling the lining and looking for secret compartments. Eventually, when they couldn't find contraband, the officer said;

"Would you come this way?"

"What's wrong, officer?"

"Just come with me, Sir."

Holder followed into a back room and was ordered to strip. Then he was body searched. Finding nothing they asked him to get dressed again.

"Now, I demand to know what you were looking for."

"We are not required to answer any questions. You may go."

He was furious. When he finally emerged from customs at the arrival area Lynn was near to panic.

"God, I thought I had lost you."

"Let's get out of here, quickly."

They piled into the first taxi available and drove to Twickenham.

"What do you think they were looking for? You were so long, I thought they had arrested you."

"I think they were after the notes."

"Do you mean to say they have that much power?"

"You'd better believe it and much more."

"Then they suspect you have their secrets?"

"Maybe, or perhaps they wanted to scare me. They just make me angry and more determined."

"They certainly scared me."

The taxi pulled up outside his house. Holder paid and they entered to find a pile of the usual junk mail clogging up the doorway. He took the luggage upstairs and came down to listen to messages on his answering machine. Just by the phone was a written message from his son saying; "Hi Dad. One day we might meet." Holder laughed and switched his answering machine onto playback. The first message brought him down to earth. A young digital communication expert working on a defence project had allegedly committed suicide by driving his BMW at a wall. He was only twenty-two years old and his name was Stewart Turner. He listened to the other messages, then he phoned John at the fountain of knowledge.

"Is that you, John?"

"Yes, dear boy. So we are back safely from paradise. How is the angel of my desire?"

"She is now an ace investigator, a needle finder extraordinaire."

"You obviously worked her too hard. How cruel of you."

"Now John! Could you put the name Stewart Turner in the pot and see what brews?"

"Just a minute..."

"A young man of twenty-two, snuffed out in his prime. Worked for Advanced Electrical on MOD contract work. Killed when his car crashed into a brick wall at the end of May."

"Nothing else?"

"No, that's all."

"Now can you put the name Ivan Karovski in your mistress and polish your crystal ball."

"OK dear boy, just a minute...He is listed as a defendant in a court case. He avoided prosecution by pleading political immunity, supported by the Russian embassy."

"That's interesting. He must be a Russian agent. Thanks John."

"Give my undying love to Lynn."

He put down the phone. So the death of Daniel Kershaw was preceded by a Russian agent following him. That was getting near the truth. Russia was becoming the odds on favourite in Holder's book.

Lynn came down and heard the news.

"By the way John sends his undying love and thinks I am overworking you."

"Bless him, he is obviously a good judge of character. But I wouldn't have it any other way. I am going round to the shops to get some food. Is there anything you want while I am out?"

"No, we have enough wine, haven't we?"

"Yes, plenty."

Lynn departed on her shopping spree while Holder unpacked his bag, showered and changed into something more comfortable. On returning Lynn asked if she could ring her parents and tell them about their trip. He agreed immediately but warned Lynn to consider the possibility that his phone might be tapped. She was careful, after phoning her news through she went into the kitchen to prepare a meal, while he collected his notes and collated them with his previous work.

Soon the meal was ready, the wine opened and they were together, alone at home, in candle-light; all work forgotten. Their interest turned to each other and as the night grew older, they abandoned reality together for what seemed to be several eternity's. Their love expressed itself, delivering a passionate degree of single minded joy at the orgy of pleasure they experienced.

Next morning the work of assembling notes and writing the story began in earnest. For the next three weeks he planned no other work. He wanted to get everything down in order, with his concluding summaries, so when the time came, it was up to date and ready to go to press.

As he prepared the script Lynn typed it into the word processor. They were about half way through, after two and a half weeks, when he answered the

phone one morning and learned of another death in the defence industry. That night a weapons engineer, Michael Barker aged sixty, had died of a heart attack. The news came to him via his friend in Reuters.

Holder dropped what he was doing and they both drove to Chippenham in Wiltshire. They arrived in the early afternoon and checked out Michael Barker's address. Twenty minutes later they parked outside his house. The police were present as Holder walked up the drive of the spacious bungalow. The garden was well kept, with a profusion of rose beds flanking the winding drive. A detached double garage on the left contained a workshop and storage space with room for one car on the right. The inspector came up to them and asked politely, "Can I help?"

"Yes. I am David Holder. I am here to investigate the death of Michael Barker. Can you tell me what you know?" He said, showing his police press pass.

"His name was Michael Barker as you know. He worked for Advanced Electrical in Christchurch. The police doctor tells me he died of a heart attack. He was sixty years old."

"Can I see the body?"

"I am afraid it has already been removed, but if you go to the local mortuary I am sure they will accommodate you with that pass."

"Did he have a wife?"

"No, he was a widower."

They were just about to leave, to interview the neighbours, when two plain-clothes men came out of the bungalow carrying a large box. Holder recognised the familiar icy stare of the man from the security service.

The neighbours, Mr and Mrs Wells, were a retired couple in their late sixties.

"I suppose you want to know about Michael. Well, what's to tell?" Said Mrs Wells. "He was a quiet man that kept himself to himself, but very friendly. He was a widower. His wife died some time ago and he has led a quiet life since then. He lived for his work. Physically he was very fit. He had regular health tests, which are standard practice for senior staff. We know, as we both worked at Advanced Electrical."

"Did anyone know him well?"

"The best person you can contact, if you want to know about Michael, is his colleague Jenny Crane. She worked in the same department as Michael and probably saw him yesterday. She lives in the end house on this side, number fifty-six."

"Tell me, from what you know of him, was he a candidate for a heart attack?"

"Well, until this morning I would have said no, but I seem to have been proved wrong."

"That remains to be seen. Thank you, Mrs Wells."

They drove to the local mortuary to view the body and waited half an hour before permission came to see the deceased. Holder had already tried to persuade Lynn to stay behind, but she insisted that she should experience her first slab case. The body was on a table, not in a compartment, so the pathologist must have been examining it. The face was whitish-grey colour and drawn, the muscles rigid from rigor mortis. The limbs were difficult to move. In this short time all life had gone and just a solid mass remained, the sad finality of death.

First he examined the hands and the arms, then the face and neck. Hidden in the hair at the base of the skull he could just make out a red singe mark. He parted the hair and there it was, a distinctive burn mark on the flesh, surrounded by a circle of reddened skin. He had only seen this unusual mark once before and that was about a year ago when he attended a murder. The thug attacked the victim with a stun gun. He remembered being told that the American version of this aggressive weapon produced a shock in the region of eighty-thousand volts for a millisecond. It was enough to induce a heart attack in the healthiest of men and might simply kill outright. The mark was small and easily missed specially if no one suspected foul play. He was certain he was looking at another murder.

The time was now five-thirty, they decided to interview Jenny Crane, Barker's colleague from work. As they pulled up Jenny was just getting out of her car. They introduced themselves and Jenny asked them to come inside.

"It was a terrible shock to learn about Michael's death. I saw him about two hours before he died and he was a picture of health then. He was a man who really looked after himself. He ate sensible food. He was not overweight and he took plenty of exercise. I can usually tell a candidate for heart attack and he certainly was not one of those."

"Go on," said Holder kindly.

"There are quite a few of us at work who are certain that he did not die naturally. The project that occupied him was so secret he couldn't even tell us any details. He used to disappear for one week in six. He never told us the reason for his absence. However, just recently, he did show concern about the deaths in the defence industry. Daniel Kershaw was one of his colleagues. He mentioned that he met with a horrific accident last April."

"I know. I investigated that death and I can say, with fair certainty, that it was not suicide, but murder. I also know the project. It was a laser defence weapon that was being developed by Advanced Laser Technology combining a total defence program for the American and British governments. How would Michael have fitted into such a program?"

"Well, that's a big question. His greatest skill was to take electronic development and adapt it to the specific needs of any given project. So it could be that his job was to marry components from two sources, or modify something to suit requirements. He was a quiet genius, really."

"You're confirming my worst fears."

"Why, do you think the Russians did it?"

"It has to involve the KGB - why else would the police have orders to keep quiet? Why else were British security involved at every death?"

"This is frightening. Listen, if you need any other help please contact me. Don't use my name, but I will help if I can. I appreciate the risk you are taking and I am fully behind you. It's obvious that the security services and police can't protect any of us on this project."

"Thanks," said Holder, getting up; "be in touch!"

On the way back home they both agreed that it was murder for three main reasons, the health report, the mark on the neck and the connection with Daniel Kershaw. Speed was of the essence in this job. He impressed this on Lynn as she was recovering from seeing her first body.

In mid August Holder had an assignment in Sweden that he couldn't side-step. He was filling in for a colleague on holiday covering the trial of Captain Grey on drug smuggling charges. The case was due in court in the middle of August. For the next ten days they worked uninterrupted. It was becoming a very timely investigation.

Lynn was doing a brilliant job with the word processor and the work was nearly up-to-date when the time came to depart for Sweden. He decided to take Lynn along as he came to rely on her ability to support him in his work. He had to admit that he would now be lost without her.

CHAPTER 16.

Next morning while Lynn collected the return tickets to Stockholm, Holder arranged with John to compile all information available on the preliminary hearing of Captain Grey. At eleven o'clock he went to collect the information that was to give him a background to the investigation.

"Good morning, dear boy. Where is the angel of my desire today?"

"She is busy preparing for our trip. How did you get on?"

"Found a lot of coverage. I hate to think what I will have by the end of the trial. I have collated and dated it, so you can easily see the order of events. Seems a strange case. Don't get mixed up in the drugs World - Even more dangerous than defence."

"I am only covering for a colleague who couldn't make the trial. He's on holiday and I need the money. This is not part of my own case, but I will be looking into drug trafficking later this year, in South America. I'll have an expert with me then and I will take the greatest of care to stay out of trouble."

"Give my undying love to Lynn, you lucky chap. Take care."

"Thanks. I'll ring you when I get back."

"The road to hell was paved with good intentions."

"I mean it. I just forget sometimes."

With that, Holder made for Twickenham, where he sat down to sort through the cuttings. He wanted to spend the rest of the day familiarising himself with the case. Twenty minutes later Lynn called him to the dining-room. Afterwards, they each compiled their own appraisal of the case. Studying the political manoeuvring, between the British and Swedish governments, which gave the case its character. They ended up with the pertinent information.

Grey was twenty-eight years old at the time of his arrest. He gained his commission in nineteen-eighty. He was arrested on the sixteenth of May eighty-seven, in Stockholm. The Swedish police charged him with smuggling two hundred and fifty pounds of cocaine into Sweden.

He was accused of hiding the drugs in secret compartments in his car. The car in question was, according to Grey, on loan from a friend for his holiday. He stated that he knew nothing about any drugs hidden in the car, a Mercedes. He was held without charge for three months before the trial and was not even allowed access to his family accept through his local lawyer.

At the first hearing, Mr Eriksson represented him in court. He was not granted bail as Sweden's system did not operate this system. They held him in solitary confinement to await his trial. By June considerable concern was being shown at home about a system that treated a prisoner as a criminal before his trial and his family applied pressure to relieve his suffering. The solitary confinement and lack of bail were, according to his lawyer, affecting his health.

His commanding officer stated that he could not believe that Grey associated himself with such a sordid trade and that there must be some mistake.

They postponed the date of the trial many times, amid rumour and denial of evidence and frustration began to tell on both sides. The latest date to be fixed was the fourteenth of August. The court's estimation was that the trial itself would last for four days.

Holder suspected that this would turn out to be a gross under-estimate. Lynn came into the room, rubbing her hair with a towel. Sauntering up to him, she gave him a long, if slightly wet, kiss and said;

"It's time for a hard working boy to come and show a wayward girl how to enjoy herself."

They landed at eleven thirty Swedish time, reaching their hotel in Stockholm in time for lunch. It was a large friendly place with an old fashioned atmosphere. The room on the third floor was spacious, with all the essentials, but lacked the refinements found in American hotels.

The trial started the next day. Holder decided that they should do some sightseeing and shopping as this would probably be their last chance. They toured part of the old city. One thing that particularly impressed them was the tidiness. There was no sign of litter in the streets, or of waste bins overflowing. People here took a pride in their city.

That night They visited a Swedish night club. Later they dinned and used the club casino. Holder, to his surprise, started a winning streak on the roulette wheel. Having enjoyed a night of action they returned to their hotel exhausted and ready for a good night's sleep.

They were in the courthouse by nine-thirty for preliminary investigations before the trial started. Then, at the appointed time, they entered the courtroom and sat in the benches reserved for the press. The room was filling up, which was not surprising, as the case had received an unusually large press coverage. Grey was not in court, which prompted Holder to ask the journalist next to him for a reason. The answer surprised him. This was a preliminary hearing, for committal proceedings, to lodge the case with the court. It did not require the presence of the defendant.

The defence council sat on the benches opposite. By now the courtroom was full. He noted the strange absence of Grey's girlfriend.

The judge entered. He was a grey-haired man in his early fifties and the assembly rose in respect until he was seated. This preceded a shuffling silence as all the participants prepared themselves for the battle ahead, shifting their papers into some order.

The judge opened by formally announcing the charges against Grey and outlining the procedure to be followed during the trial. By the end of the summary it was time for the lunch break.

Johansson, the Swedish journalist sitting next to Holder, was in his early thirties with short cropped, light mousy hair and a thin elongated head. Holder asked him to lunch with them to explain the Swedish justice system. He agreed and they went to a local restaurant. For a while they discussed the pre-trial and then Johansson described the system of justice in Sweden.

"First of all our legal system assumes guilt until the defendant and his state appointed defence, prove innocence to the presiding judge. It seems to be at this point that Grey found himself at a disadvantage. He assumed that the legal system of the two countries would be similar. Your law says a defendant is innocent until proven guilty. In your system a conclusion is reached by the court after examination and cross examination, by prosecution and defence barristers. The jury have the final word and they are led by the judge's summary."

"Your system sounds similar to France."

"In Sweden, the decision of guilt or innocence is made before the trial, with only the public prosecutor, the police and the state elected defence lawyer present. It was at these hearings, that have taken place since his arrest, that the state prosecutor decided to press charges. The trial will commence today, or be set to start later. Having established guilt the chances of getting him off, judging from experience, is about one-hundred to one against. This trial is not to determine guilt or innocence, but rather to make records of the evidence and to decide on an appropriate sentence, once both sides have had their say."

"You mean to say that no cross examination of the witnesses takes place to establish the facts in public?"

"That is all done in closed preliminary hearings."

"Dangerous system," said Holder, "and rather medieval to my way of thinking. Much of this evidence would be disallowed or discredited in an English court."

"Yes, I am afraid it is not to our credit. Some people are actively trying to change the system, but that won't help this poor bastard. However, I could tell you a great deal you don't know about this case if you could spare an evening. Now we must get back. The judge will not allow us to enter the court during the hearing."

They arrived back with a minute to spare before the judge entered to start the next session.

The public prosecutor rose and formally charged Grey with smuggling two hundred and fifty pounds of cocaine into Sweden.

He claimed that Grey had lied to him in his first statement, given to the public prosecutor's office, when he said that he came to Sweden to meet a friend. He later changed his statement to say that his friend asked him to take the car to Malmo. This was the highlight of an otherwise boring day in court.

At the end of the day they announced that the trial would start on the twenty-first of August, next week. They cleared the courtroom. This was a total surprise to Holder who understood the trial would continue. He realised that this was going to be a long job with no predictable end date. The court had estimated a four day trial, but when would it start? He began to think he had lost something in the translation, until

Johansson assured him that he hadn't. Holder loathed reporting on trials for this reason.

Johansson left with Lynn and Holder and asked if he could drop them off at their hotel. They welcomed the offer and asked Johansson in for a drink on arrival.

"All you have seen today is the charge being lodged. The trial proper will start next week, unless they postpone it again." He smiled an apology.

They went into the lounge bar and took a quiet corner while Holder went to reception and faxed his report to London. Lynn had already ordered the drinks when Holder joined them.

"Right Svere, you said you could tell us the background to this case. Let's have a long drink and hear the facts."

"Well, along with several other reporters, I have been working on this case since last April, when Captain Grey was first arrested. I started before that. I was already onto the syndicate operating this supply route and what I have to tell you is supported by knowledge gained in my quest to expose drug trafficking in Sweden. As you know we have already gaoled another army officer for smuggling cannabis into the country."

"Yes, I have studied the case for similarities."

"I have to declare an interest, at this point. My younger sister became an addict because of this type of criminal. When the drug squad first stopped Grey they only found a few ounces of cocaine in his car. Suspicion led the drug squad to continue their search and they found another consignment of commercial size. This made them more curious, until one of the other prisoners arrested at the same time exposed the details. Apparently he disclosed Grey was a courier for drugs destined for Amsterdam supplied through the CIA from South America via Marseilles in France."

"Keep going," said Holder.

"A simple reason may explain the supply of drugs. The Iran Contra affair blew up in the face of the President and the funds made in five years of arms trading, held in a Swiss numbered bank account, dried up. Therefore the only payment available for this large amount, without Congress finding out, was in drugs from South America. The company supplying mercenaries had the choice of taking drugs as payment or nothing. One theory is that they seconded Grey from the army to carry out this mission. It was a favour to America."

"Better cover - possible, but very risky."

"They asked Grey to carry two consignments to Sweden as they were behind schedule. What he did not know was that the international drugs ring supplying the cocaine was already under investigation and surveillance by the Swedish drugs squad. Perhaps they watched Grey all the way, but they also knew of his immunity, so they had to be careful only to tackle him if he dealt in Sweden.

"My theory is that, It wasn't till he picked up his contact that they knew for certain that it was a local drop. That was when they moved in."

"That doesn't make much sense. His contact could have been anyone."

"Now came the most ironic part of the whole sordid affair: the IRA cell in Malmo owned the consignment, purchased through a Russian middleman according to a reliable informer. The IRA trade in drugs to buy arms to kill British soldiers in Northern Ireland. Isn't that a cruel joke?"

"If that is true it is sensational."

"I am sure Grey did not know and I am equally sure that he would have refused the job if he had known the facts. Probably his contact was all he knew. That is the normal procedure for a courier."

Holder thought hard and long about this account. It answered some of the questions that had been pre-occupying him, but opened up others.

First, he knew the contact from a previous investigation and he was not a member of a Swedish drug ring. He was an ex-SAS officer. He may have been involved in the CIA operation but he was certainly not involved in the local Swedish distribution. He was most definitely not a distributor to the IRA cell in Malmo. If the drugs were destined for the Malmo IRA cell it was without his knowledge.

"Grey had an impeccable service record." Said Holder still doubtful. "He had been an undercover agent in Northern Ireland for the last eighteen months. This was a dangerous position and trusted only to the cream of SAS intelligence."

Holder thought. If he was right about him getting into Grey's car it would have no significance to the Swedish drugs squad. It would not have provoked an arrest. It was stage-managed, but for what reason? This was the question to which he must apply himself, but he was not going to divulge these thoughts to his new Swedish friend.

"That is a remarkable account of the situation. Do you believe it is true?" Holder continued.

"We have no way of knowing for sure how much of it is true, but my journalistic feeling is that most of it is."

"Have another drink."

"No, I must go. I am already late for my girlfriend."

He thanked the Swede for his help and turned to Lynn and said:

"Can we go upstairs? I don't want to be overheard."

"Oh David, I can't wait," replied Lynn, not realising he was being serious. Once In the room he outlined his thoughts to Lynn, watching for her reaction.

"You have a devious mind."

"Nothing is ever as it seems, especially when you are dealing with stratosphere politics."

"From what you have said it seems to be a laundering operation to pay a security company for mercenaries and somehow Russia is involved. Another link with a security company and the KGB maybe?"

"Lynn, you are spot on my thoughts. You are as devious as I am. Do you think thc security company could be our old friends Sentinel Armed Securities?"

"Possibly."

"Sentinel Armed Securities always seem to participate in all our enquiries. If it is them it adds another illegal activity to their long list of crimes. I must say I never expected this trial to link with our enquiries? Now we will keep this theory strictly to ourselves, until we have hard evidence."

"OK, but what can I do next?"

"I want you to contact Grey's girlfriend tomorrow. She may not want to talk but she could be our first lead."

He rang his office and asked for all information available on Grey and his girlfriend, leaving the hotel fax number for the reply, which they promised within the hour. The trial would start in Stockholm's Central Criminal Court on the twenty-first. That gave Holder five days to do some research, more than enough time.

Meanwhile Lynn rang round the hotels to find out where Miss Pierson was staying. She succeeded on the fifth attempt and decided to visit her that evening, while Holder arranged their schedule for the next day.

Lynn asked at reception to speak to Miss Pierson. The receptionist rang her room but found that Miss Pierson refused to receive visitors. She suggested Lynn should call at eleven o'clock the next day. She went back frustrated in her endeavour but sympathising with the girl's predicament.

Holder received his fax from London and his first lead, supported his theory. There wasn't much he didn't already know on Grey. However his girlfriend, Miss Sarah Pierson was a retired army officer assigned to the SAS. On leaving the service she joined a security company, Sentinel Armed Securities, a photo existed of her outside her company office. What a small World. A confirming lead. Was she in charge of Grey's operation? That would place Captain Grey in the same camp. That information places Sentinel Armed Securities firmly behind illegal drugs dealing.

Holder, having listened to Lynn's frustration, consoled her but warned she must become used to rebuffs. It happened all the time in this job. A good investigative journalist never gives up when he is on the scent.

Next morning he made an appointment with the police chief, while Lynn went back to the hotel to interview Miss Pierson, only to find that she had left unexpectedly. It wasn't till Holder came back at six o'clock that she knew that he had failed as well. Although he had achieved an interview nothing new had come out of it. Their bad luck continued for the next four days. None of their efforts came to anything. There seemed to be a policy to exclude the press, as if a secret agenda was controlling the affair.

They arrived in court on the morning of the trial only to find that the prosecuting council requested another postponement and the defence lawyer agreed. For the next few days, they checked the court every day, until, on the twenty-sixth of August, it finally started.

The courts were a monument to the past. Long marble pillars supported the high rafts and ceiling. The floors, also marbled and shining, gave the feeling of solid permanence. The courtroom, was oak panelled and the benches and seats made from solid oak.

Just before the proceedings started Grey entered the courtroom, escorted by two detectives and took his place. He looked much fitter than reports suggested. Beyond the courtroom entrance security guards from the anti terrorist squad searched all those that wished to enter.

At the very back of the courtroom, in the public gallery Holder spotted his man from state security. Now what was he doing at this trial? What could state security possibly want at this trial? Or had he been mistaken all along in thinking he was from them? Maybe he was the elusive Major Strange from Sentinel Armed Securities. If that was the case, why was he present at the police enquiries after the scientists died? Looking at it from both angles it answered questions but it also posed others. He must get a positive identification on his return.

The trial started with the prosecution's evidence that was boring, to say the least. The proceedings were interrupted only by the whispering voice of the court interpreter and followed by a denial of the charges by the defence.

The only part that was of any interest to the audience was when the chief prosecutor attacked Scotland yard for their refusal to let their drug squad give evidence. In reply to this the defence produced a letter from Scotland Yard. It stated that they could not attend as their evidence was hearsay and not admissible in an English court. Then Grey took the stand, raising the interest considerably with an account of his part in the affair. The rest of the day was Swedish legal mumbo-jumbo.

Lynn was relieved when the strain of the day's hearing had ended. Holder faxed his report back to his office and then he took Lynn out for a meal. Next day they were back in court. Grey was cross examined by the prosecution and managed to turn the evidence into a clear affirmation of his innocence. This man was not running scared. This was an act and he was commanding the stage, but why?

His defence seemed to sway the court in its eloquence and precision but the court turned when faced by evidence presented by The Swedish drug squad that was to successfully seal his fate. Holder knew that if his theory was right Grey was on his own. His backers would not publicly show themselves, therefore his spirited defence was to gain a lenient sentence. The third day saw testimony from his father, who looked pale and troubled as he entered the hushed courtroom to give his evidence. He presented more a character reference than a defence.

A string of character witnesses came forward to support Grey. They were fronted by his commanding officer who gave him a glowing reference.

The defence claimed most of the evidence presented by the prosecution was hearsay and would not have been allowable in an English court.

It was Friday evening. The final day of the trial was Monday. Johansson invited them to a party on Saturday evening and arranged to collect them at eight o'clock. He hoped to have someone to interest them.

Johansson arrived early. After a quick drink they left. The party was in the flat of a fellow journalist in Stockholm. He introduced them to their host and hostess and then took them to meet a man who was sitting on the sofa talking to an attractive blonde.

"This is the contact in the drug squad that I told you about Carl, meet Holder and Lynn." The blonde, as if instructed, faded into the crowd.

"I hear you are over for the case."

"Yes. I am covering for a colleague. Tell me, why is it that you did not arrest Grey until he made contact with his friend?"

"We had strict instructions that we must not arrest him till that man appeared and made contact."

"So it was not knowledge of a contact that prompted you but an order from above. Was that order from the Drug Squad or was it political?"

"The way the order came I suspect it was political."

"Did you ever get the feeling that there was a conspiracy that you were not party to?"

"Now it is funny that you should suggest that, but yes I did and I was not alone in this. We pointed out several matters to our superior that did not seem to tally. We were told to forget it and get on with our job. This was not like our boss."

"Do you know anything about the conditions in which the contact and Grey were held after their arrest?"

"Peter Naylor pleaded guilty, so he was held in normal gaol conditions, which are very comfortable, but I heard that he had special privileges. This was probably organised by my boss in return for his co-operation. Strangely enough rumour says he was seen with my boss in a restaurant, but that is only a rumour. Grey was held in a special cell used for pre-trial detainees. He had a small bed-sitting room and seemed quite content when I saw him."

"Do you know if Peter Naylor was part of the Swedish end of the drugs syndicate?"

"We have no evidence. We were as I said, instructed from above."

"Has either prisoner been treated in anything other than a normal manner?"

"Peter Naylor seems to have received privileges that the normal prisoner could not expect, but he was an important prosecution witness. I don't know about Grey, except his food seems to have been special on the occasions I have seen it."

"Thanks, you have been a great help." Johansson signalled the blonde who returned to her police officer.

"Those are not the questions that I expected, is there something I don't know?"

"I'm not sure yet. It is too early to tell. It is only a theory at the moment. I like your persuader for Carl. Do you pay her?"

"Now as if we would do that. She just enjoys her pleasure." Said Johansson, grinning.

The party was a swinger and they enjoyed the rest of the evening, eating, drinking, conversing and occasionally dancing, until Johansson offered them a lift back to their hotel.

"Now tell me what is on your mind regarding Grey?" Said Lynn.

"Although he was definitely carrying drugs to launder into cash, I believe he was sent in to clear up the IRA cell in Malmo and this trial is the cover but I doubt if we will ever prove it."

Monday came. Grey looked drawn by the ordeal but was still alert. His Father, having given evidence was sitting behind him. The prosecutor made the winding up speech for the State. He called for a long sentence on the officer who had lied to the court.

He launched a stinging attack on the British criticism of the Swedish legal system, by pointing out that there was no time limit on Grey to put his case. The defence, rose to make his closing speech. He dismissed the bulk of the prosecution's evidence as trivial hearsay. He read a letter from a senior officer in Scotland Yard, which stated that all the evidence heard from the drug officers was unsubstantiated and therefore not admissible in a British court.

It was then time for Grey to make his final plea. It was a five minute oration, short and to the point, not the rambling of a man in despair. He made a spirited attack on the Swedish Legal system that ignored his innocence till proven guilty. This curtailed his ability to prove his innocence. At the end he made an impassioned plea for leniency.

The trial ended on this plea and the father was seen to give some final words of encouragement to his son. He left the court to await the judgement, due in a week. Holder faxed his report to London and took Johansson out to dinner. He thanked him for his help and arranged for him to fax the result of the judgement to his London office. This gave him the following week to do some important follow-up work in London. Johansson arranged to take them to see a fellow journalist the following evening. He felt Holder should learn a little more about quiet Sweden.

CHAPTER 17.

The trial of Captain Grey was over but the verdict yet to come. The frustration was telling on everyone. Johansson took them round to see a colleague that evening, who was investigating the murder of the Swedish prime minister. Holder recalled that the news of this death had shocked him but could not remember the details.

Johansson drove them to a flat in the suburbs of Stockholm to meet Jan Petersson, a top free-lance crime reporter, six feet tall with icy blue eyes. His striking feature, a constant frown built into a rugged complexion. His hair was curly, short cropped and blonde. They sat round a table, with a bottle of wine to refresh them while they learned about Petersson's investigation into the death of Curt Hanson and the search for his killer.

"As you know Curt Hanson was gunned down in the street, during his homeward journey from the Theatre, on a cold evening, on the twentieth of April eighty-six. This is a date most Swedish people remember and indeed they can also recall what they were doing when they heard the news. Curt Hanson was a crusader for our nation and he died in a terrible manner."

"There is no disagreement on that." Exclaimed Holder, warming to the huge Swede.

"To understand what I am going to tell you it is essential first for you to know Hanson's background and his way of thinking. This will help you to understand why he died in such a way. He had galvanised the Swedish people into a crusade for peace and disarmament. We really believed that this man could bring the World to its senses and indeed the World was using his enthusiasm as a bridge between the East and the West. He had also opened Sweden's doors to many refugees and unfortunately, terrorists from Palestine and even Ireland. He hoped to give them a home to call their own. Instead they abused his hospitality."

At this Johansson intervened. "Being a pacifist and an idealist, his understanding of the real World was sometimes naive to say the least. That could well be the reason he did not even consider the danger that his policies constituted to his own safety. He continually shunned protection. It is this lack of realism that exposed him to the assassin's bullet. Since his death we have heard many claims that this or that organisation ordered his death. Our theory takes into account all of the important clues left after the murder."

"So first let's look at the murder." Said Petersson.

"He was walking down a snow-covered street on his way home. A lone gunman came from behind and fired two bullets into him, having produced a pistol from under his long coat. One of the two bullets penetrated his chest and ultimately killed him. The assassin ran off into the night, chased by several witnesses. The police set up a cordon too late and covered an inadequate area, failing to trap the killer. In our view, he was almost certainly a professional hired assassin. The description given by several observers, including The Prime Minister's companion, was of a man about six feet tall, wearing a long dark coat. He had dark hair, was about thirty-five years old and European. In the panic he escaped by bike, car or train."

"So what were the police doing?"

"Stockholm's Commissioner of Police, carried out the enquiry. He clashed with the public prosecutor's office throughout the investigation, often enabling arrested suspects to go free. There were many other incidents of discord between the two sides. This case has brought the whole system into disrepute in most Swede's eyes. The chaos in these proceedings has hampered the real task of finding the murderer. Even changes of the players in this farce have had little effect."

"This sounds like an effective ploy to hide the truth."

"Knowing the type of friends that surrounded Curt Hanson gave important clues to the pattern of his thoughts. The attendance list at his funeral is another useful source of information. Among the usual representatives and heads of state that always attend such funerals were several interesting guests. Yasser Arafat, there as a friend. Fidel Castro from Cuba, who only ever attends funerals behind the iron curtain; and Daniel Ortega from Nicaragua. Ortega is a significant thorn in the sides of all right wing antagonists. These examples gave an idea of Hanson's political stance!"

"What this indicates is that he was well to the left of centre in his political thinking." Holder observed.

"After two and a half months of fighting, the public prosecutor in charge of the case resigned, through utter frustration with the police chief and they appointed a new prosecutor. Meanwhile rumour of his association with a society name, came to the surface, but alongside so many other rumours that all seemed unlikely. They accused the PKK Marxist Leninist Kurdish worker's party and the usual hostility against the Kurdish population started. They also accused the CIA without much proof."

"This all smacks of a concerted state dis-information attempt to spread red herring's. I have seen it all before."

“They named General Pinochet's secret police - hiring an American hit man called Michael Townley. A Neo-Nazi group claimed that they had killed him and would kill Herr Brandt at his funeral. They also named Abu Nidal's terrorist group as likely suspects, because of Hanson's friendship with Yasser Arafat. Many other factions that he might have annoyed along the road to World peace fell under suspicion. He was in the United Nations Peace Team trying to bring an end to the war between Iran and Iraq. He had meetings with Bani Sadr, former president of Iran. After the last meeting he ordered a halt to arms

dealings between Iran and his own arms manufacturers."

Petersson sank his beer and poured another round of drinks.

"Now this was in line with his policies, but the arms dealers of Sweden took exception to this interference and started trading through middlemen, to overcome this ban. Arms manufacture is Sweden's largest industry and a very powerful political lobby. Sweden's prosperity depends upon the arms trade. It was this fact that Curt Hanson did not seem to recognise, or chose to ignore. Strangely, since his election, he fought a campaign to strengthen the Swedish economy. His policy of arm's sales restriction was frustrating this effort."

"He even adopted right wing monetary policies to bring this about, compromising his socialist principles." Said Johansson.

"The threat to the arms manufacturers was the last straw. Industry was a tight group of conservative power barons who did not take kindly to being ordered around, especially by a communist-loving pacifist. Hanson was a threat to their interests and bad for business. War made them fat profits and gave jobs to the population. They saw nothing wrong with that principle."

"Arm's manufacture," said Holder, "is a catch twenty-two situation. Firms spend a fortune developing them and need a large market to recover their investment. Their own country alone can't provide an adequate market, so they have to find markets elsewhere. This is where the morality issue finds its ground to complain."

"Up to this point in my investigation I believed that the Iranians were behind his murder. Everything seemed to fit except he left no clues and the assassin was European. This much we knew from firm evidence. The one point that went against this theory was that the Iranians always carry out their own executions. We therefore changed our minds and began to look in a wider field. Then we had a stroke of luck. I met a man who had left SAPO, our Swedish secret police. Curt Hanson had reorganised his state security, reducing its scope and personnel to a much smaller and less effective unit and with this went its power. Morale was low and many lost their jobs. My informant stayed on, but left later. Before he left SAPO he learned of a plot being prepared by a group of right wing officers disgusted by the virtual annihilation of SAPO."

Johansson interrupted, "At the same time some members of the arms industry decided to defy the Prime Minister's request only to sell arms direct to user countries approved by the government. When Hanson realised that his arms manufacturers were ignoring his directive he decided to test his strength. He ordered a snap election with the arms trade as the central issue on the platform."

Petersson continued. "A dissident right wing group within industry was informed of this decision. Some of the concerned members held a secret meeting. At this industrialist's meeting they decided not to risk the possibility of Hanson getting an electoral mandate to force them to stop arms supplies to Iran so they contacted the right wing, non-executive group within SAPO to discuss their mutual disquiet."

"Was this how they hatched the plot to kill Hanson?"

"Yes. Secretly they removed a gun from within the police compound and the assassin used it as the murder weapon. It was a Smith and Wesson magnum revolver. SAPO, because of its depleted state, did not have a suitable candidate for the job and our informer overheard one side of a conversation to place a contract. They recommended a British firm to carry out the job, but as they did not repeat the name he could not give me this information. So we think the assassin came from England and was hired by a group of industrialists, with the help and guidance of an element inside SAPO."

"There is a security company that I know that does work under contract for governments. I'll write the name down for you. You never know, it might help."

"Thanks. That will be followed up. Who knows?"

"Be careful."

"Point taken. When you actually study the efforts of the police in Sweden you realise they are getting nowhere fast and have been chasing every red herring dragged before their noses. In the end, to save their credibility, they will probably charge some poor vagrant, or hapless criminal, just to show a result to a population that wants revenge. If I am right, this will be a fix not justice. I am convinced that the assassin will not be caught now, especially if he was a professional, as all the evidence leads us to believe."

"We have several leads that support the allegations of our SAPO officer." Said Johansson.

"The dissident element within SAPO leaked several reports before and after Hanson's death. The one before his death related to tax evasion. This emphasised their readiness to try to topple him. This ploy did not generate as much scandal as they expected. After his death they leaked the story of his liaison with a heiress. SAPO started this story using the investigating team lead by The police chief. They also leaked rumours to the press that Curt Hanson had liaisons with a famous model. He was, in the eyes of the right wing element, a puppet for Moscow."

Petersson continued. "He appointed a hard left man as Minister for Defence, who, by his own admission, knew nothing about defence. All these leads set the scene for the result. It was his decision to test his power against that of the arms manufacturers that triggered the final decision to assassinate him by an element within his own industrial base. If you ask any police investigator he will tell you there are four main reasons for murder: sex, money, a grudge and random chance. If you discount sex and random chance, you end up with money and a grudge. Our 'suspect' stands up on both counts. The industry would have lost billions of Kroners if Hanson tamed our arm's industry. This element would have spent any amount of money and stopped at nothing to prevent this happening. Hanson effectively annihilated SAPO."

"That makes sense." Stated Holder.

"They had very good reason to help the dissident element, to get revenge for their demise. It doesn't matter which way we look at this analysis we find it stands up. You can't say that about any of the other theories."

Holder challenged, "So why haven't the police come to the same conclusion? Perhaps they don't want to solve it."

"They want the mystery of Hanson's death to become less of an issue in the minds of the public. It won't do that without a culprit. That is the dilemma Hanson left for them. They know that they must give the public a fall guy and SAPO cannot be that guy. They are now back to strength, with the most modern equipment money can buy, so now they are untouchable."

"So they are looking for a scapegoat to quell public opinion?"

"Yes. Any allegations that included SAPO would devastate the confidence of the Swedish people. Industry is in a similar position. Sweden's position and her prosperity rely on trading arms. So to attack it is to attack the economy. Without the arms trade the economy would collapse. In the end realism wins very easily and the State is always capable of ignoring crime or even committing it to protect the status quo. So a fall guy will be found, one who has no power to answer back and the people will be partly satisfied, but it will be a miscarriage of justice, a crime."

"Well," said Johansson, "I told you it would be a night of surprises."

"Yes, it's certainly a powerful case you present. I hope you can make it stand up and the truth comes out, for that is what we do all this work to achieve."

Holder then told them about his investigation, as briefly as he could, which left his audience completely speechless. It was one-thirty before Johansson drove them back to their hotel ready for their journey back to London in the morning.

CHAPTER 18.

Glad to return home they found the usual heap of mail waiting. To their relief there was no news on the answering machine of further deaths. They hadn't been in ten minutes when the phone rang.

The caller stated, "You are investigating matters of interest to us and we would like the opportunity to meet you and discuss your investigation."

"Who's speaking?" Asked Holder.

"We'd rather explain matters face-to-face. We think you would wish to hear our point of view. Where would you like to meet us?"

"At my office." Replied Holder.

"No that would not suit us at all. Perhaps a hotel or restaurant of your choice?"

"I only meet strangers at my office."

"It will be to your advantage to meet us. We can clear up many points you have been investigating. You will be safe, you have my word."

"The answer is still the same. As a voice your word is worth nothing."

"We don't make offers twice."

"Are you from Sentinel Armed Securities?"

"Don't lets name names. Keep it impersonal. Did you enjoy your trip to Sweden? It is better you forget what you heard for the sake of your own health. We have an interest in silence and that is what we advise for your own good. Don't meddle in things that should not concern you if you wish to grow old."

Holder put the phone down as the implications of the call startled him. He didn't like threats. The first and most worrying factor was that they now knew his address and second, they had up to date information where he had been. They had accurate security information. It must be Sentinel Armed Securities but how did they get state information so easily? He now had them positively tied to Jane Armstrong's death and now it seems Grey was laundering drugs for them. What other dreadful acts connected them to common crime? The deaths of the scientists? He still backed his hot favourite, the KGB team and this mysterious Russian private agent. When one of them went so far as to threaten him it must mean that he was already too close to the truth for their comfort.

He told Lynn what had just happened and she showed concern. However, Holder decided he would bide his time. It would be impractical to move immediately, anyway. They decided to be very careful when entering and leaving the house and to check the car for any bugs or explosive devices.

When he thought of all the different ways in which they had already killed their victims, he realised that whoever was behind the deaths could easily target him. The only way he could really protect himself was to disappear. He was angry. That sort of 'friendly advice' was the last way they would ever gain his co-operation.

He wanted these people nailed and he wouldn't be happy until that happened. He would not let it get to him.

"Lynn, don't you think you should take a trip home till this blows over?"

"Not on your life. I want to stay with you and get on with the work."

"Thanks, Lynn. I do appreciate your support, but when I go to South America I would feel happier if you went to your parents till I'm back."

"That's a deal, Boss. I will have earned a break by then. Now I am going to make a meal, so I want you to go upstairs, have a bath, change and come down for an evening away from your worries."

He looked at her and marvelled at her coolness. Threats like this had never occurred before, yet Lynn had brushed it aside. He complied and prepared for a long soak and some contemplation. Then he dressed for a casual evening at home.

When he came downstairs, Lynn had already changed, laid the table and lit the candles. The meal would be ready in fifteen minutes. He opened a bottle of wine and they toasted their success, in spite of threats. The candle light, glistening in the crystal cut glass and flashing in Lynn's eyes, brought his thoughts to matters of an utterly different nature. She was certainly beautiful, but they were not only lovers, they were also close friends. Holder could not believe his luck. He had found that girl in a million.

"Lynn, I want you to know how lucky I feel to have you and I hope you will stay with me. I do not wish to think of life without you." How amazing that a threat concentrated thoughts, he reflected.

"David, thank you for telling me, especially at this time. Come, dinner is ready." Lynn kissed him tenderly and they sat down to a meal of English hot pot, cooked in an unusual wine sauce.

After the meal they sat in front of the coal fire and enjoyed each other's company. Holder played some of his collection of traditional Jazz and light classical music. Eventually desire took them up-stairs, to release the emotional pressure that had built up inside them since that unscheduled phone call.

Their desire seemed more immediate, more intense, than ever before. Each caress accelerated the pleasure. Each kiss became more passionate, more urgent. Their whole bodies seemed charged with desire, intensified to a fever's pitch by the threat to their personal safety.

It seemed to Lynn an age before Holder touched her tenderly between the thighs. The explosion of delight was instantaneous. Time scale vanished and Lynn was absorbed in a World of accelerating, compulsive joy, so intense, so immediate, so acute, that it took her breath away as she groaned with pleasure and gasped for breath at the same time. The feeling was so great she hardly felt the physical union, only realising their joining of bodies as he powered to a climax. The impossible for Lynn happened. An eruption of passionate desire enveloped her senses as she vibrated from her pinnacle of satisfaction.

Completely fulfilled and physically exhausted, they lay together, held tightly in each other's arms, as if to let go would invite danger.

They worked all next day preparing the report dealing with their visit to Sweden. Holder was going to meet his SAS contact that evening and they both agreed it would be best if he went alone, as Lynn's presence may restrict the flow of information. At the appointed hour He drove off to the Admiral Codrington in Chelsea, to meet Michael Neville, a serving SAS officer. He had prepared himself well before leaving, lining his stomach with milk to absorb the alcohol. Those boys really knew how to knock them back. Holder drew up a stool at the bar and sat down next to Neville, who seemed if anything more dejected than the last time he had seen him. He ordered a triple bloody mary and a pint.

"Well, how's tricks, Michael? You look a bit down in the mouth."

"I am. You know that I was worried about my reaction tests. Well I have just heard. I failed my last test. Now I am waiting to hear that I am out of the SAS. I accept that but then my worries really begin."

"You knew that day would come - nobody gets younger."

"Yes, of course I did but I only now realise I am not trained for any worthwhile job in civilian life and to remain in the army would be too much of an anti-climax. Most of us agree on that."

They went into the garden room and found a seat. It was a warm September evening and would not be quiet for long.

"What I predicted last time you saw me, has now come true. It's like a nightmare. It is only a matter of time before I enter a completely unknown World. My feelings seem to boil up inside me like a cauldron. On one hand I hate most jobs that are available to ex SAS men. On the other hand, I know, I may be forced to accept a job of this nature to survive. There are jobs in Nicaragua as mercenaries, Sentinel Armed Securities are recruiting men for a group supplying arms and manpower to the rebel forces.

Congress has vetoed it and therefore made it an illegal interference in the affairs of another state. My conscience would not allow me to do this work. Nobody wants to know if it goes wrong and the money, while good, doesn't cover that risk level."

"In America, Michael, I was told that Grey was, laundering drugs for Sentinel Armed Securities, as payment for mercenaries supplied?"

"How did you hear of that? It is only gossip inside SAS, but that is often correct. Grey, as you may know, was in the SAS. He had been in Northern Ireland for eighteen months, as an undercover agent. The strain tells on anyone over a period of time, even a highly trained man like him. They gave him a break, lined up another job, a rest from the strain of front line work, but enough to maintain the adrenaline and pay well."

"Did they second him to Sentinel Armed Securities to launder drugs?"

"Yes, the reason, I guess, was to turn drugs into hard cash to pay the mercenaries supplied to the rebels in Nicaragua. My opinion is that requests for help came from America. They had lost their source of revenue from the Iran arms deal and the money in the Swiss bank, that had been paying the bills, was exhausted."

"That seems logical."

"The group dealing with the mercenaries arranged several consignments of drugs through CIA contacts in South America and rumour says Grey was one of the couriers chosen to carry these consignments. He had already done other trips and carried diplomatic clearance through the countries concerned and authority to trade in Amsterdam's drug market, a well-known distribution point for Europe. A delay in France required a change of plan. So to meet his appointment with Peter Naylor, he decided to go to Sweden first. This meeting was nothing to do with drugs."

Holder nodded. There was a growing pattern. "The most ironic thing that we were told is that the IRA cell in Malmo had already bought the consignment that Grey carried in his car. They were dealing in drugs to make money, to buy arms, to kill our troops in Northern Ireland. He paid the price for a rash decision."

"Who's we?" Grinned Neville.

"My new Help mate," Holder smiled back.

You can see why I don't want to become mixed up with these kinds of people. I oppose drugs. It revolts me to even think that our governments are using this vile trade to make money, to do things their parliaments would never condone."

"Tell me, what do you know about Miss Sarah Pierson?"

"She is, as you probably know, an ex-SAS operative now working for Sentinel Armed Securities and was in charge of Grey's operation."

"Then she wasn't his girlfriend?"

"Not as far as I know, unless, through association, she became entangled. We heard he took his orders from her."

"Tell me is it possible that Sentinel Armed Securities work for both the British Government and the KGB?"

"Yes, theoretically it is but practically it might stretch a point. I can make some enquiries if you wish?"

"Could you please?" Holder got up to get them another drink. At this point he changed the subject. The room was getting full and he did not want an audience.

"Going back to your problem. I will have a word with a friend of mine who owes me a favour and see if we can find you a job that will suit you better. I know someone that has been looking for an insurance assessor, but I think that would need previous knowledge of the trade and it's not really your scene. I am sure we can find something more lively."

"Thanks Holder, you are a good friend. Sorry to burden you with my problems."

"Tell me something else, do you know anything about the murder of the Swedish Prime Minister, Curt Hanson?"

"Only what I read in the papers. Except I seem to remember a rumour going around our barracks that an ex SAS man was hired to kill him, but it was only a rumour."

"There is a favour I need if it is at all possible. I must identify Major Strange. I think I have been fooled into believing he was a man from state security."

"I'll see what I can do. It's my turn to get a round."

"I'll have a scotch, thanks."

"Coming up."

Neville again seemed his normal self. He was not totally brainwashed. He thought and felt, perhaps too much. He was a man pleading to be normal. His cries went unheard by the authorities. They made him into an efficient killing machine and were now too busy training the next generation of men to worry about the last. Neville came back from the bar with the drinks. The place was now full and the garden room crowded.

"Now, if I meet you tomorrow, at say the same time, I hope to have a picture of Major Strange. This will depend on getting hold of the right contacts."

"Why don't you come round to my place for a meal instead - Lynn would love to meet you, and she is a great cook. I will ring my friend in the meantime and set something up."

"Sounds great. It's a long time since I've been to someone's home. Strange isn't it?"

"Think of it as part of your de-programing process." Joked Holder.

"You really hit the nail on the head." They left together. Holder dropped Neville at the barracks and gave him his address.

"Expect you about seven-thirty tomorrow then. Don't worry, we will sort something out I am sure."

"Thanks again Holder. I am looking forward to it."

Next morning Lynn continued with the documentation of the information while he phoned his friend about Neville. By mid-afternoon Lynn stopped to prepare the meal for their guest. By seven o'clock everything was ready and they sat down together for a quick drink.

Neville arrived with flowers for Lynn. Smart, in cavalry twill slacks and a tailored sports jacket, his shoes bore a high shine from the endless application of polish.

"An offering to my hostess. Holder, you did not tell me she was so beautiful."

"Thank you, that's sweet, full marks to the army."

"Now, first things first. Your usual?"

"Yes, a bloody mary, please, and I have the photograph you asked me to find. It's taken when he was much younger but I think you should be able to recognise the basic features."

Holder examined the photograph under a magnifying glass.

"Although the photo seems to have been taken when he was a young officer. It is undoubtedly the man I thought was from state security. This means Sentinel Armed Securities are deeply involved with the government in covering up the traces of the scientist's assassins. But why?"

"The usual reason I suppose - to protect the public from the truth."

"That's putting it kindly! Another mystery solved, thanks Neville. Now, I have some good news for you. My man is looking for a serious bodyguard-cum-chauffeur for an Arab client. Here is his card. If you give him a ring he is waiting to hear from you and you can arrange a suitable time for an interview. It's a start. I don't know how good the job is, but it is worth a look."

"Thanks, Holder. That's the best news that I have had for a long time. It has lifted a weight off my shoulders. You know Lynn, you have a twenty-two carat guy. He really cares, behind his joking image."

"Michael, he got to me the first time I met him. It gives you a wanted feeling, doesn't it?"

"Yes, that's just how I feel."

"Now stop this! You two are embarrassing."

"Well boys, I've got a surprise for you. Come this way if you please."

She led the way into the candle lit dining room. Holder poured the wine. First they had a hot dish of sea fare in a delicious wine-based sauce. Next, her father's recipe for Beuf Stroganoff, now Holder's favourite meal and to finish there was a traditional sherry trifle. Holder decided to tell Neville about his investigation, which took most of the evening and it was very late when He finally rose to go home.

Now relaxed, Neville was smiling and happy. Holder had not seen him so full of spirits for some time.

"Lynn, you are a wonderful hostess, only surpassed by your culinary skills, which are only shadowed by your beauty. I cannot tell you how much I have enjoyed this evening. As for you Holder, I can only say thanks for helping me to get back on board the human race. Your research fascinates me and I will certainly see if I can enhance your knowledge with extra evidence before I leave. There are things about Captain Grey that are not apparent. Just bear that in mind. I can say no more at the moment."

"Neville, drive safely and keep in touch. If that contact is no good let me know and I'll try again. As regards information, obviously I will welcome anything you can get on the security company or the deaths of the scientists. Be careful. Don't get caught."

"By the way I haven't got the answer on Sentinel Armed Securities yet but I am still trying."

Neville left and David turned to find Lynn behind him.

"He's nice," said Lynn quietly, "but I saw the tension pour out of him as the evening passed. I now understand clearly what you told me about the plight of SAS men and I can see it is real. I hope your exposure will help them, I really do. I think that man is desperate inside. I felt the tension at first."

"He said in so many words that our theory on Captain Grey might be close, but where does that leave the Russians? Why all the dead scientists? other than slowing down Star Wars."

"Lets leave the washing-up. Come upstairs and hold me. I am feeling emotional."

He picked her up in his arms and carried her upstairs, putting her down carefully and just holding her for several minutes as her emotion subsided and passion so powerful, so immediate, took over her body. She found herself clawing at Holder's clothes in a desperate attempt to rid him of the last obstacles between them. Somehow, without planning it, they found themselves, naked and on their bed, urgently seeking the ultimate pleasure, which, when fulfilled, left them at peace together.

CHAPTER 19.

Holder knew that it was important for him to understand the origin of the drugs trade, before he embarked on his journey to South America. He realised to understand the full implications of the business and its power over people, he needed to know the history of the trade and the devious methods used to launder the hot money. He must research how the top dealers like the Mafia and the South American drug's barons cleaned their money to use in the real World.

Although drugs go back to ancient times their commercial potentials were first realised by the early colonisers in India. The research led him back to before the beginning of the Opium trail. He wanted to find out how it was that drugs took hold of a whole continent. It started with the Dutch explorers, who landed on Java and set up a business exporting spices, in the late Sixteenth century.

Their main source of trade was China. Energetic traders, the Dutch wanted to monopolise the spice trade. This required complete control of the source and production. They set up a base at Batavia, building themselves a fortress ready to control their new found empire. Next they befriended the rich landowners of the region and then, to achieve their aim, massacred over fifteen thousand people on the Banda Islands.

After the massacre they controlled the trade and enslaved the natives. This trade continued for eighty years, becoming a source of great profit. Trade with Europe was particularly lucrative. They carried spices round the World on a constant stream of Dutch galleons.

Then, in the eighteenth century the shift in the global economy, specially in Europe, started a move in preference, away from spices to plantation based products. The new demand was stimulants, chocolate, tea, coffee and sugar. The settlers tried to shift their production to a plantation based economy.

Some natives, particularly the Chinese traders, who had helped them until this moment, revolted against this change of course. So difficult did this make their position that the settlers, who had used them as the brokers between the islanders and themselves, decided they must eliminate the opposition. In seventeen-forty they massacred a further ten-thousand in Java. This effectively quashed all attempts at resistance.

It was at this time that the British explorers followed the Dutch, setting up their base in India, where the Dutch did not have such a strangle-hold. The British staked their claim in a similar way and were good pupils of the Dutch. They learned how to take over and control the local population, using opium to sedate and manipulate them. They opened up the opium fields of India, at first using the product to control their workers. Soon they were exporting their new product for medical uses. Later they realised its potential as a stimulant, greater than that of coffee or teas. It was the power over the brain that made this drug so interesting to the colonisers.

The use of drugs went back in history, large scale marketing and consumption only started in the seventeenth century. By the eighteenth century it was developing into a large business. The Dutch colonisers were the first to realise the potential of opium and were followed by the British who used slave labour in the fields of India to grow the poppies and extract the gum to make opium, to satisfy the ever increasing demand for the drug, specially from China.

It was against a cloak of respectability that these early colonisers plied their foul trade. They moved into China with their greedy eyes fixed on the culture and wealth of this burdened land. Most people think that China corrupted itself by self-inflicting this most terrible drug. Opium induces a craving for constant supply. The user becomes a skeletal shadow of his former self and eventually dies. It was the Dutch and the British who introduced it to China. The purpose was to rob the people of the three main products of their culture, these being tea, silk and porcelain, all of which were fetching good prices in Europe.

The colonisers pursued their trade with vigour. A famous cartoon in Punch depicted the colonisers forcing opium down the throats of the poor Chinese. They quickly became addicted. Heroin is a purified form of opium and still creates havoc in the World today. This dependence of the population ensured that the colonisers were able to buy their wares at a give-away price. So low was the price that they made vast fortunes out of the misery they perpetrated upon the Chinese. Once hooked on the drug they had to work like slaves to produce the goods to feed their craving. As the demand grew for these products so the colonisers spread their evil grip over the continent of China.

The Chinese generally chewed opium, but the Dutch showed the natives how to smoke it. The drug induced a lack of hunger and increased physical awareness. Thus they managed to make their slaves work harder and require less food. Production costs fell dramatically. The population was vast: as each man died there was another to take his place. They never suffered from labour problems, despite the way they treated their slaves. The seeds sown by the colonists in China and other Eastern countries, still bear hideous fruit. Some are addicts before they are born, contaminated by their addicted mothers.

Today the Triads replace the early colonisers, who roam the streets of Hong Kong and Singapore. They distribute the misery that heroin inevitably brings in its wake.

Like the colonisers, the Triads are motivated purely by profit and greed. The price of Opium or Heroin is such that the addict quite often has to turn to crime to pay for their habit. The Triads kill to get their way, eliminating anyone or anything that opposes their interests.

The drugs scene has not really changed since the early days, motivated by greed, managed by criminals and bought by the losers of the World. Today it is the World's second largest business, controlled by powerful people in influential positions. To overcome an entrenched power base of this nature would be a massive task. It would require an educational campaign of global proportions to bring the weight of public opinion behind the issue. This will only happen if agencies like the CIA withdraws their support from the drugs barons, taking real action to seal off the routes of supply. Then and only then would the World see the changes necessary to break the backs of these vile dealers in misery.

Holder became depressed after a few hours study. However he pressed on, knowing that the trip to South America was an expensive investment and he must gain the maximum value from his efforts.

The next question was what happened to the vast profits? To understand the operation in its entirety was to realise an unlikely connection, that between the Mafia and God's bank in the Vatican.

In the sixties a man named Sindona offered Pope Paul the VI, his skills as a financial expert who could handle the large dis-investment programs that the Pope was planning. He was changing his management of assets to come in line with his policy dictate 'Popolorum Progressio' announced in sixty-seven. This stated that the church was the protector of the poor and should dis-invest in capitalism. The same edict proclaimed that the land of the World belonged to everyone, not only the rich.

At this time the Roman Catholic Church was the largest real estate owner in the World. Something the Pope failed to mention or act upon. In reality the Pope was trying to take a step away from capitalism, as a public relation's exercise and to appease the poor of the World.

His idea was to dis-invest in the church's direct control of its assets. Then re-invest abroad where the wealth of the church would be less apparent. There was no real intention to hand wealth to the poor. He appointed Sindona as his financial adviser with instructions to work closely with the director of 'God's Bank,' Bishop Marcinkus.

Around this time Interpol was showing great interest in two men, Sindona and Gelli, the head of P2, a notoriously corrupt lodge of Italian freemasonry. In November of sixty-seven they telexed the Italian police in Rome. They asked them to investigate the possibility that these men were dealing in drugs, between Italy, the United States and possibly other countries. The police replied that there was no evidence to show any such dealings.

Sindona received copies of all the relevant records of this interchange within a week. Sindona and Gelli had already woven their web around both the police and the politicians of Italy.

Meanwhile the CIA had been compiling a file on Sindona's links with the five most powerful Mafia families of New York; Gambino, Genovese, Lucchese, Bonanno and Colombo. These families were all inter-linked in the running of various rackets; prostitution, gambling, pornography, usury, protection, fraud, large scale theft from banks and above all, the manufacture, distribution and retailing of drugs.

The Gambino family led this group of misery brokers and their financial adviser was none other than Sindona. These families were all dealers in heroin, cocaine and marijuana. Sindona not only helped to control the Italian and Sicilian side of the business, but also laundered the vast profits made from this trade. In controlling every stage of this trade, from the manufacturer to the user, the Mafia stood to make millions, as long as they could clean the money. Sindona, with his connections and understanding of the banking World was the best man to handle such vast fortunes.

Heroin that started life in the Lebanon ended up in Southern Italy, some as raw opium and some already refined. From there it went to Sicily, to the two Mafia families of Inzerillo and Spatola. They had several factories that refined and exported the finished product to America. At one time the Mafia infiltrated Alitalia and was shipping unaccompanied suitcases of heroin to New York, for collection by Mafia associates - each receiving fifty thousand dollars a time for their services. The revenue of these two Sicilian families alone reached five-hundred million dollars a year in the late sixties.

The strange thing was the CIA did nothing to halt this illegal trade. This is the key to understanding the whole affair. They accumulated a mass of indictable offences against all the families, also against Sindona and Gelli. They made no move to curtail their foul trade. Their political masters in the White House decided it was prudent to allow this trade, as long as it held back the chance of a communist government in Italy.

Thus it was that the CIA, who could have blown these operations apart, did nothing, while Sindona built his empire through the Mafia and laundered his money through the Vatican assets. This was how the CIA, P2, God's bank and the Mafia collaborated to each other's advantage. Meanwhile Sindona continued to build his personal fortune, buying Vatican assets and manipulating their share values on the Italian stock market.

He boasted that he always used ninety-five per cent of other people's money to finance his grandiose schemes. That was probably one of the few truths he ever uttered. So the Mafia provided the money he needed, while the Vatican provided a means to cleanse the proceeds.

The real irony came when the Vatican offered for sale a pharmaceutical company called Serono, among other products manufactured they produced contraceptive pills - banned by the Roman Catholic church for use amongst Catholics.

The church was not alone in holding double standards. American politicians were decrying the spread of the use of drugs, while allowing traders to expand their markets, illegally. America never lifted a finger to stop them trading, even though the CIA had enough against them to indict them in any court. Why?

Two answers were apparent by the mid-seventies. One, as stated, the dread of Communism taking control in Italy. The other was that the Mafia had

control of many politicians. Many of them owed their election to Mafia based funds. Congress, could if needed, come to the support of the Mafia, when faced by an onslaught from the CIA; after all, congress owed a great deal to the Mafia!

Sindona used Mafia money to buy companies, both from the Vatican bank and on the free market. He often bought companies that were foundering. He showed no concern about the health of the firms he was buying. His one aim in mind, to artificially boost the share values of new companies, creating a false market for them. Sindona achieved this by the devious transfer of assets, with the assistance of his friend Calvi.

On one deal alone Calvi and Sindona made six-and-a-half million dollars each. Calvi shared his spoils equally with bishop Marcinkus, illustrating again the corruption they spread in their wake. Pleased with Marcinkus's management of the bank, the Pope promoted him to president in the early seventies, little knowing the fate that was eventually to befall their affairs.

Sindona and Calvi became richer and richer. They openly boasted that they controlled the Milan stock market, as indeed they did, through falsification and deceit. Large holes were appearing in their bank accounts, hidden only by large telex transfers in time of crisis. Meanwhile they continued their purchases, sometimes inadvertently helped by such institutions as Hambro's Bank and Gulf and Western. Gulf and Western - who financed Paramount pictures; made 'The Godfather.' Ironically enough, the moneys that

came from this expose of the Mafia helped to fund their dirty dealings.

Italy's economy began to show signs of strain from the onslaught brought upon it by the two criminal dealers. The church, although skimmed by Sindona, had also profited from his dubious deals, benefiting them beyond the Pope's wildest dreams.

Sindona started a complicated cost invoicing export system. Paying all profits into the Finabank abroad, while paying the cost price invoices through the bank of Italy. They sent these to the tax office and taxes were avoided. They then tried invoicing at a loss and got away with that as well, not only avoiding tax, but getting tax credits from the government. Sindona bribed politicians to allow the situation to continue unhindered, with a feeble argument that it would keep down unemployment.

They even worked a fiddle on imports. It seemed that the Mafia had no trouble with borders, moving drugs and money wherever required, unrestrained by customs, Interpol or the CIA. In the seventies Sindona opened a bank account for the Christian Democratic Party, putting three quarters of a million dollars into it for the party funds. He was an avowed anti-Communist but to hedge his bets he opened another account at the Finabank for the Communists. He put three quarters of a million dollars in this, with further payments to follow, but carefully made sure that it went in under another name.

He speculated against international currencies, shifting large blocks of money around. The dollar, the lira, the mark and the Swiss franc all suffered. The speculation against the lira alone was a six hundred and fifty million dollar operation. They awarded Sindona the 'Man of the year' award in seventy-four that honoured his steadfast work in the service of his country and against communism. The American ambassador presented it, despite the large file held by the CIA covering all his activities.

The CIA itself was in a spot of bother due to expenditure that they could not explain. In an attempt to put things right they offered to sell 'The Daily American,' a propaganda paper controlled by the CIA. Sindona agreed to buy it. They considered him to be a staunch anti-Communist and sold the paper to him, confident that it was in good hands.

Sindona, however, knew how to keep politics on the boil between left and right. This kept the heat off him, so he plied the money into both sides to assure his freedom from attention. This was not the first favour Sindona did for the CIA. He bought, on their request, two million dollars worth of bond issue from the national bank of Yugoslavia. He also moved money on request within Italy and Greece.

He offered one million dollars to Nixon's presidential campaign. Due to the new regulations that related to election funds they refused the money. This illustrates that he was a man that went right to the top with his bribes, a well-practised Mafia policy.

Bishop Marcinkus attended a United States attorney's investigation into the counterfeit securities operation managed by Sindona. He praised Sindona at the hearing, but, at the same time he paid three hundred and seven thousand dollars fine for an illegal transaction for the Vatican bank. When they paid the fine they sold the shares at a profit. Even Bishops turn a blind eye when it is to their advantage.

If the Vatican was still blind, sight was returning elsewhere. The holes in Sindona's bank accounts were getting larger by the minute. He decided to merge his two banks into one, calling it Banca Privata. Two large holes made one unmanageable crater created by his illegal manipulation of assets.

It was no better at the American end, where the Franklin bank was suffering a similar fate. It needed the Federal Reserve to step in and save it from crashing. If it did go it would take many other banks with it. This bottomless pit absorbed two billion dollars of federal funds, enough to save it from ruining other banks, but not sufficient to avoid bankruptcy.

Back in Italy the Banca Privata suffered a similar fate, crashing with an enormous shortfall of funds. Many small investors lost their life savings. It also signalled the beginning of the end for this master of World finance. The debts of the Banca Privata, estimated at around three hundred million dollars sealed its fate. Twenty-seven million dollars of this was Vatican money. Their share holding in the bank was more than thirty million dollars. To this day they deny they lost a cent.

Yet this was a crash of massive proportions. The demise of the Franklin bank was the largest crash in banking history of the United States. Soon they signed an order for Sindona's arrest. As usual, a tip off passed to Gelli found its way to his friend Sindona the day before they came to arrest him.

He turned up in Switzerland and six months later was back in the United States. Finally they arrested him in America and a request was made for his extradition to Italy. He was no longer of any use to the United States as an anti-Communist, if he ever had been. His position looked critical.

Even then Sindona wriggled. He proposed an extraordinary plan to annex Sicily as the fifty-third State of America. This was the last desperate ploy of a remarkable con-man.

Holder sat back and considered this account of one side of the drugs business that he had never understood. He had never been able to work out how the drugs barons laundered their high profits and put them back into circulation. This account gave him perfect insight into their operation, showing how they colluded with the World banking system and bought legitimate assets that returned clean money to the system. Meanwhile it made vast fortunes for the Mafia, Sindona, Gelli and Calvi also of course, in its wake, God's Bank.

It amazed him to see how countries, politicians, ambassadors and banks, to say nothing of the Vatican, all became involved in the largest swindle the World has ever known. A single man can control the World's powers, by clever strategy and the adroit disguise of his wrong doings. Sindona relied upon America's fear of communism.

Everything he did to promote that fear advanced him and promoted his continued freedom. That is why he funded the Christian Democrats and the Communists at the same time. Holder suspected that America had no interest in stemming drug trafficking.

Surely, if they had treated him as the criminal that Interpol and the CIA knew he was, the Vatican would never have become involved in laundering Mafia money. Italy would not have fallen in financial trouble. The Communists would not have had the funds they needed to promote their ideals. The Mafia would not have had a laundry for their dirty money.

This man had created many of these problems and the Americans had fallen for the bait, communism. With a little foresight America could have protected Italy from communism and defended NATO's interests, with far fewer repercussions and at a fraction of the cost.

Holder thought of President Marcos. His people said He stole his country's wealth, murdered the opposition and then went into exile with still more of his country's assets. America supported this man to the last, even giving him the right to live in America until his corruption became so public that they had to withdraw their support. Marcos was a man the Americans funded to fight Communism.

Would she ever learn from her mistakes? It seemed at the mention of Communism they forfeited all the principles of the nation to combat this paper tiger, or more cynically to hide other activities. Drugs will, however, eventually be America's Waterloo.

CHAPTER 20.

He had to understand both sides of the drug's business to fully realise the truth behind the lies of convenience released by government to suit their selfish, short sighted agenda's. Now his main research found Sentinel Armed Securities mixed up in this sordid trade. The second largest trade in the World; Drugs.

It was a cold grey September day when, having said his farewells to Lynn, Holder climbed aboard his flight to Los Angeles to meet his fellow journalist, Danny Fisher, in California. The direct flight to Los Angeles, arrived mid-afternoon American time. Passport control seemed to take unnecessarily long and when he finally emerged, having passed through customs without incident, he found Fisher asleep in the waiting area.

"Wake up Danny. They haven't arrested me."

Fisher yawned and rubbed his eyes, then looked at his creased jeans.

"God, I nearly gave up hope. You are staying with me tonight and we are flying to Peru tomorrow evening."

They hailed a taxi and drove to Fisher's large apartment in the centre of Los Angeles. It seemed to be suitable for a family rather than an overworked bachelor. It had two bedrooms and three other large rooms. One, a fully equipped gym and the another an office, with a computer, a word processor and every other device you could imagine, including a modem link with his office. The living room was enormous. It had a panoramic view over the city from full length patio windows that opened onto a long balcony.

Los Angeles was still very warm. Danny fetched some beers from the cooler and they sat out on the balcony. The flight left LA late Friday evening, arriving at Lima around mid-day Saturday. They were going to see for themselves the picking fields and the way in which they extract cocaine from the leaves. Peru supplies around sixty per cent of the cocaine base made from the cocoa leaf. The majority of its produce went to Colombia, for the Cali or Medellin cartels for processing into cocaine sulphate. It would be from this visit that they would acquire a feeling of the business and some idea of how it operated. Next, Bogota, where Fisher had arranged to speak with a disenchanted member of DEA, the American Drugs Enforcement Agency.

This was going to be a difficult trip, with many hazards, whole areas were under the control of cartels, particularly in Colombia. Cartels have armies of thugs that kill anyone who looks like a DEA agent, so guides were essential if they wanted to see around a region. They must live rough, grow beards and wear dirty clothes. It was going to be more demanding and more dangerous than any consignment either of them had ever undertaken. After a planning session they went for a meal in Danny's favourite Italian restaurant. They continued to talk about their trip and what they might find.

Holder felt reasonably fit but wondered how the gourmet Fisher would cope with jungle heat. They returned to the apartment for the last comfortable night's sleep they were to experience for a month. Next morning Holder started to shave when Fisher reminded him about disguise. If there was one thing Holder could not stand it was growth on his face, but anything for a story and this was no exception. They spent the day in restful pursuit of pleasure, allowing some time for sun-bathing on the sun-drenched beaches of Los Angeles. They drank their last good wine and soaked up the atmosphere of wealth in the city.

There was one mission that Fisher wanted to complete before they left. His aim was to show Holder the American end of the cocaine trail, the destruction of human life. It was his first hand knowledge of this suffering that drove him on and he thought Holder should share this perspective.

He took him to a rehabilitation centre run by an extraordinary Priest, who had dropped out of his church to help these addicts regain their self-respect. It was the most revealing two hours Holder had ever spent on an investigation. He came face to face with the reality of despair. He saw a great man who truly cared for his fellow beings.

The Priest was one who would reach out and offer his soul to save anyone from death's door. Holder spent time with a young girl of seventeen who looked haggard, old and suffered acute bouts of depression. He saw a man of fifty-eight cry like a baby. A child of eighteen months still hooked on drugs from its mother's womb. He met two teenage lovers who had formed a suicide pact, nearly died from despair, but were saved by the fast action of this Priest. In another area of the hostel he met the parents of addicts; many, were ordinary people. One was a police officer and another a lawyer. Then there were the twilight souls of the city slums. All no hope addicts.

This poison did not respect the boundaries or structures of society. It cast its ugly shadow wherever a weak mind or a rash spirit allowed its presence. First it thrilled its victim with enhanced senses and strength of limb. Then it attacked the body through that most vital organ, the brain. It quelled fear and enlivened the imagination. Pleasure gave way to depression and paranoia, allayed only by further intake.

Cocaine is not addictive, it is compulsive. Those poor parents did not know what they had done to deserve this. Each of them was asking how it was that their child had sunk to these depths. This great Priest had taken their suffering on board. They could get comfort and hope from each other by realising that they were not alone; so he ran regular awareness sessions for the parents and friends of the users. This was every bit as important as helping the users themselves, as anyone who is close to an alcoholic or an addict knows.

That evening they ate early and then had a drink while Holder wrote a card to Lynn. Leaving Los Angeles at night was spectacular. The lights of the city formed patterns like the stars in the sky twinkling in the distance. They settled down to sleep, waking in time for breakfast at seven, it was already a bright morning. The heat even penetrated the plane's air conditioning. They could just make out the shape of the coast far beneath them. Soon they were descending and the tropical jungle became visible. On the higher stretches they observed terraced cocoa plantations.

Peru was the largest producer of cocaine base, providing over sixty per cent of the US import. It was in these plantations that the process began. Soon the plane was landing at the airport in Lima. The facility was modest by international standards. The first of many signs they were to notice belying the poverty of this country. Legal trade was declining in Peru, while illicit trade was booming. Cocaine had become a secondary currency, one that provided access to much needed dollars. They checked through customs and collected their baggage without incident. The next job was to find a hotel that would allow anonymity and the taxi driver earned his commission by finding them a suitably shabby abode on the outskirts of Lima, an ideal place to disappear for several days.

The room was squalid and dirty, with two ancient single beds. There was a basin and toilet, but no shower or bath, no television or safe. This would be their home for a while. Holder started counting the beetles racing around on the dirty floor. Far worse than the accommodation, the heat was almost unbearable. He could feel the sweat pricking up on his face, before rolling and dropping off his chin. He wondered how he would bear the constant humidity.

"I am meeting our first guide this afternoon," explained Fisher, "so relax till then, or take a look round Lima."

"Let's relax." Replied Holder.

"Thank god you said that. It's unbelievably hot, but that's the price of invisible life."

"Yes, it will take some getting used to, I imagine?"

"I think so. A few days at least."

After a rest in the humid room they went downstairs, called a taxi and drove to meet their first contact. The chosen bar was not much better than their hotel. It was in need of complete renovation. While waiting, they sipped cold beer. Fisher became impatient. They were about to give up when a short, slight figure entered, looking around, he came up to them.

"My name is Carlos. You are Mr Fisher please? I am sorry I am so late but there has been trouble, much trouble. The plantation that I have just left received a visit from the drug squad. They have burned the crops and stolen their chemicals. This means ruin for this farmer. So, I am taking you to another farm. For every farmer they destroy three more appear elsewhere so they are not winning. We will go later when it is cooler. My sister's man and his brothers own the farm. It is North East of Lima, in the hills, at about two thousand feet. They grow the best crops in this area. I am your passport to enter. Remember this. They hate the DEA. They sometimes shoot first and ask questions after. OK? Understood?"

"What can we take as a gift to your sister and her family?"

"Come with me and we will buy provisions. That's better than money"

They walked to a local market through the squalid streets of the area. The place was full of people trying to scratch a living, signs of poverty were all around. Addicts stooped to this level through the very plant that brought a glimmer of hope to the people of Peru. It was indeed a very mixed-up World. They bought food and canned drinks to take with them and set off on their first journey, to a cocoa producing farm in the hills of the Peruvian jungle. The first part of the journey was reasonable, on roads of a passable standard. The vehicle, a rather old battered van, gave them reason for concern.

As Lima faded into the distance, so the road became worse, until it was a track, the van bumping up and down with the terrain. How the van survived neither of them could understand, but Carlos assured them that he did the journey regularly. After three hours of torturous buffeting they stopped outside a settlement that looked like a cattle barn.

"This is my sister's home."

Holder glanced at Fisher who shrugged his shoulders, smiled and stretched his weary bones.

Carlos' sister, Maria, came out to greet them. She was short, with jet black hair, parted in the centre, falling straight to the nape of her neck. Her dark hazel eyes revealed the strain, but also fortitude and strength; characteristics that were necessary to deal with the turmoil in this ravaged land.

"My sister, she speaks no American. She greets you to her humble home. She has a meal prepared specially for you."

"Thank your sister and show her the food and drink we have brought as a gift." Said Fisher. They unpacked the van and took the gifts inside.

Holder noticed an area in the yard outside, covered in green leaves drying in the sun. A man was turning them on the rack. Behind this stood a shed with an open front, containing more leaves stacked in neat piles. To the left was another open shed, where a man was wading in a vat of leaves treading them down to extract their juices.

At sundown a sudden coolness fell over the Country, a relief from the unbearable heat. The darkness fell suddenly.

The family slept inside the main building. The toilets and washing area were outside in the yard. They had no luxuries, for all their drug trading, only the basic necessities. However, they were well-off compared to most farmers in the area. The hut doubled as their home. They slept, ate and lived in the same room. They cooked on a calor gas unit. During the heavy rains they collected water in large barrels and used it in the vats for turning the leaves into cocaine base and for cooking, washing and drinking.

The meal was ready and the men collected to meet Holder and Fisher. Introductions over they sat on the floor to have their only meal of the day. They had the appearance of slightly modernised Inca Indians. Short in build, they had shoulder length jet black hair, parted on their crowns. Their noses were straight and long with high cheek bones. They looked weather worn and a strange sadness in their faces, reflected a struggle to even survive. They sat on the floor to eat.

Maria passed round bowls made of clay, full of a rich brown bean preparation, together with a flat pancake type bread. They all watched Maria's husband break the bread and use it to scoop the food into his mouth. All followed suit. After the first mouthful Holder's eyes began to water. He turned to Fisher who was in a similar predicament. It was a kind of chilli-con-carne made with the hottest pepper he had ever tasted, burning him as it descended, leaving him almost gasping for breath. After the initial shock, it was delicious, the flavours of the dish exploded in the mouth and the sweat it provoked cooled him from the heat of the day.

Fisher offered drinks all round to douse the fire left raging in their bodies. That night they slept well, a deep satisfying sleep although the bed was merely a mattress of cocoa leaves on the floor.

Next morning they rose at dawn, washed in the tubs outside then studied the process used to change cocoa leaves into cocaine base. This family was richer than average because they turned the leaves into cocaine base themselves, rather than selling the leaves to a processing lab. As Cocaine base they sold it to a merchant, who in turn sold it in bulk to a cartel member in Colombia. There it underwent a further process to produce cocaine sulphate.

Next they went to look at the slopes where the cocoa plants grew in the rain forest, about seven-hundred meters above sea level. The plantations were on the slopes of the Tingo Maria region. The leaders used machete knifes to carve a trail through the jungle terrain. It was hot but not unbearable. The forest gave way to long pampas grass and shrubs and between them cocoa plants grew in abundance. The cocoa plants, one to two metres tall and one metre in diameter, grows leaves' three to ten centimetres long and bright green in colour. The pickers were stripping them bare, putting the leaves in bags ready for transportation back to base. The bags weighed twenty-five pounds when full, carried on the back, or on the nape of the neck. Local tracks required that they carry their crop on foot or by Llama.

Farther up the slope a man was planting a newly cultivated area with cocoa cuttings. They ridged it to protect the new saplings from the heavy rains, which can sometimes be of monsoon strength. Rains were the secret behind the frequent cropping of the leaves and responsible for their bright green colour.

It was possible to harvest up to ten times a year, though on average they managed around six pickings. Nature here was such that the environment supplied all that they needed to propagate. The heat, the rain and the drainage were all perfect.

There were no tractors to carry the leaves. Everything was done manually. The farms were small, unless the family was particularly large. This family, with three men, cultivated around ten acres of cocoa trees and a further six acres of cereal and food crops for their own consumption.

Breathless, Fisher explained. "The cocaine industry requires five hundred kilos of leaves to produce a kilo of base paste, which is twenty-five to fifty percent pure. It would be a massive job to eradicate these farms. It would only be possible spraying chemicals from the air. This would kill everything it touched. Not surprisingly the Latin American countries rejected its use much to the annoyance of the DEA. These farmers were really only filling a demand. They were not criminals. They received barely enough to raise their quality of life, let alone make them rich. To wipe out the cocaine trade would be to devastate over one-hundred and fifty-thousand people in Peru alone."

"That would be totally unacceptable." Holder insisted. "You can't start another Vietnam with Operation Orange in Latin America."

"I once saw a cartoon drawing, depicting a South American President speaking to Uncle Sam. He was saying, 'It's not that we are corrupt, it's that you corrupt us.' How prophetically accurate that turned out."

"I was just wondering how this whole business could be stopped without harming these hard-working people."

The heat was unbearable when they loaded up, both lending a hand to carry the harvest back to base.

They laid the leaves, collected that day, out to dry in the heat of the midday sun, not for cocaine but for local consumption. They did not refine it for their own use, but to sell for local users who chew the leaves. This was a traditional local pleasure, like smoking, handed down through many generations. It was still legal to use it that way and therefore openly tradable. Because it was legal it was also cheap, bringing only pin money to the growers.

Back at the sheds the process to make cocaine base was about to start. First they washed the leaves in a mild solution of sulphuric acid. At intervals each day they trod it down to extract its cocaine elements. This was repeated several times a day, for four to five days. The farmers had to take care not to stay too long in the solution, or they would suffer blisters on their legs from the acid. The next process took the resulting liquid from the treading process and mixed it with lime, ammonia, gasoline and a few other chemicals. The result was a soft paste-like substance called cocaine base.

Then they transported it to Lima for sale to a go-between. They made their trip to Lima five or six times a year, depending on how many crops they harvested. It was Carlos that took it to Lima for them and naturally they paid him for the job.

Fisher continued, "Multiply the production of this farm by sixty-eighty thousand you get some idea of the size of the problem. There is a vast network of peasant farmers providing the raw materials for this appalling trade."

That evening, after a rough journey back to Lima, Holder and Fisher prepared to meet the go-between. He was the link between the grower and the laboratory, usually a merchant of some kind, who would collect consignments until he had a large quantity of base. Then he would transport it to Colombia, by a safe route, bribing officials on the way. He would move anything from one-hundred to five-hundred kilos at a time, to the Cali cartel. Their annual production was in the region of four-hundred tons of cocaine sulphate a year. Sixty per cent of the base came from Peru and fifty-five per cent ended up in America.

They pulled up at a filthy cafe and waited inside, drinking coffee, by now so grubby that nobody would take them for gringos. A telephone call invited them to a small grocer.

The merchant was a flabby man in his early forties. He was always on the move, darting around the store like a fly waiting to settle. His eyes penetrated his guests, as if trying to read their inner thoughts. Carlos introduced Holder and Fisher to the merchant assuring him it was safe to speak freely.

They presented the merchant with about ten kilos of processed paste. He examined it and then dissolved a small sample in a liquid already prepared. Satisfied that it was pure he turned to Carlos and shook his hand agreeing to pay four hundred dollars per kilo. They weighed the paste and the deal was agreed. Then they sat round the table for a drink of sugar cane liquor to celebrate the sealing of the deal. The merchant was leaving for Colombia within the week. He had three more quantities to collect. Then he could leave, with two-hundred kilos of cocaine base worth one-hundred and sixty-thousand dollars to him. The price had already doubled and the process was far from complete.

The merchant, displaying the adornments of wealth around his neck and wrist, wore an expensive chunky gold watch, one of the status symbols favoured by those who become wealthy in this way. Another was a point two-two automatic slung loosely round his gross proportions.

The deal done they thanked Carlos with a generous tip and left to prepare for the flight to Bogota.

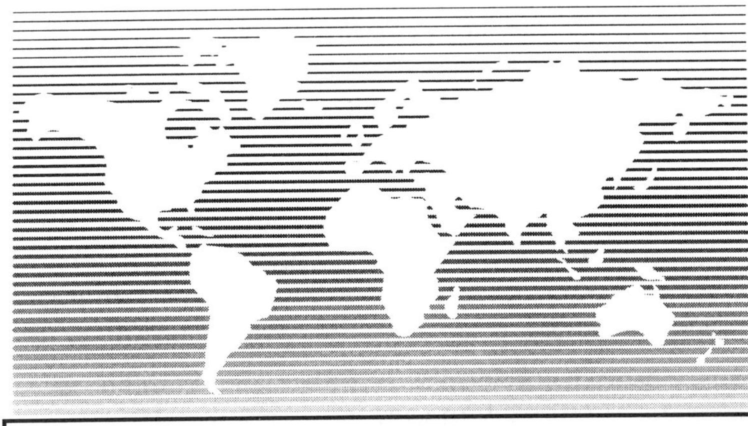

CHAPTER 21.

Their flight was late leaving Lima due to a minor engine problem but would land in Bogota mid-afternoon. They used the time to analyse what they had seen and agreed that the problem of drug trafficking was far more complicated than they had appreciated. Before leaving their homes they had never even considered the lives of the growers.

They had seen how hard these farmers worked, for their frugal lives, how little the farmers made from their work. Four hundred dollars was apparently a good price for a kilo. Yet a kilo of cocaine sulphate, made from three kilos of base, fetched between twelve thousand and twenty-eight thousand dollars in America and nearer forty-five thousand pounds in Britain. Traversing the two countries there were the traffickers, the couriers and large buyers, like the

Mafia families of New York, all of whom took a substantial cut. The retailers mixed the product with all sorts of impurities, like sodium bicarbonate, doubling the volume thus halving the strength, before it reached the streets. Diluted cocaine sold in grams, or at most in ounces, for the equivalent of three hundred and fifty thousand dollars a kilo, a fortune away from the farmer's meagre four hundred dollars.

The huge mark-up attracted people to this trade. Vast profits were for the taking. Nobody considered the wake of misery that they left behind.

Holder and Fisher knew they must see the laboratory that converted base into cocaine sulphate and then study the routes used to smuggle the powder onto the World market. Finally they must find an informer to describe for them the activities of the CIA and the DEA in their control of drug trafficking. Neither task looked simple.

The plane landed at Bogota, bumping up the uneven runway till it came to a halt at the airport terminal. They waited in customs for what seemed hours while customs officers searched everyone's luggage. Suddenly the police surrounded two passengers, who had been sitting opposite and marched them off to an office behind the customs zone. Holder found out that they had been in transit to LA. On searching, the customs found a consignment of cocaine sewn into the handle of a bag. Catching the small fry while leaving the big fish to get on with their business undisturbed, seemed to be their approach, because it was visible.

Eventually they cleared customs and took a taxi into Bogota, after which they found and settled into a small hotel. Fisher rang his contact, a free-lance journalist, based in Bogota who spoke Spanish and some Indian dialects.

They went into the city to get the feel of the place. There was a bizarre combination of poverty and affluence intermingled into an odd alliance with examples of cocaine wealth sprinkled round the bastions of the old city. Never far away evidence of poverty surrounded the richest citizens.

Nevertheless it was more prosperous than Lima, where poverty spilled out in the streets at every turn. Here it was more private, but still present. The ancient Spanish architecture was a constant reminder of colonial times and the modern part told the tale of wealth generated by this more modern form of colonialism, the cocaine trade. Back at the hotel they waited in the bar for Fisher's contact.

A large fan rotated lazily above them, giving welcome relief from the sweltering heat. Cold beer was a welcome habit. A man in his early forties entered, looked around and came over to where they sat. He had long mousy hair and an Edwardian moustache. He was of slight build and wore spectacles dangling from his neck. His crumpled suit, exposed his bachelor status. Fisher rose to greeted him.

"David, this is Jerry Littner."

"Pleased to meet you, Jerry."

"You guys come to see how the other half lives?"

"What can I get you to drink?"

"Bourbon on the rocks please."

"So you haven't changed your habits. Coming up." Fisher went to the bar and returned with more cold beer and Littner's drink.

"Now Jerry, before we hear what you have lined up for us, it would be helpful for both of us to understand how Colombia came to be involved in the drugs trade."

"Well, it is difficult to know where to start, but perhaps it should be in the early sixties, when Colombia was producing a vast quantity of Marijuana. About two thirds of their production went to the United States. The quantity grew larger and larger as usage expanded, creating many problems back in the States. America put pressure on the government of Colombia to destroy the fields where it grew, threatening them with the withdrawal of aid if they did not comply. The president, Betancur, loudly proclaimed a fight, to the death, against the drugs trade. By this time the traders of Colombia were a force to be reckoned with, run and controlled by the barons of the Medellin and the Cali cartels. They are living a life of luxury surpassing Hollywood."

Fisher took up this remark. "Fabio Ochoa Restrepo is a typical example. This man has won every prize going in the World of horses. His stables contain over five hundred high bred horses and each has its own groom. His son, Jorge Ochoa Vasquez, is one of the wealthiest traffickers, a multi-billionaire."

Littner nodded agreement and continued; "By seventy-nine the market for marijuana was dropping off and the demand for cocaine was growing. The barons started running down their crops of marijuana and looking for cocaine to replace it. There was little cocoa being grown in Colombia at this time. So they struck up trading agreements to buy base cocaine from Peru and Bolivia who, between them, now supply about eighty-two percent of the base. This was a much more convenient and profitable trade for the barons. It is ideal for processing in factories hidden in the forests, or in part of a larger factory, away from the public gaze."

"Remember they had established their marketing policy with marijuana." Added Fisher.

"Yes. They applied their knowledge to expanding the cocaine trade. It wasn't till five years later, when cocaine established its market and marijuana was disappearing, that President Betancur declared war on the drugs trade. The DEA backed his battle with advisers. The knowledge that all they were declaring war on was a trade already dying through change in demand remained un-mentioned to the public. It was a PR exercise designed to deceive Congress. They duped the public into believing that they were succeeding in their war against drugs."

"The campaign was successful in persuading America that congress had won a great victory against their evil trade." Intervened Fisher.

"However cocaine was fast replacing marijuana." Continued Littner. "They failed to mention this. The first battle with the barons in eighty-four, was named 'Operation hat trick.' The Colombian government came off worst and the justice minister, Rodrico Lar Bovilla, was assassinated by the cartel. The DEA then concentrated on the eradication of the marijuana fields by spraying glyphosate herbicides from the air. They waged war on the growers and the transporters, mainly peasant farmers from the Chapare area. The growers, badly equipped, fought along side the so called left wing guerrillas. They presented an easy target for the DEA with their ample resources and firepower. Many guerrillas died, but the cartels remained unscathed."

Fisher reminded, "They were able to continue with their new business quite freely, while the government agencies concentrated their attention on the far less dangerous trade in marijuana. This satisfied the States. They had appeased the public demand for results. Colombia had done enough to ensure that aid continued to flow her way. Everyone was happy."

"What a con!" Exclaimed Holder.

"In this way the elite of the cartels grew even richer and ever more powerful, controlling the areas that they lived in with their own private armies. They also controlled the people, by building them houses, schools, churches and playing fields. No one could touch them now. If you went into their area alone you risked being stopped. You could end up dead if they chose not to believe your story. Worse still, Colombia was a reasonably rich trading country, but its manufacturing base had long been in decline."

"The cocaine trade must have adequately compensated for the loss of trade but the problem comes in cleaning the money."

"Yes and no. Now there were two economies, straight currency and the cocaine dollar. Cocaine was generating three times as much currency as licit trade! So strong were the cartels that they controlled many of the financial institutions. A Law passed by the Colombian government threatened the cartel members with extradition. They responded by declaring the American presence to be illegal and threatened the Ambassador with death, forcing his resignation and the exodus of over two thousand American citizens. They even had a tap on telephone calls between the Colombian Ministry of Justice and the US embassy, giving them advanced information of any manoeuvre that might occur."

"Amazing. Governments seem to be devious the World over." Commented Holder.

"Peru, Bolivia and other countries, uncertain of transporting cocaine to America, were selling their base to the Colombian Cartels who finished the process. This is how Colombia came to supply most of the refined cocaine, because she had the best methods of delivery without detection. She had many officials on her pay list, from customs officers to politicians. They looked after the cartel's interests and turned a blind eye."

Littner continued, "Now the Colombian banks, supported or owned by drugs related money, practise a 'Ventanilla Siniestra,' which accepts and exchanges foreign currency, effectively laundering money for the cartels. They had their routes tied up and the base product supplied almost exclusively to them. They put the government in a catch twenty-two position and the finance of the country was in their pocket. This was all because the DEA, ordered by the CIA, chose to oppose the communist factions in the country, rather than take on the barons."

"Surely it is now far more difficult to halt the cartels?" argued Holder. "They wield immense power. The help they provided in eradicating Communism in Colombia and neighbouring states, have earned them the support and protection of the CIA."

"My contact, who worked for the DEA, will be able to tell you much more about this." Said Littner, "He saw it all first hand."

"In America alone official figures estimate the number of users at six and a half million. It is probable that the real figure is at least double this. In one year over sixteen hundred people died from the use of cocaine. This gives you some idea of the size of this trade. The USA takes about sixty percent of the total production. One interesting fact is that, in eighty-four, after the marijuana wars finished and Colombia's export was reduced by ninety-five percent, Mexico took over where Colombia had stopped. They were dumping large supplies across the border. Customs caught one syndicate taking ten thousand tonnes into America. This was eight times the official DEA production figure for a year. There were many red faces around the day this figure came out!"

"I'll bet there were."

"The two barons arrested admitted in court that they had around eight hundred police and officials on their regular payroll."

"We have already discussed Colombia. Bolivia next door is the largest supplier of cocaine base." Said Holder.

"A declining economy had brought its budget near to bankruptcy and forced it to rely more on its cocaine based economy. Bolivia became the first to openly recognise such an economy. She produced some hundred and seventy thousand tons in Eighty-five. Peru, although she resisted an open acknowledgement, was also running two parallel economies."

"How do you stop that after years?"

"You can't," laughed Littner scornfully, "look at Jamaica. She produces cannabis. Her legal export potential is seven hundred and ten million dollars, including revenue from tourism, but her revenue from cannabis is over one billion dollars a year. This also applies, in varying degrees, to the economies of the Bahamas, Belize, Afghanistan, Eqypt, Honduras, India, the Lebanon, Morocco, Nepal, Nigeria, Pakistan, Senegal, Sri Lanka, Swaziland, the Philippines and Thailand to a lesser or greater extent."

"The magnitude of these organisations is frighteningly real. Do they exert any political pressure?"

"Off course they do. Wealth bribes power, always has. It is, therefore, understandable that the growers and traffickers exert considerable covert political and military pressure as well. Politicians often earn more from the traffickers than they do in their official capacities.

In eighty-five America spent over fifty million dollars on the control of narcotics while the United Nations spent under seven million dollars. Much of the US budget goes towards supporting their DEA agents abroad, in countries such as Colombia, Peru and Bolivia. Countries like the Bahamas and the Turks and Caicos islands, are strategic posts in the drug's delivery network. Over sixty percent of cocaine entering the States flies over or comes in by way of the Bahamas."

"We are meant to control the Bahamas, can't we stop this immoral trade?"

"The DEA arrested the Prime Minister of the Turks and Caicos islands on charges of accepting bribes to allow drugs to land in transit to America. They are still trying to indict the Bahamian Prime Minister and other Ministers, for reportedly accepting similar bribes." Littner laughed. "It is ironic. In seventy-four America cultivated four thousand tons of marijuana. California showed concern that it was surpassing their top crops. It became one of the most profitable crop in twenty-two states and lead the field in ten. At that time America was growing fifty-five percent of the marijuana for home consumption."

"The Jamaican government took the attitude that if it acted against drug production the economy would collapse and Communism would take over. Ganja was profitable. Seaga, the prime minister, encouraged banks to accept drugs money, known as Ganja dollars. A comprehensive report showed conclusive evidence that, between seventy-one and seventy-eight, the Bolivian military regime played a major part in establishing the trafficking syndicates. It showed how the health minister, Carlos Valverde, made sure the industry obtained the chemicals and solvents they required. He also tipped off the drugs barons by leaking many DEA reports and plans to them."

"Panama is now taking some of the heat off the Bahamas as a staging post." Interposed Fisher.

"The Bahamas are under strict observation. Panama returns something like a billion dollars to the US federal reserve each year, governed by a right wing military dictatorship which seems to give them immunity. She launders money to her heart's content, no doubt lining the pockets of her rulers. The most mysterious part of the whole business is the routes the drugs take from one country to the next. The explanation of the control of these I will leave to my DEA contact as it is a complicated political issue."

Fisher nodded. "Bogota supplies to San Diego, Los Angeles, Tucson, Phoenix and Vancouver. Antigua delivers by land through the Panama, Honduras and Mexico to Brownsville, Corpus Christi and El Paso.

Sierra Nevada De Santa Marta area delivers by air and sea to Jackson and Mobile. Key West and Marathon via Haiti and Bahamas to Miami, Fort Lauderdale, Tampa and New York, Washington, Detroit and Chicago. Guyana delivers to New York, Montreal and Europe. The base of the Amazon delivers to Europe. Caracas delivers to Puerto Rico and the New York area and so it goes on."

"They seem to have enough routes to ring the changes if something goes wrong."

"I have already said that sixty percent goes over or through the Bahamas. This is a mass of Islands, with private moorings and facilities for thousands of boats, going between the mainland, around Fort Lauderdale, to the Bahamas islands every month. It is a perfect cover for smugglers, shielded from watching eyes. The methods used are too numerous to name, but large consignments, of up to one thousand kilos at a time, usually go by boat, in a container in the hold, or on deck. They carry drugs alongside legitimate cargo. I have gone on too long, but it is a massive subject. The more I study it the further I seem to be from any conclusions. It comes down to a choice of either ruining several already poverty-stricken countries as well as their economies, or else legalising the trade."

Holder thought over Littner's grim story while Fisher voiced his own conclusions.

"The second alternative would bring revenue to the treasuries involved which could bring help for drug addicts. At the moment it is plain that the agencies are pulling against each other, not solving the problem. Legalisation may be a better alternative. It couldn't be much worse. I feel that until we can understand the users, the dealers, the peasant farmers and the producers, no drugs policy will succeed. Anyway Jerry, that's a hell of a book of facts you have given us. You need another drink."

"I won't say no. I am parched."

"Bourbon on the rocks?"

"Yes. Thanks."

Fisher waved to the barman.

"Tell me," asked Holder, "what do the people feel about the cartels?"

"Well, the money rubs off down the line, so they generally approve of them. The cartels have killed a lot of people, a Minister of Justice, some judges and officials, DEA men, police whom they couldn't corrupt, informers and anyone that opposed them. The people turn a blind eye to that, as long as some of the wealth rubs off. Some of the barons actually do a lot of good for their communities."

Fisher came back with the drinks and for the rest of the evening they discussed the press and their experience of working in Colombia. Next day Littner collected them for their journey to a remote factory making cocaine sulphate. The facility was Hidden in Cali cartel territory deep in a forest with only a dirt track leading near to the entrance. Two armed guards stopped them on the roadside, some two kilometres from the entrance. Littner rolled down the window and talked to one of them in Spanish. The conversation was curt. The men stood menacingly aiming their guns at the car.

Littner turned and said, "Get out of the car, slowly, without making any sudden moves." They obeyed and found themselves being searched. Satisfied, the guards ordered them away from the car and that too was searched. The soldier in charge then seemed assured and they continued their journey.

They parked their car in the forest. Littner led them to the factory, where they were greeted by a man with grey hair and a slight stoop. A pair of spectacles perched on the end of his nose made him look like a scruffy professor. "Hi Jose. How's the cauldron today?"

"It's like hell as usual, especially near the drying room. So these are your two friends who want to see our little factory. Pleased to meet you." Jose offered a sweaty hand then led them to a refreshment area under a thatched roof.

"We can offer you a Coca-Cola, or I have a special bottle of stronger liquor. It's made from sugar cane and very strong, about one-hundred and forty percent proof by your ratings. It's made in illicit stills, locally, but it's really a speciality of Jamaica. Would you like to try it?" Holder accepted but Littner and Fisher stuck to coke. After the first mouthful Holder knew why. It set his throat on fire and burned down to his stomach. Jose laughed.

"I did say it was strong. Now, this is not what you have come all this way to see. Let me try and explain what we do at this plant. First, I should tell you that I am a chemist by training and I am in charge of this unit. We work deep in this forest to protect ourselves. The authorities have closed many plants, so we have to hide well. You may have seen our guards on the road?"

"We thought they were going to shoot us."

"No. They are there to protect our interests. At this plant we receive base cocaine from all over Latin America and we convert it into cocaine sulphate. The base comes from Peru and Bolivia. We also get small amounts from Colombia and Venezuela. It comes to us direct from the growers, or through middle men, in the case of the smaller farmers. We get between one hundred and five hundred kilos at a time. It arrives in all sorts of containers by many different forms of transport, by truck, llama, or on foot. You name it, we get it."

"Why doesn't the government raid you?"

"You will notice that nothing is visible from the sky. This is most important as the DEA conducts regular aerial searches. Of course we have to watch out for informers too. We kill them when we find them. This is an expensive operation and we can't have it spoilt by informers. Chemically, what we are trying to extract is C17 H21 NO4 that is, pure cocaine sulphate. Anything over seventy-five percent pure satisfies us. First we take the paste and wash it in chemicals, so, if you follow me, I will show you the process."

In the first hut they saw several men stirring cocaine in plastic buckets of lime water, gasoline, acid and potassium permanganate.

"They strain off the liquid and add a drop or two of ammonia to purify it and bleach the finished product. At the end of the process they add the last ammonia to the reddish liquid, it turns white and crystals begin to form."

"What quantity per acre can you expect?" asked Holder.

"We get about a pound of cocaine from an acre of land per cropping. The next stage is this way. Please follow me." They moved to the next shed.

"Here filtration takes place, removing further impurities and whitening the product. Next I will show you the final process." Before they were within thirty yards of the last shed Holder felt the heat.

"This is the drying process. We lay the cocaine crystals on this tray and subject them to special, high-powered white light. As you can feel, this is hell on earth. These bulbs dry the crystals completely and also bleach them further. This crystalline powder is the final product. We weigh it into kilos and then seal it in airtight bags to protect it from detection in transit. From here it goes to all the corners of the World, but most of it ends up in the States."

"Does it worry you that it depraves and even kills people?" Asked Holder.

"No. So does alcohol and cigarettes, if used in excess. This is no more harmful than anything else if used in moderation. There will always be people who abuse themselves, but if they didn't have cocaine they would find something else, don't you think?"

"How much do you produce each week?" Asked Fisher.

"About two to three tons, depending on how much base we get."

"How do you dispatch it?"

"That, I am afraid to say, must remain a secret. Many different ways are used. That is all I am prepared to disclose."

"Thanks again for the tour." Commented Holder as they left to return to their car.

Back in the car they discussed their next move.

"Tomorrow I hope to speak to my DEA contact." Said Littner. "Then you can get the story behind the research to add meat to your investigation."

"That's great. Tomorrow. Same time?"

"Can't see you till after twelve-thirty, amuse yourselves till then."

Next day was exceedingly humid and Holder found it difficult to breathe. There was thunder, preceding a storm the like of which he had never experienced. The down-pour was an opening of the heavens, flooding water into the equatorial cauldron, as if to douse its flames. It was this combination of heat and heavy rain that made the jungle a place of rapid, luxurious growth, allowing frequent cropping of the cocoa plant. It was like one vast greenhouse. At two-thirty Littner arrived in a state of frustration.

"Sorry I am so late, but Ed has disappeared. I have searched all his usual haunts, I can't find any sign of him. I am afraid you can't finish your investigation until we find him. He has the information you need and he is the only one I can trust. Don't worry. He will turn up."

"Can we help you search?"

"Not at the moment. It is better that I do it alone. If that doesn't work I will call you in."

For five days they waited, not daring to go out together in case they missed their chance. Having written up their notes, boredom began to set in to add to their frustration. The heat was unbearable and they noticed it even more with nothing to do. Finally, in despair, Littner called them in to help. They scoured bars and clubs.

By the third day they were ready to throw in the towel. As they drove towards their hotel Littner thought he saw Ed disappearing down a side alley. The car screeched to a halt and they ran down the street.

They saw their man enter a bar at the far end. Half-way down the street they came to an abrupt halt blocked by two ugly looking men brandishing long knives, who stepped out of a doorway in front of them. One of them shouted some obscenity. At that moment Holder knew that they were in great danger. If these guys had friends they were out-numbered, never mind the fact that they carried weapons. There was no way that they could reason with them, so they must disarm them. Holder indicated this to Fisher and they dived on one of the men, catching him completely by surprise. Holder caught a glimpse of the other man bearing down on them and kicked upwards at the knife he brandished. Astonished, they disarmed both men, who fled, leaving their knives lying in the gutter.

Fortune had favoured the bold. Littner just stood in amazement, shaking visibly. They continued down the road knowing that they were lucky to be alive. Arriving at the bar down at the end of the street, they found Ed sitting in the corner. He was completely oblivious to the danger they had just overcome to reach him.

"Where the hell have you been, Ed? We have searched all over town for you for eight days!"

"Sorry. I had to go out of town on urgent business. I left a message for you with my assistant."

"He disappeared, too."

"Oh dear. He isn't very reliable! I am sorry, but it couldn't be helped."

"We were nearly killed just now. It's only thanks to these two that I am still alive. Two aggressive youths in leathers attacked us with long knives. We were in this wretched alley looking for you."

"What can I say? They were probably cartel henchmen. They are totally unpredictable. Let's go to your hotel where we can get down to business before something else happens."

Back at their hotel they settled in the lounge, complete with drinks, to hear the inside story of the DEA. Ed was a man with a quiet crusade.

"It all began with a commitment I made to eradicate drugs from our streets. My sister is now in an institution having driven herself mad through using drugs. She was a lovely girl and had the World at her feet. She was about to go to university and would have had a perfect start to life. Then she met a man who introduced her to 'good times.' We all warned her, but she fell for his charms. He was a drugs dealer. Soon he had her hooked.

Then he tried to turn her into a prostitute. She went mad, knowing that we had warned her and that we had been right. She couldn't cope with that and went down hill fast. Eventually, we had to have her committed, for her own protection. This made me determined to help to fight this evil. That was twelve years ago. I joined the DEA team, thinking that they were 'knights in shining armour.'

I am here now because I found that they did not measure up to my image."

"Has it helped you reach a conclusion, Ed?" Asked Fisher.

"After twelve year's experience I have come to believe that we should not be here at all. We should be blocking the entry of drugs to the States, not interfering with another country's way of life. Politics have been a major factor in my disillusionment. When the DEA started we tried to control drug distribution inside the USA, but we soon began to realise that it would be easier and more cost effective to attack the traders on their home ground. So, in the late seventies, we began to tackle the problem at source, with the reluctant co-operation of the governments concerned."

"But, surely," protested Holder, "their co-operation is essential!"

"We misguidedly thought that, because we were formed to eliminate drug production, this is what we would do. Alas, politics took over and we found we were being manipulated not only by the authorities within the countries where we were operating, but also by the CIA. It seemed at first that there was method in their games, so we played along with them for a while, pulling our punches where our consciences dictated otherwise."

"What changed your mind?"

"As time went by a pattern began to emerge. We were busting the traffickers and growers that belonged to the left wing element, but leaving the right wing groups to operate un-hindered. This sickened me. I saw our opportunity to end this vile trade disappear, as load after load was allowed through. We had strict orders from the CIA to leave well alone. Now the cartels are so powerful, especially round here, that to beat them would require a huge army. I have seen some good men killed on duty, while we pulled back and I have gradually realised that we are nothing but a pawn in a political game."

"You're being used as agents against communism." Said Fisher dryly, "Drugs are a secondary issue. The CIA controls you!"

"They are the ones who pull our strings." Said Littner.

Greenshaw's book, 'Flying High,' exposes some of the hypocrisy inherent in US policy. It tells the story of an international marijuana and cocaine trafficker who claimed to have paid thirteen and a half million dollars, over a ten year period, to the Semoza regime in Nicaragua. This had been to guarantee un-impeded landing facilities for his planes on route from South America to the USA. After the revolution he moved his operation to Nicaragua."

"The CIA sanctioned that?"

Ed nodded and continued.

"Greenshaw interviewed a CIA agent who confirmed that the right wing guerrillas in Nicaragua had cut airstrips in the jungle so that planes could land there. The CIA had helped in the construction of these airstrips, with the knowledge that the planes were landing from Colombia. Their official task in Nicaragua, to oppose the Sandanista government that overthrew Semoza! So with one hand the CIA is fighting Communism and with the other it is supporting the right wing dealers, who in turn assist them in their main mission, killing commies!

How can we expect to solve the drugs problem this way? The American people are being duped by propaganda."

"You mean they are being led to believe America is winning the drugs war."

"Yes. Another example, on the other side of the globe, is the Afghan war. The Mujahideen forces use the sale of drugs to obtain arms for their war against the Russian occupation. They use drugs openly to buy arms, in sight of and with clearance from the CIA. The drug that is being traded in this case is the worst of all, heroin."

"So Nicaragua is not a isolated case?"

"No. Nearer home, in Bolivia, the CIA used the drug issue to de-stabilise Garcia Meza's regime. They undermined the Stroessner autocracy by similar methods. Interpol disclosed how the health minister, Carlos Valverde, made sure that the industry had free access to the chemicals they needed and kept the barons informed of all our moves. The most devious thing that happened was the propaganda con on the American people. They announced, in nineteen-eighty, that they had won the war on drugs by the assault on the marijuana fields. We had already filed our reports about the move towards cocaine and indeed, had busted some of their plants. They chose to ignore this back at the White House."

"It seems so pointless to waste so much money operating the DEA if the CIA can overrule their every move."

Ed continued. "At this time we received orders from the CIA to wage war in the Chapare area, where cells of communist sympathisers were growing their crops. Meanwhile, of course, we were to leave the wealthy ranches of the Santa Cruz and Beni alone. That convinced me that our government had no intention of eradicating the drugs barons. They used us for publicity when they needed it and as a weapon in their fight against Communism. The CIA controls the routes for drugs leaving central America. I don't mean to imply that they are running the drugs, although we know they do, when necessary, use drugs to finance the fight against communism."

"You mean they actually trade drugs?" Questioned Holder hoping for a lead.

"They used drugs to buy arms for the contra rebels in Nicaragua and to pay for mercenaries for the same battle. Some consignments went to Europe, to an English company called Sentinel Armed Security."

"That's interesting," said Holder, "so the evidence is also available out in this neck of the woods that supports something I have been researching. Why don't the CIA just pay for the mercenaries?"

"Simply because their covert fund has run dry in Switzerland. This was due to the press exposure of the Iran-Contra affair. Drugs were their only source of payment due to the clamp-down on covert funding."

"You have given me the reason to be here. That confirms my findings." Replied Holder.

Ed sipped his drink and continued. "The incident that finally provoked my resignation involved me personally.

We spent a long time getting to know a member of one of the cartels. Naturally this exposed us to considerable danger, but it had been worth it. We built up a fat dossier of information about their operation and had everything in place to bust it wide open. It would have also netted a few of the big boys on our side of the water. Two of our operatives lost their lives for this fat cat. We reported that we were ready to move. After considerable delay we received orders to call it off."

"Why was that?" Asked Holder.

"This man was apparently helping the CIA. I was so mad that I almost gave the go-ahead on my own. This baron had a vast operation going. He sat in his luxurious palace in Medellin, administrating his dirty deals and laundering money at will. We really had an opportunity to crack a large nut and the CIA blew it,

purely for political gain. We found out later that he had paid for a huge consignment of arms for the Nicaraguan rebel forces. I was sick to the pit of my stomach. That was when I decided to resign."

Fisher agreed. "The politics of the drugs business are such that as long as the cartels are useful to the CIA they are safe. Occasionally there are big busts, but you can safely bet your bottom dollar that the right wing cartels never get touched."

"I despair of the situation." Sighed Ed. "This is why I have resigned. Now I am working to have the CIA brought to book and made accountable for their actions."

There wasn't much to add or even ask. He had told the full story. They all sat and sipped their cool drinks in silence. Holder was the first to speak.

"Ed I have come a long way to hear this. Can I use it in the book I am writing?" Holder now knew he must turn his investigation into a book to expose all the details of his findings.

"By all means. I hope it has more effect than all my years with the DEA. If the government would only realise how irrelevant their campaign against Communism is to the real World. The Communism that most of these poor folk practice is only the co-operation born of necessity. It is to protect themselves against us, the fat cats, by which I mean the power houses of government and the Barons.

We are not dealing with the evil type of Communism practised elsewhere, although Cuba is perhaps an exception. Nicaragua uses drugs, to buy arms and to fight the rebels, of necessity. The rebels derive much of their income from drugs too. Drugs have become a part of politics. They have become

integrated into our economic system but they are still more important to the third World, where they are central to survival.

It would not be practicable to break the chain now. I have reluctantly come to the conclusion that legislation for legalisation is the only way ahead. Where this has taken place usage has fallen, as well as the price. Taxes contribute towards helping the users, in much the same way as we help alcoholics. Most importantly, it cuts out some of the criminal element and trade passes into the hands of legitimate businessmen."

CHAPTER 22.

It was a cold, damp November morning when Holder arrived back at Heathrow, a far stretch from the almost unbearable humidity and heat of South America. He had been away for a month and it was a strange feeling coming back to this cold climate.

They stopped him at customs and searched his case, but they did not strip him this time. Instead they removed the notes from his bag and disappeared with them into a back office. He did not have Lynn to carry them, but as they were in shorthand he felt safe. He complained loudly about being kept waiting and was ushered into an office, where a severe, grey-haired man sat studying his notes.

"Sit down, Mr Holder."

"I have no wish to sit down and you have no right to read my notes. I am an accredited journalist and these notes are my work. Kindly return them."

"I am afraid you are ill-informed about your rights. We have the power to do anything we wish if we suspect someone and I do mean anything. So I suggest you sit down and explain to me what your business has been for the last month."

Holder sat down in disbelief and the official continued.

"Now perhaps you would be good enough to tell me what you've been doing in South America?"

"What right have you to question me about my research? It is nothing to do with you until I write my article. Then you can judge it's quality."

"I will repeat this once more, so that you completely understand me. We have full powers, under the customs and excise act, to question you, detain you or charge you, if we so wish. Do I make myself clear?"

Holder was beginning to suspect that this man was from the security services or even Sentinel Armed Securities and not customs as his uniform indicated.

"I have been doing two months research to establish the routes that the drug barons use to distribute their products around the World. That has been the extent and purpose of my visit."

"Very commendable. Have you any exposures that we should know about?"

"None that you don't already know, I am sure."

"I notice that the CIA is mentioned several times in your notes. For what reason?"

"It relates to their attempts to control drug trafficking in South America."

"An endless task, I am sure."

He bought that one, thought Holder.

"I have taken the liberty of Photostatting your notes so that I can have them studied by our experts. You may go."

"I must make a formal protest about the intimidation I have been subjected to during this interview. I am also seeking legal advice about photo copying my notes."

"I shouldn't bother. No one has ever succeeded with such a wasteful complaint. Just be glad we are not holding you."

Holder left, in a state of inner fury. He picked up his case at the customs desk and called a cab. The drive took thirty-five minutes, due to a road accident. He arrived home, paid the taxi and studied his seals, to check for intruders. He found both the front door and the garage seal disturbed. He went to the rear of the house, unlocked the patio door, which still bore its seal and entered his living room. His first thought was that the place might be booby-trapped, so he moved carefully, examining all possibilities as he went. He reached the front door without incident. The usual heap of junk mail lay in a pile, but pushed away from the door. This established unwelcome visitors.

He went straight into the dining room, which doubled as his work room, to find chaos awaiting him, papers strewn all over the place. The most important thing was missing. His computer discs, covering all his work for the last two years, had gone. His heart sank low as the full implications hit him. He rushed into the hall, lifted the phone and then had second thoughts. He unscrewed the head and looked inside it. Hidden in a corner he found one of the smallest bugs he had ever seen. He ran out of the patio door, frightened and furious and dropped the bug on the stone slabs, grinding it into the concrete as hard as his weight allowed. The bug, now in a thousand particles, lay shattered and harmless.

He took a deep breath of the cold air to control his emotions and went back into the house. He searched the rest of the house for listening devices. Then, when he had satisfied himself that there were no more, he rang Lynn to confirm that he was back.

"Hello darling, how are you?"

"David you don't know how pleased I am to hear from you. Are you all right?"

"Yes, I'm fine. Just a few problems. Tell you when I see you."

"I'll be with you by ten o'clock this evening, so light the candles and be ready."

"I'll collect you at the station."

"OK. See you then."

Holder went into action, tidying up the dining room and checking the mail. Then he went to the garage and opened the door, carefully and slowly. He inspected the car thoroughly, using a light to see underneath the car and round the wheel arches.

A magnetic homing device was very carefully concealed under the front near-side wheel-arch. Again the blood boiled inside him and he went outside to simmer down. He was only doing his job as a reporter. It was the penalty for investigating state business.

He pulled his car outside the garage and gave it another thorough inspection. It was obvious that they now wanted to know his every move. The box of discs would tell them exactly what he had been doing and the bugs told them where he was going. The custom's operation had been another form of open interference to make him run scared.

The train was twenty minutes late. He waited, impatiently, yet hopeful, with one red rose, to greet Lynn. As their eyes met in the half light Holder's heart quickened.

"You waited. I'm sorry I'm late," exclaimed Lynn, running up to him. They held each other, long and hard.

"You're certainly worth the wait," said Holder, giving her the rose. She blushed as she thanked him, on the way to find the car. She didn't stop talking on the short journey home.

Then he told her the bad news.

"I was searched again at the airport. They read and copied my notes. So, if they can decipher them, they will know everything I did in South America. I am sure that the guy was from British security, although he wore the uniform of a customs officer. When I arrived home I found the seals disturbed and our discs stolen. That's all our work gone and they bugged the car and telephone as well. I have destroyed the bugs."

"David darling, they haven't got our discs. I have. There is also a back up copy at the bank. They only stole the blank discs in the box, which I labelled to confuse a burglar. I also left a pert message on one of the discs."

"Lynn, I don't know what to say. I didn't know how to tell you. that's just wonderful."

"Reserve that for later. You must be hungry."

"I have prepared a meal for you, out of posh packets," replied Holder, looking doubtful.

He went into the kitchen to heat up the food, while Lynn, for a change, sat back and relaxed. Twenty minutes later he came in and asked her to come to the table. The lit candles directed flickering light through the crystal glasses, giving a warm and exciting atmosphere.

She sat down and knew she belonged. She was home. Lynn lent over the table, clutched his hand and thanked him with her eyes.

"Now it is my turn to show appreciation." She poured a cold bottle of champagne she left in the cooler. Later she led him upstairs into the bedroom.

They stood for a long time, just holding each other closely as if to make up for all their time apart. Slowly they undressed and showered, gently soaping each other's bodies, transfixed by the other's presence and full of wonder at the feelings that flowed between them.

Separation had strengthened their mutual awareness and answered their remaining doubts, putting them where they belonged. They were closer, in body, mind and spirit than either of them had ever believed possible.

It was well past noon by the time they had talked and then dressed. Holder taught her how to seal the house, so it showed the entry of an intruder. In future they must use this ploy whenever they were both out working. He still worried about Lynn, but she would not consider going away till it was all over and in his heart he didn't want her to leave.

At two-thirty the phone rang and a voice asked for David Holder. Lynn passed the phone to him.

"David Holder speaking."

"My men were very disappointed that they did not find your work on the Advanced Laser affair when they called. It would have saved us all a lot of time and energy, don't you think? It wasn't very nice of you to find our bugs. It will make our task of keeping track of you much more difficult. However keep track of you we will, of that you may be sure."

"What right have you to break into my house and abuse my privacy?"

"Why can't you be reasonable and have a meeting with us? We can clear up all matters to both our satisfaction and then you will know exactly where you stand."

"I have already told you I meet strangers only at my office, nowhere else. What's your problem?"

"It's a pity you don't see it our way. We are both on the same side. After all Communism is the common enemy of the West, isn't it?"

Holder decided to test a theory.

"Don't you think you overplay that hand Major Strange?"

"Never underestimate your enemy old chap. Now will you meet us for a friendly exchange?"

He had scored. That confirmed the photograph. It was Major Strange. He was the man with the staring eyes. Not a man from security.

"Only at my office, where I am in control."

"It's a pity you are so stubborn. You are going to cost the taxpayer a lot of money, if that's the way you want it. By the way, it was an interesting investigation you did in South America. Our friends at the CIA don't like publicity. Best forget it if you know what's good for you. You see you can't escape us. We can get to you whenever and wherever we want. Be warned. Be wise. Be quiet."

Major Strange put his phone down, leaving Holder reeling like a goldfish in a bowl. He ignored the laws governing ordinary people. No one policed his firm, even the politicians. He said and did what he liked and justified everything in the name of the national interest. It was obvious to Holder that he could kill him at any time if he so wished. Therefore he must have good reason to keep him alive so far. He must make sure that the reason, his discs, did not fall into his hands.

At last he knew the identity of his antagonist, Major Strange of Sentinel Armed securities. This posed a much larger question. If he was working so closely with state security it would be most unlikely he was also working for the KGB. So who was killing the scientists. It must be a Russian team.

"Lynn, they are closing in on us. That call was from the same man who spoke to me before I went to South America. I now know who he is."

"Let me guess, Major Strange?"

"As usual you are spot on. They are good, very good. He had already read my notes from the airport incident and wanted a meeting. The one thing that they want is our discs. From now on in we must not let them out of our sight and we must burn all our loose notes after they have gone onto the computer. It is most important that we keep our back-up copies up to date and secure, at the bank. They must not get a full set. If they succeed they will kill me. Frankly I think you should go back to Wales until this is over."

"Don't worry David, I'm not quitting now. We must just be more vigilant and a little smarter than them."

"That's easily said, but you would have to have a very devious mind to outsmart them."

"That should be easy then."

"I don't know if I approve that remark."

Holder ordered a whole series of new locks and security devices to protect his home, until, in the end, he wondered how he would cope with it all himself.

Over the next few days they continued their investigation, frequently disturbed by the locksmith fitting the new security system. Now they had no freedom of movement around the house at night. No more late night snacks. The place was a network of beams, to detect any movement inside the house, with a high decibel alarm outside, to warn of intrusion. Before they entered the house there were switches to disarm. There was a switch in the hall for the downstairs rooms that they had to remember in the mornings. They had done everything to ensure their safety.

They were well on the way to learning the truth behind Captain Grey's mission. His so called girlfriend was an ex-army SAS operative now working for Sentinel Armed Securities. His colleague, Peter Naylor was an ex-SAS officer. There was a strong link between him and Sentinel Armed Securities backed up by photographic evidence.

The security company were very proficient at picking on a subject and maintaining the pressure as long as necessary. This impressed and frightened him, as he had now become a hot target. That morning Fisher rang from Los Angeles, to check that he had arrived home safely. He was concerned to hear the trouble experienced on his return. These faceless men seemed to be able to break the laws at will and had no regard at all for human rights. Everything they did was illegal but they were protected by the state system.

The next six weeks went by uneventfully. In mid-December, Holder had a call from Michael Neville, who was just about to leave the regiment and wanted to meet before he retired. They arranged to talk that evening at the pub. When they arrived at the bar Neville was already in his usual position. He greeted them and bought the first round then they retired to the garden room.

"First I must tell you that the man you introduced me to has landed me a job with an Arab, as a body guard and chauffeur. I am indebted. I wanted to thank you for your concern and help."

"That's great news. Congratulations."

"Yes Michael, I'm pleased for you too." Said Lynn.

"Now I have some information for you, that I came upon purely by chance, a mistake really. You know you told me about your investigation and also your suspicions about Captain Grey's trial? Well, I stumbled upon some information on the computer relating to an IRA cell in Malmo. It seems this cell has been very successful in raising funds to provide arms for the IRA. Our computer lists details of a undercover operation being mounted to break this cell and the details correspond exactly with the facts you gave me. It does not mention either Captain Grey or Peter Naylor by name, but it does say that the operation is in go mode."

That's very interesting."

"Supplies have been sent to an agent in Malmo for our operations. It looks as it's being done with co-operation from SAPO and Sentinel Armed Securities. It is such a secret operation that I can't find out any more about it. I hope you don't use this until they have an opportunity to clean this cell up for good."

"Don't worry, I won't rush to print. It will all be over by the time I hit the press but it confirms a theory I had about Captain Grey. This is the sort of operation I would support and the proper use of our security service."

"I also found out that Sentinel Armed Securities have started recruiting mercenaries again and the word is that it's for the CIA. They are looking for ex-SAS men who have had at least seven years operational experience and are offering eighteen thousand pounds for a three month period, as front line trainers for the Contra rebels. They reckon recruits have a twenty-five percent chance of return. They will have the most modern automatics available, plus all the usual back up power. The first batch has already been recruited and the next batch is due to go in January."

"Have any of you been approached to apply for the job yet?"

"Several of thc boys at the barracks have shown interest. I suppose the pay is so good it would tempt many trained soldiers, who think they can cheat the odds and get to the pot of gold. They even get each man to make a final will before he leaves. I can't confirm Sentinel Armed Securities work solely for the British security service yet"

"I can't either, but it is looking more likely they do, leaving me with a big problem; who kills the scientists.

It must be the KGB but who does the dirty work for them? Thanks Michael for your help. That gives us a stronger case for our report. Now when do you start your job?"

"I leave the barracks at Christmas and start my new job in January."

For the next week Holder concentrated on his work for the paper, while Lynn tidied up the script on their investigation, the foundation of the book.

For a Christmas break he drove Lynn to Wales, where they found peace away from their work. They went to Megan's lakeside cottage, where Dr Steiner had met her fate. They rang the bell and waited. The surprise delighted Meg. Lynn absorbed the quiet tranquillity of the scene.

They spend New Years Eve at Lynn's family hotel near Little Haven. The short break was soon at an end and they drove back to London.

Before entering the house they checked all the seals and to Holder's surprise they were all intact. The usual pile of junk mail greeted them when they opened the door. After switching off the alarm, they searched the house. Everything in place, he started to relax. He checked the mail and played back the messages on the answering machine. The last message brought him down to earth. The voice of Major Strange wished him a trouble free Christmas and a healthy New Year, as long as he minded his own business.

Holder smiled at his adversary's gall, but shuddered nonetheless. Early next morning he had a call from his paper, who advised him of another death in the defence industry; Tony Mather, a laboratory technician in atomic energy research.

Unfortunately, Holder was too late to view the place or get a feeling of the atmosphere at the scene. He had allegedly fallen down a cliff to his death, but this had happened some three days before he came back, so it was passed his early bird tactic.

They did, however, visit his parents and neighbours and came back convinced that this had been a genuine suicide and had nothing to do with their investigation.

CHAPTER 23.

Holder woke with a call from his paper, advising him of the death of another defence worker. Lynn rushed breakfast and they were both on the way to Portsmouth within fifteen minutes. The drive, through the rush hour, took longer than expected but they eventually arrived and parked by the house.

The police investigation was well under way by the time they arrived. The body was still in the car. He died of carbon monoxide poisoning. Holder had now seen this scene several times and was able to search economically for the clues. First he spoke to the police inspector in charge of the investigation.

"Can you tell me everything you know about this death?"

"So far we have his name, Roger Symms aged fifty-two. He was a computer expert working at Advanced

Laser Technology. He was unmarried and that is about all we know so far."

"What is your opinion about his death?"

"It looks like a simple suicide to date. This is one of the most common forms of suicide and we have found nothing so far to make us believe otherwise."

"May we look inside, readers want atmosphere." Said Holder, waiving his police press pass.

"Help yourself - but don't touch."

Holder started his search, telling Lynn what he was looking for at each stage. He found a tiny clue on the garage floor. Half hidden under a piece of wood, he saw a leather-covered black button, un-observed by the team of police investigators.

He checked the coat Symms was wearing, a sports jacket with plastic buttons. It could be something or it could be nothing. He sniffed the face. The air was still thick with the lingering exhaust fumes and the same stink clung to Symms skin, but he detected another smell around his nose.

"Lynn. Smell round the nasal area and tell me what you pick up."

Lynn hesitantly bent over the body and sniffed near his face. She stood up abruptly, exclaiming decisively,

"Almonds."

"Now we must wait and see what comes up at the autopsy."

"Why almonds?"

"It's the smell left after cyanide has been used to kill or stun someone. I would like to study his wardrobe, to see if he has a jacket to match this button."

He went up to the Inspector and asked if he could go inside and look around. He granted permission provided a constable accompanied him round the house. They looked in his wardrobe and found no leather coat or any jacket with black leather buttons. They searched the coats in the hall, again with no result. He put his head into the living room to find two men searching through papers in the desk. As the shorter man turned, to see who had entered, they recognised their old acquaintance from Sentinel Armed Securities.

His steely stare broke slightly as he recognised Holder from previous encounters.

"You seem to get to the scene very promptly. Who tips you off?" Asked Major Strange.

"Direct from the horses mouth." Replied Holder, coldly.

His face cracked momentarily, but resumed its blank stare so quickly that only the sharp eye could have detected any movement.

"Mr Holder, you have been warned not to meddle in our business. Why do you persist?"

"Major Strange, it's my job for a start and mysteries fascinate me."

"I suggest you deal with this death as a suicide."

"Why? Were you here to make sure when it happened, or perhaps it was one of your Russian rivals? you can't stop them - right?"

"Now Mr Holder, don't be so facetious. The facts speak for themselves."

"They certainly do and suicide will certainly be rejected, if the facts are reported by the autopsy to the coroner."

"What makes you say that?"

"Facts."

"Be more precise."

"Well, for a start, take the black leather button on the floor of the garage. It's from a coat very similar to yours."

Major Strange immediately inspected his own as if to clear himself of blame.

"What does that prove?"

"Whoever lost that button could be the murderer of Mr Symms. Why not confide. The Russians are behind this because of star-wars."

"Your imagination is too vivid."

"If the police do their job, this death will be found to be murder and an investigation will ensue."

"I doubt it."

"Do you mean you will suppress it?"

"This isn't Russia."

"Then why do you interfere and threaten the press when they are doing their job?"

"National security is paramount to our freedom."

"Curtail the press and you curtail freedom. Then we become a police state. Are we a police state?"

"Of course not."

"Then let me do my job un-hindered. Stop telephoning me with threats."

Holder turned and walked away. The constable, who had heard the conversation, turned to him and said;

"Thanks. Our freedom depends on people like you."

Encouraged by this comment, Holder counted yet another reason to proceed.

Next he tried both neighbours, but to no avail. He found that they did not want to talk about Mr Symms.

He went back to the police inspector, asked for and received, all the information relating to the autopsy and the eventual coroner's report and left for London. Sometime, he knew that he must go to the firm for their comments.

It was, again, a murder and he awaited only a negative coroner's report to know that the authorities were in on the deceit. So, most likely, was the private security company, who must be working with the state security otherwise they would not be allowed behind the scenes.

How could the State influence police, coroners and medics who were otherwise honest? The answer was, unfortunately, a simple one. Pensions. The State pays pensions and therefore it can influence citizens who would otherwise be honest.

They arrived back, completed their security checks and entered the house.

Holder spent the rest of the afternoon writing records of their morning's work. What became clear to him was an arrogance in the attitude of Sentinel Armed Securities that told him they could deal with him whenever and wherever they wished. This was to have an increasing effect on his actions and would eventually, if allowed, control his thinking. It would be disastrous for this investigation. Their stupidity confused him. Why cover their tracks? Unless, through these murders, Russia was severely damaging Western defences. The British government was so secretive, much of which could be attributed to covering their own mistakes and short-comings.

For once he did little but assess his career and his new found happiness with Lynn, but in the end journalism won the day. After all it was his life's work and he had reached the top the hard way. He must go through with the investigation until he reached a conclusion and published his findings.

Lynn, realising that he was torturing himself, decided that it was best to allow him space to think. She assured herself that he would make the right decision when the time came. She longed to re-assure him that she was behind him and that he should ignore all threats and proceed. She also knew that he was thinking of her in making his decision and that also had to take its place. So she put up with the silence and busied herself round the house until he was ready to share his thoughts with her.

"We've received innumerable threats to our safety since we returned from Sweden and recently I have been very concerned for your safety. Lynn I love you, I must think of you first. I've decided that I must see the investigation through to the bitter end. I know no other trade, but you do not need to take this risk."

"Before you go any further please understand that I am now part of this enquiry and I care for you and our project far too much to leave because of these threats."

"Lynn, are you so sure? It could be fatal for you to stay."

"That's a risk that I'll take. I am involved in this now and I am going to see it through."

"I don't know how to thank you enough for your loyalty. Many would have wilted at this point, but you have remained resolute."

Just as he finished, the phone rang: his office asked him to go to Hampstead, where the police were arresting Edwin Schmidt on spying charges. They rushed out of the house, setting their security and drove to Hampstead to cover the story.

The address was a second floor flat at Stanmore court. When they arrived Holder went straight up to a police officer, whom he knew and took him aside.

"Bob, how's tricks. this story is very important to me. What can you tell me about this man?"

"My God Holder, long time no see. Let's make it quick. His assumed name is Edwin Schmidt. Our Security service caught him red handed, passing and receiving messages to and from Prague. He was working at a London Store until eighty-five. Then he resigned to become an estate agent, as a cover for his real activity, spying for the KGB. As we are old friends I will give you something that is not on my schedule, but don't use it till after the court case. A very important defector from the Eastern block, exposed Edwin Schmidt. Security knew for the last two and a half years and he has been under observation for all this time."

"You can rely on me," promised Holder.

"There is a second person that may turn out to give further evidence and that is his twin sister. She came into his life a while back, after some years of trying to trace her long lost brother. The State will want a blood test identification. It will destroy that poor woman when she learns who he really is. Can you imagine what will go through her mind?"

"Tell me, what was the purpose of his spying?"

"We have not received a complete picture yet and I can't release some of the information we have obtained. If I tell you it concerns defence secrets and Jewish organisations that should give you enough for the moment."

"Would it have anything to do with Advanced Laser Technology?"

"I am not at liberty to say!"

"Anything else you can tell me?"

"Not at the moment. The Security boys are in the flat now, sorting through his belongings. The tools of his trade have been found, transmitters, receivers, code books and lists of all sorts which have yet to be examined. I am afraid only part of this will come out as some of the information is classified."

"Thanks Bob. See you for a drink one of these fine days."

They went home and he faxed a report through to his office.

Holder's mind tried, as usual, to analyse the implications behind the sketchy details. He was beginning to formulate ideas that could solve the last remaining mystery in this long investigation. Was Schmidt the link between the Russians and the contract killer?

He decided to make a list of all the deaths combined with their skills so he could take a look at their collective capabilities. For two hours he moved his bricks around till suddenly he saw clearly.

"Lynn, I have been blind. All along I have been looking for the ultimate weapon as I was convinced they had an advanced laser gun that made other weapons redundant. They have, but it was not the reason for the deaths. The answer has been staring me in the face and I never considered it till now. It's not the secrets of the weapons the KGB want. It's the computer software that controls, guides and deploys them. That's the secret that the Russians so desperately wanted and the scientists that died nearly all had at least part of that knowledge. It was the advanced command and control system they needed so desperately so they could catch up with Western technology. Their computer technology is known to be well behind the Western powers. What a fool I have been. I should have seen this clearly when the Russian journalist told me in so many words, Russia was broke."

"Sometimes," said Lynn, "when it stares you in the face, it blinds you to its existence."

"You're absolutely right, Lynn, what do you make of this Edwin Schmidt affair?"

"Would you like a question as a answer?"

"Try me."

"Could this case lead us to the missing link in our investigation?"

"God Lynn, you do think like me! Why they were killed. If we hadn't been called to investigate this arrest, we might never have connected. So there are two possibilities, firstly that Schmidt contacted a contract killer to slow down the development or steal the secrets of the command and control program. Secondly the unthinkable that I have persistently put in the back of my mind. That our security service contracted Sentinel Armed Securities to stop them talking. The implications of which are horrific. That is the last brick we need to build our case."

Holder started to prepare his written sketch on Roger Symms. An hour and a half later he approached Lynn.

"You've a glint in your eyes," Lynn exclaimed, puzzled yet curious.

"Take a look at this." Holder passed Lynn the sketch he had written on Symm's death. "It helps my thinking-there's one for each case I believe is murder."

It was a cold March evening when Roger Symms drove home from his work at Advanced Laser Technology's factory in Portsmouth. He arrived at his small cottage on the outskirts of town. He decided to service his car that evening ready for the Easter break, having arranged to visit his sister's family one hundred and fifty miles away. He had to make sure he would have no problems on the way as the car service was slightly overdue.

Roger was an accomplished computer engineer, working on sensitive defence projects. His high degree of expertise had assured him a good position in the company and he was working on several top level programs.

He was fifty-two years old and a bachelor. He belonged to the local dramatic society and his social life revolved mainly around this hobby. His neighbours considered him to be a bit of a hermit, but rudeness was not his intention, he followed a very heavy domestic schedule. He was of medium build, with dark receding hair and weighed in at one hundred and fifty-five pounds, fit and trim for his age.

Roger parked the car in his double garage and went inside to change his clothes. Ten minutes later he was out in the garage and preparing the car for its service.

He reckoned it would take about two hours if everything went as expected.

He finished his work on schedule and went inside to wash. Then he took the car out for a short drive, to

check that everything was satisfactory. When he was sure, he returned to the garage, parked the car and switched off the lights. He emerged from the car and as he turned he noticed a man in a long, dark coat approaching him. He swung round to greet his visitor. The stranger drew near, took his hand out of his pocket and sprayed an aerosol into Roger's face. He collapsed immediately as the stranger fitted a mask to protect himself from the fumes.

He then moved the limp body back into the driver's seat, taking the car keys out of his hand and starting the engine. He noted that the tank was nearly full, turned off the garage lights, closed the doors and melted into the darkness of the night.

CHAPTER 24.

Informed about another tragic death, they drove to the flat of Colonel Andrew Sinclair, the first senior manager to die in suspicious circumstances. Holder recognised a police inspector and asked him for the preliminary details.

"Ex-para and SAS officer, worked as an assistant sales director at Advanced Laser Technology. He was found in the flat this morning by a colleague. Died from electrocution."

"Was there any suicide note?"

"Not that we have found."

"Any sign that another person was present in the flat?"

"No. We are sure he was alone."

Holder examined the body, the room and then looked round the flat. At last he turned to Lynn and delivered his verdict;

"I think this one is actually suicide. The only odd thing that I have noticed is that his ankles are swollen. Perhaps a clue, but I can't see where it leads. What is it meant to tell us?"

Turning to the inspector, Holder asked:

"Can you give me his home address?"

"We are not allowed to release his address yet, but as a friend, they live very near the centre of Wiltshire. I didn't say that Holder, OK."

"Thanks, friend." Holder turned to Lynn and said,

"Let's wrap this up."

As they turned to leave Major Strange entered the flat. When they passed Holder quipped.

"What, couldn't you get up this morning? You're too late. Lets talk - soon."

They left before he could reply.

On the way to Wiltshire Lynn studied the map and they decided Chippenham should be their first stop. They entered the town. A quick glimpse at the directory gave them Sinclair's address. Holder was astonished. Murders by the barrow, a killer squad on the loose and still not one of these people was ex-directory.

On arrival they stopped the car outside the entrance to a small estate. It was a beautiful grey stone house, in the style traditional to the region. Leaded windows graced the front and a thick oak door finished the solid appearance. A wall, hand built in Wiltshire stone, surrounded the estate, undulating

along the slopes of the surrounding meadows. A long avenue of beech trees led up to the house.

Holder rang the bell and a well-dressed lady in her early fifties answered the door. He introduced Lynn and Mrs Sinclair asked them both inside. She seemed composed, almost in complete control.

"How can I help you, Mr Holder?"

"I have just come from the flat. Your husband's ankles were very swollen. Can you explain this? I didn't understand why."

"Oh dear. I was told that the press would be here, but not so soon. My husband had a very bad road accident some three weeks ago. He was in collision with a tipper lorry. His legs were trapped and he had to be cut out of his car. He showed signs of being disturbed since the accident, although his legs improved." She paused then decided to continue. "About a week ago he tried to commit suicide. That accident killed the better part of him. He never recovered his old self."

"Where did he have the accident?"

"Half way to Bath. My son was with him at the time. By luck he wasn't injured."

"Would the Bath police have the details of the accident?"

"I suppose so."

"Do you think he committed suicide?"

"I am sure he did. He was in a terrible mental state."

"Was his car crash an accident?"

"So the police say. I was not there, but Paul thought it was."

"Was your husband working on a defence project?"

"He spent all his time on high security work."

"Star Wars related?"

"I can't say. There was one thing he left in his jacket pocket. It's a car number I think. It was written on the back of a receipt. I only found it an hour ago when I was sorting out his clothes. I'll fetch it."

Holder smiled encouragement as she re-entered the room. "Did your husband give you any hint, when he left for London, that he would not be returning?"

"He was in such a state, Mr Holder, it was impossible to read him. Almost as though he was sleep walking. There you are. It may be nothing."

Holder didn't have to check the number. It was the Russian private detective again. Once more Holder put the KGB back at the top of the list.

"Thank you for your time Mrs Sinclair."

Their next stop was Bath police station. They were evasive, refusing to give the name and address of the lorry driver. Why refuse him this information unless they were party to the deceit? What could the authorities - government security gain? Surely, if the Russians were taking out scientists like shot rabbits, the government ought to seek his co-operation? Not threaten.

They drove back to London. Next day he rang the personnel manager at Advanced Laser Technology. He confirmed the state of Colonel Sinclair after the accident. Holder was almost ready to believe he was looking at a suicide, despite the presence of Major Strange at the flat and the attitude of the police. However something about the accident bothered him. This man was probably head of the project They were investigating. Was he in charge of all the dead scientists?

That evening he rang Michael Neville to find out how he was getting on in his new job. He arranged to meet him at the Admiral Codrington at eight o'clock. Lynn prepared a quick meal and they left, taking due precautions, to line their stomachs.

Neville was a changed man. He greeted them cheerfully and bought the first round.

"Michael, I need help. Any contact inside that you can trust?"

"I have a long-time buddy. What are you after, David? Because whether we can tap it, depends on it's sensitivity."

Holder told him all about the latest death.

"I can get this guy to put it in the computer and see what comes out. What's his name?"

"It's Colonel Andrew Sinclair.

"Thanks Michael and how is the new job?"

"Not bad. The Arab has no manners, which is quite humiliating, but he gives good bribes. A hundred quid for parking outside Harrods! That Colonel shouldn't be a problem, he is ex-SAS so we have good access to his details."

They drank and talked till closing time and arranged for Neville to come round with the answer the next evening.

The following day Holder tried to find the name of the lorry driver, but it seemed to have slipped everyone's memory, including the local press. In a normal accident this sort of information was always available, so he knew it was part of a cover up operation. That evening Neville arrived with a broad grin on his face.

"I think you will like the information that I bring. The computer listed the Colonel's accident as a failed operation. Another attempt had been ordered, but not executed. It seems he beat them to it."

"Go on."

"Secondly, Sentinel Armed securities work under orders for the security executive on defence sensitive matters. They do not work for Russia. Do you want the rest?"

"Try me."

"Colonel Sinclair's details came from Edwin Schmidt's file, whoever he is and Sentinel Armed Securities are contracted to handle this case file."

"Good God we killed our own scientists."

The shock of the discovery that somewhere, deep in the grey area of government there was someone who decided the defence scientists must die to protect our secrets left Holder reeling in horror and disbelief. He began to check his evidence up to date and found this disclosure, which was one option he rejected all through his research, fitted into his evidence so far perfectly. He had rejected the possibility that state security would be involved in such an act, as it would be against all the cherished rules of a democratic free state, apart from being a terrible own goal. Now he could see the reason for many unexplained events he had investigated and it put the whole roll of the state in a different light. It was, without a doubt, true the state had used a private security company, lead by an ex-SAS officer, to carry out their heinous acts of personal sabotage.

They did this foul deed because, someone with the power to decide, instead of trying to protect the innocent scientists, ordered their deaths as the only sure course to silence. This took place when their names were transmitted to the KGB by a master spy. Worst of all, the state cowered away from doing its own dirty work and sub-contracted it to a private company for profit. Then tried to cover up the trail of their wrong doing.

Holder knew his case was drawing to a close. It was a matter of time till the last list of scientists transmitted to the KGB would be eliminated, then the slaughter should cease.

He had to continue to log his research. So he prepared his written sketch covering the death of Colonel Sinclair.

They left their home near Cippenham and took the unusual route across country to Bath. It was a happy journey and they both enjoyed the delightful countryside, until Sinclair noticed that a car seemed to be following, the driver talking into a microphone. Sinclair was security conscious and this presence disturbed him.

He remembered he had already written down the number of a previous car that had been following him. Due to the strange demise of several of his colleagues, he was edgy. There was little room for manoeuvre on country lanes, he could only go on and hope that his fears were ill-founded. He drove on for two miles down the twisting, turning road. Then the car behind turned into a side road and he began to relax again.

Suddenly, as he negotiated the next sharp corner, a tipper lorry came hurtling forwards. He had only seconds to avoid a collision. There was no room to manoeuvre. He glared at the lorry driver, realised that he had no intention of giving way, ignoring the brakes, aiming at head-on-impact. Slow motion action followed, his brain raced, the strange deaths of scientists on his project flashed through his mind. Daniel Kershaw's was uppermost. This was a set up. That car behind led the lorry to this place, timing the position of impact perfectly. They murdered his men, now it was his turn. His son? How could they do this to his son? The lorry crashed head on into his Volvo, stopping it dead and driving the engine back into the cab.

Miraculously and with much help from his Volvo, his son, dazed, incoherent, suffered only minor cuts and bruises. Sinclair lay unconscious, legs trapped in the foot well by the engine. Paul, recovering his senses, reached to help his father. After several long minutes he came round to find his son caring for him, his greatest prayer answered. The police had just arrived and he could hear an ambulance in the distance, clearing a way to the scene of the accident.

He heard the lorry driver making his excuses for not stopping and knew he was lying. Without proof what was the point? He was a marked man and do what he may, crippled as he was, how could he take on the might of the state. It was hopeless and he knew it. Now it was just a matter of time. They cut him out of the car, his ankles dreadfully swollen. The nurse administered pain killing drugs. That helped. They held him in hospital for two days and then sent him home to rest. At first he used crutches: gradually he learnt to walk again.

It wasn't long before he realised that this was not the only damage he had incurred. He couldn't get the face of the lorry driver out of his mind. It had been the face of an expert concentrating on his job, not one of fear. He trained at Hereford or some other camp, but in the armed forces without a doubt.

The days went by and his ankles showed a marked improvement, but his mind remained tortured by the memory and its implications.

As a trained soldier he knew the score. He couldn't tell his family, but he knew it was only a matter of time before the end and gradually this turned his mind upside down. He began to look inwards and resemble walking death. His family noticed his decline, but put it down to shock and opted to let time do the healing. Time was not on his side. He suspected every person he saw of being the assassin and every car driven by another homicidal driver. Without knowing it he was colluding with those that wished to kill him.

Two weeks of this living death went by. His thoughts began to turn to suicide. He desired nothing more than to release himself from this mental strain. He knew in his heart that he was driving himself crazy and had no resistance left.

What effected him most was waiting. In desperation he tried to kill himself, but to no avail. He resolved to do the job properly next time and planned his death for his next visit to London, in the company flat, away from the family, to save them from the pain of finding his body.

On a warm August night he took his own life with the precision it had taken him a lifetime to perfect. A colleague found him next morning, electrocuted. The real man had died in the lorry accident three weeks before.

CHAPTER 25.

On Sunday afternoon, they finished their work, when the phone rang and his editor asked him to cover another suicide, in Addlestone, Surrey. The victim's name was John French and he worked at Advanced Defence Systems. Another defence related death, but the killings would stop shortly, as the list of scientists supplied by the Czech spy must come to an end.

If he was right, by December eighty-eight the deaths in the defence industry would have run their course. That would prove his theory. He insisted that Lynn stayed within sight so he put her in the car and rushed off to Addlestone. They arrived to find the police busying themselves around the garden shed where John French lay dead.

It was a large detached house set in a well-stocked garden. Holder went up to the police inspector.

Introducing himself, he asked for full details of the case.

"John French. Fifty years old. His family consists of a wife and two children. He took his wife to work this morning, then the dog for a walk. This was the last time he was seen before his wife found him dead in the shed."

"Where did he work?"

"Advanced Defence Systems."

"May I see the body?"

"I don't see why not. Got a press pass?" Satisfied the Inspector showed him in to the shed. A wire, connected to the main's supply was attached to the body whose eyes stared wildly. Another electrocution? Holder studied the body carefully and then searched the shed for clues. He found a hole in the shed door freshly cut.

"Was the shed closed when the body was found?"

"Yes and locked."

He went on checking and found a window closed but not locked. It was the only escape route.

Where was Major Strange from Sentinel Armed Securities?

"Lynn, can you interview the neighbours while I have a look round?" Turning to the Inspector he asked;

"Can I speak to Mrs French?"

"She is under sedation. Can you come back tomorrow? I am sure she will see you then."

"I'll do that. Thanks for your help." Holder began to search outside the shed and round the door for clues. Neither the scene nor the neighbours were forthcoming with anything of substance. They drove back to London knowing they would have to return the next day to interview Mrs French.

Next morning, Holder went up to the door and rang the bell, Mary French answered. He showed her his press pass and entered.

"I am sorry the house is a bit of a mess, but I am not up to cleaning it at the moment."

"I quite understand. May I say how sorry I was to hear of your husband's death. I was here yesterday, but I decided to come back today, rather than to bother you at that moment."

"That was thoughtful. It's all a shock - I can't believe this is happening."

"Do you think your husband committed suicide?"

"No way, he was a happy family man. He loved me, his home, our children. He had no worries. We were well off by anyone's standards and a very close family. No, he was got at by the same people that have killed all his colleagues. It was only a week ago that his boss died. He would never have done this to his kids. He doted on them and would not have chosen to put them through this misery."

"Tell me, did you know there is a hole in the shed door?"

"That door is brand new. I don't recall seeing a hole in it."

"Was the shed locked when you found him?"

"Yes, but the window latch is faulty. It can easily be opened from both sides, so an intruder could have got out that way."

"Do you know what work your husband was undertaking for Colonel Sinclair?"

"He never told us much about his work. I do know it was a very high security project."

"Mrs French, I must tell you that I am of the same opinion as you. It's a long story, but I believe that they murdered your husband. My investigation, which has been extensive, has made me sure of this. He died to stop information on his project from reaching the Eastern block.

I believe when the scientist's names became known to the Soviet Bloc intelligence, as people with expert knowledge of the new total defence program, the KGB would compromise them. In the opinion of those I'm hoping to expose, their only option was to silence the source, permanently. At first I thought the KGB were the killers."

"Then who did it?"

"Now I believe the KGB targeted him. Our security found out and ordered their execution. If I am right, he will be one of the last to die, because our security arrested the spy. Only those on his last list of names will be in danger."

"You mean our security arranged the death of my husband?"

"Yes, but nothing that I can say will bring your husband back, but it might help you to understand why he died. You may have noticed that the deaths came in clusters. I believe that these corresponded to lists compiled by the spy. I am determined to expose this scandal and I will do everything in my power to achieve this."

"Turning to Lynn, she almost broke down. "He cares. Look after him."

Three weeks later he was attending a press reception at the Savoy, when they paged him.

"David Holder speaking."

"David darling, sorry to disturb you but we have just had a call from your office. There's been another death, at Bracknell."

"Lynn, get everything ready. I will be with you in about thirty minutes. Thanks for calling me."

"OK boss, bye."

Holder arranged for cover at the conference, drove quickly back to Twickenham and collected Lynn. The inspector was the same man that attended the scene of Jane Armstrong's death, a lifetime ago. Had the case gone full circle?

"Good morning. We meet again and once more under sad circumstances." The inspector looked at them both, not quite sure how to carry on the conversation, plainly moved, seeking words.

Holder was gentle, "I'm sorry too. What can you tell me so far about this death?"

"His name is Brian Wells. He was thirty-three years old, married, no children. Worked at British Space Projects as an engineering manager. He died from carbon monoxide poisoning and circumstances lead us to believe it was a suicide. There is no evidence of an intruder to make us think otherwise."

They looked around the scene. It was very similar to the layout of Edward Purcell's death, except that Wells had made no bid to escape from the car. A hose pipe placed through the back window fed the obnoxious fumes to the motionless body. Holder examined him carefully, but could find no tell-tale mark to suggest any attack. However, the style was too similar to dismiss and Holder's mind still leaned towards murder.

Again he noticed Major Strange missing from the scene. Was he pre-occupied planning another death?

He went to interview the neighbours knowing he already knew the facts behind the case. A conclusion would soon be achieved. On the Drive back to Twickenham he told Lynn about his feelings and she just sighed;

"I hope so."

CHAPTER 26.

It had been a long winter for Holder. The last scientist died in September. No further deaths occurred. It supported his theory that they eliminated the last list of scientists and the sequence of assassinations had come to an end.

He now knew the reason for the deaths. He foresaw the result of Edwin Schmidt's trial. All he now awaited was confirmation that Edwin Schmidt collected details of the British Total Defence program and his case would be complete. It would support and confirm information he received from Michael Neville. It was unlikely that they would name names at the trial. They didn't have to; after all they caught him red handed.

Holder knew that some of this hearing would be in camera. Parts of the information involved was much too sensitive for public exposure and the part played by the private security company must be protected at all cost. While waiting for the trial, they finished work on the investigation, tidying up all the loose ends. All that now remained was the trial and its conclusions.

Then, at last, he would be able to draw this expensive and time consuming project to a close. His relief showed at the prospect of finally going to print with the story that had cost him so much and stretched him to his professional limits. It had been exciting, if somewhat hair-raising at times. He had dedicated most of his time over two years to this investigation and the work started long before that period.

He acknowledged that by far the best part of his investigation had been finding Lynn. Meeting her was extraordinary good fortune and had filled a big gap in his life. She showed so much interest in his work. There was no conflict between woman and work that had bedevilled his relationship with his ex-wife. They waited together for the trial to begin.

Edwin Schmidt was sitting with his defence lawyers. Dressed in a blue pin-striped suit he looked more like a business man in a judicial enquiry than a spy on trial. He showed no fear and seemed to be adopting a somewhat light approach for someone who was about to receive a heavy sentence.

This did not surprise Holder. This man was a highly trained agent. He had, after all, been acting a part for the last thirteen years, while he extracted highly confidential information from the state and passed it to a potential enemy. Some of the facts were about to unfold.

First the judge read out the charges. Edwin Schmidt pleaded not guilty. The judge asked the potential jurors to declare whether they were of the Jewish faith. The special nature of the case dictated that no person of the Jewish faith be allowed to serve on the jury.

The jury sworn in, the case began. The prosecution, led by Mr Ember, made their opening speech. After Edwin Schmidt's arrest he was taken to Paddington Green police station, where He asked if he could convey a simple message to the Czech Embassy. It read; 'Edwin Schmidt arrested.' Interviewed at the police station he told detectives that he was born in Holland during the war.

His mother, while having an affair with a soldier, became pregnant. Her soldier sweetheart died in battle in forty-two and her father forced her to go away when she was ready to give birth. She eventually reached Czechoslovakia, where the Red Cross found a home for her twins. Edwin Schmidt claimed to be one of those children and his twin sister backed his story. She had searched for him since the war and eventually tracked him down when in seventy-seven, she received an address in London, through the Red Cross. It had all been an elegant ruse. After his arrest a DNA test showed conclusively that he was not her twin brother.

Edwin Schmidt acquired her brother's identity and cynically persisted in the deception after Miss Schmidt contacted him in seventy-seven. He was indeed a cool customer, an actor of skill and deception. On arriving in this country, in seventy-five, he found a job at a store, where he quickly rose to become a purchasing officer. In October eighty-five he left to become an estate agent. This was a move of convenience, a front for his real business: he had been triggered.

One of his first orders was to spy on the Jewish organisations and to feed back information to his embassy. When special branch caught him transmitting messages in groups of five figure numbers, they found all the materials and equipment necessary for sending and receiving messages carefully concealed in his flat.

Over the past thirteen years he had received more than three-hundred coded messages. They were of a type that could only be de-coded by a method known as a one time pad. In the flat They found six of these pads, some concealed in a bar of soap, for receiving instructions from Czechoslovakia, but using several other methods to send messages back to his masters.

He controlled other agents, through a number of dead letter boxes for receiving and sending instructions and information. They found a list of contacts in his wallet. On examining his bank accounts, special branch discovered that he received large sums of money from undisclosed sources.

He joined organisations concerned with the plight of dissidents. In October eighty-five he travelled with a small group of Jewish activists, to Moscow where they visited the homes of people who wished to leave Russia. All the time his hidden agenda was passing information back to his government. There was much more to it than that. He spied on firms who were participating in the Total Defence program. How good was he? Their best man in place. The type of information that he was transmitting was hard to obtain.

Schmidt was the link with the complicated investigation that had cost Holder so much effort. This was the final confirmation Holder required. The facts would stand up to all the huffing and puffing that he expected from the state. Holder suspected that it was a foregone conclusion that Edwin Schmidt would go to jail and for several years. Schmidt knew far too much about the government's counter-actions.

This was the final brick that finished the house of facts. Edwin Schmidt's spying had caused somebody to hire a private security company to eliminate all the software designers whose names were obtained by Edwin Schmidt. These scientists were all involved in the total defence program. It was as simple as that.

Less simple was, who sentenced them to death. Holder was convinced the order, however coded, came right from the top. It was most likely that the order given to the Chief Secretary to the cabinet was as simple as: 'On no account must the secrets of the Total Defence Program fall into the hands of the KGB.'

The Chief Secretary would call a meeting of the Security Services and pass on the Prime Minister's request verbatim. Whether he would comment or not is guesswork. He probably doesn't have to add comment. This was correct procedure up to this point.

Therefore the dccision to kill the scientists rests within the security services. The main components are Internal security, external security and special branch. It is also possible there is a non-executive cell that makes decisions but this is guesswork and not substantiated. Holder concluded he might never know the identity of the man in charge of the group that signed the scientist's death warrants as the decisions were made deep inside the grey area of government.

The fact that this heinous crime was master-minded inside the system but carried out by a private company for profit was the last straw. Holder's case was made.

In the civil World the building industry suffers protectionism. Contracts allocated to certain companies are unfairly gained through action by these security agencies. It is also present in relation to the dirty tricks against the CND. In democracy the price paid for freedom of speech is to hear minority views. Only a weak and immature democracy has to silence speech in fear of its impact.

Now his investigation had reached its conclusion. He experienced an extraordinary empty feeling, as if half his stomach was missing. It was the void created by the release of pressure from his two and a half years of investigation.

"That wraps it up then. A masterpiece completed David."

"Perhaps. Now for the big one. We will see some waves if we get it published. I am off to my agent now."

"When you get back I'll have a big surprise for you," replied Lynn, kissing him tenderly.

"Can't wait, see you soon."

Holder left to take their dedicated research to the publisher. He opened the garage door, slipped into his car and started the engine.

The explosion threw Lynn onto the kitchen floor. Rushing out, she saw a horrifying tangled mess. He lay, half out of the car, bleeding profusely from wounds to his arm, chest and the left side of his face. Lynn cradled him in her arms and screamed to a neighbour to call an ambulance. A doctor, who was passing stopped to see if he could help. He gave him a

shot to ease the pain, but there was little else he could do.

They rushed Holder to hospital, his life hanging on a thread. The surgeon examined him carefully, to ascertain what he should do to enhance his survival, while Lynn waited and prayed for a miracle, wondering how a doctor was just passing at the right moment.

Holder sat up abruptly, his thoughts changed to the present by the urgency of the phone ringing.

"David Holder speaking."

"Hi David, Michael Neville."

"Great to here from you Michael. I trust everything is going well."

"Oh, can't complain. I ditched the Arab, he was too rude. I now work for a Japanese industrialist. He is the opposite, so polite. The bowing gets me down sometimes."

"We must meet for a drink."

"That's why I rang. I have something important to tell you, but I can't explain over the phone."

"How about in half an hour in the usual place?"

"Fine."

"Who was that?" Asked Lynn, as she came into the room.

"That was Neville. He want's to see us."

As they entered the Admiral Codrington they found Neville sitting in his usual place. Some things never change; thought Holder.

"Well, how's the liberated Neville?"

"Hi friends, I'm fine. I have come to terms with my new life thanks to you and it's much easier now."

"That's great news." Said Lynn, smiling with pleasure.

"So what's bothering you?"

"Last Tuesday I received a phone call inviting me to an interview. All they said on the phone was they were looking for Russian speaking men between twenty-five and forty willing to work for a short term in Russia and maybe the Middle East."

"Did you respond?"

"Well, I speak Russian as it was one of the skills I was taught while training in Hereford. We all learn different skills to cover all the many variety of special duties we may be called on to perform."

"So you went for an interview. Great it could be interesting."

"Guess who interviewed me?"

"Not Yeltsin was it?" Said Holder smiling.

"No. Major William Strange."

"I thought my book had put him into involuntary retirement!"

"No. He runs a firm called Specialised Security Services. Guess what they wanted to recruit me for!"

"To seek and kill redundant nuclear scientists?"

"How did you know that?"

"History is repeating itself in a very cruel way. I have just received reports of the first deaths and I therefore knew what it might be as soon as you mentioned Major Strange."

"You don't miss anything."

"Are you going to investigate this terrible crime?"

"Holder sat back in his seat in silence while thoughts and memories developed in his mind. Lynn as if spurred to action by the silence delivered the answer.

"What he means to say is yes I will, but sudden shyness has robbed him of his voice."

Once again Lynn came up trumps. How could he have told her he had already decided to go for it.

EPILOGUE.

For nearly three years British Intelligence, in league with the CIA observed every move made by Erwin Van Haarlem. A Czechoslovakian defector, Vlastimil Lubuik exposed his cover.

Realising they could catch the whole spy ring with patience MI5 observed every move, listened to his transmissions and waited. On the morning of the second of April eighty-eight they accidentally blew their cover and they therefore arrested Erwin Van Haarlem. They caught him passing sensitive messages to a foreign power. He was subsequently tried, found guilty and given a ten year sentence.

Moscow failed to obtain the top secrets of our 'Defence into the nineties' program, depriving them of their final thrust to catch up with Western command and control. The importance of this cannot be overstated and was so vividly illustrated during the Gulf war. At this encounter Western technology dealt a decisive blow to the Russian built command and control system defending Iraq.

The Soviet Union was forced into a major decision. Sweat it out with an inferior military control and move farther behind the Western technology or launch a hopefully successful damage control exercise. Gorbachev was a realist. He new the Soviet Union was effectively bankrupt. His people were demanding more and he knew that he could not fulfil their wishes. Developing a modern command and control system from scratch would take food out of the mouths of hungry people. Revolution was possible. Gorbachev tried to walk the live wire. The attempt ended in failure.

On the tenth of November eighty-nine Russia announced to an astonished World the Berlin wall, a symbol of East block repression, was to open and form a gateway to the West. A nation, all but dead, seemed to re-awaken and celebrate its new found freedom. After the dust settled, terms of unification agreed, East Germany again was re-united with the Federal Republic of Germany and they were one nation again. The policy of damage limitation was born.

One by one the satellite countries surrounding the Soviet Union fell like a house of cards. The once impregnable Iron Curtain displayed the inherent weakness of Communist domination. When restrictions imposed by the Soviet Union relaxed, these Nations claimed their right to democracy. Poland, Czechoslovakia, Hungary, Yugoslavia, all revoked their stance as the outer shield for the Soviet Union when democracy was on offer. Even Romania, ruled by an autocratic dictator claimed its freedom. The World stood back, amazed. The West, relying on the impotent actions of the United Nations, who always act too little too late, has let Russia starve, Eastern Europe struggle and Yugoslavia tear itself to bloody shreds.

If the West thought it had seen the Eighth Wonder of the World, in the words of a bit part actor, 'They ain't seen nothing yet.' The ninth was about to unfold. In the bible it says a house built on sand will surely fall. The Soviet Union thought they could ride the shifting sands but like any house without sure foundations its credibility started to crumble.

State after state demanded independence from the Union. Communism became a dirty word. The old guard of conservative communists, who knew no other way, attempted an ill-fated coup d'etat. Communism had ceased to rule by fear so it failed. The people rallied round Boris Yeltsin to form the first democratic state of the Union for over seventy years of Communist domination. Others swiftly followed. Gorbachev, the architect of the Union's demise, also fell. However his name will go down in history as the leader who blew and blew and blew his house down.

For this great sacrifice to his principles, because he was a true Communist, the World should hail him as a giant among men.

No-one should underestimate the transformation that has already taken place in the Soviet Union thanks to Gorbachev. No-one should underestimate how far it has to go before we can say it is irreversible.

The World today is safer thanks to Gorbachev, Yeltsin and Vlastimil Lubuik. Without Gorbachev's realism the eighth and ninth wonders of the World would not have unfolded before our eyes.

President Reagan claimed the glory for the defeat of Communism but in reality he had little part in its unfolding.

However, the scientists of America and Britain can justly claim their part in taming the Communist Empire and bringing it to heel. Without their dedication and far sighted research into efficient forms of defensive action controlled by computerised command and control, the Soviet Union might still be hanging on to the notion of catching up with the West. Nevertheless, insolvency would have eventually caused a similar conclusion.

That scientists had to die to bring democracy to the Communist block in peacetime is an appalling verdict on our times. Men like Barnes-Wallis, Mitchell and Roland Hill are still regarded as saviours of their nation, even fifty years after World War Two. Time would have delivered the same result. In reality today the Soviet Union is a shaky democracy. The West must act promptly to assist and guide their transition to a stable free market democracy. If we stand back and wait we may miss the opportunity for ever.

Now, it seems that the power houses of the World have joined together to kill the Russian nuclear scientists to halt the possibility of their transfer to another potential nuclear state. It is the action of nations with bankrupt minds. We must halt this senseless killing.

You have a row of dominoes set up; you knock over the first one, and what will happen to the last one is that it will go over very quickly.

President Dwight Eisenhower. 7th April 1954.